Death and the Cornish Fiddler

DERYN LAKE

First published in Great Britain in 2006 by
Allison & Busby Limited
13 Charlotte Mews
London W1T 4EJ
www.allisonandbusby.com

Copyright © 2006 by DERYN LAKE

A catalogue record for this book is available from
the British Library.

10 9 8 7 6 5 4 3 2 1

ISBN 0 7490 8296 8

Printed and bound in Wales by
Creative Print and Design, Ebbw Vale

Acknowledgements

A lot of people from the West Country helped me with the research for this book. First of all I must mention the excellent staff of the Helston Folk Museum, an intriguing place packed with treasures. They were Janet Spargo, Ieuan Harries and Kate Taylor, all of whom were more than helpful, particularly Janet who dealt with my frantic phone calls. Next I would like to thank Dominique Strover and Zoe Painter of the Cornwell Centre in Redruth, who pointed me in the right direction. Next comes Keith Gotch, retired to Devon these days, who was of great help about the state of one of the bodies. It was my lucky day when I met him all those years ago. Finally comes Moski Carlyle who went with me to Helston and ate haggis! Thank you all.

In memory of Rosemary Holbrow (Big Rose).
An old friend and a good one.

Chapter One

Spring had come: the Apothecary knew it as soon as he opened his eyes. The light filtering through the drawn curtains was different from the light of other mornings, for this was radiant and bright with a certain strange, disturbing quality. Raising his head from the pillows, he heard the sparkling notes of a thrush giving voice and was filled with a sense of relief that the long winter had finally ended and that the land was burgeoning with life once more. Moving quickly, John Rawlings got out of bed and, pulling the curtains back, stared out at the magnificent landscape that lay before him.

Far below was the river Exe, winding its way meanderingly through the green fields that banked it on either side. In the distance, to his right, stood the ancient town of Exeter, its steeples reflecting the early morning sun, its cathedral a splendid burst of gold as the rays caught its spires. To his left lay the stable block and the coach house and, peering more closely as he threw the window open, John could see his daughter Rose, fast approaching her fifth birthday, mounting a small but substantial pony. Beside her, assisting with the lifting-on, stood a familiar dark figure, today clad in a midnight blue riding habit. Elizabeth di Lorenzi, widow of an Italian nobleman and daughter of the Earl of Exmoor, was not only up but about to give Rose a riding lesson.

John, watching from his bedroom window, was suddenly taken up with the glory of the morning and experienced a strange surge of excitement which started deep in his blood. For a minute he puzzled as to what it was, then realised that it was his response to the changing seasons, that he was suffering from a wonderful, heady attack of spring fever. Closing the window again he pulled the bellrope, and as soon as the hot water arrived, washed and shaved before putting on his clothes and hurrying downstairs. But he was too late. Elizabeth and Rose had already gone off and he was left to his own devices.

Eating his breakfast solitary, the Apothecary's thoughts

wandered. This was the third occasion on which he had visited Devon since the death of his wife, Emilia. The first had been when he was on the run, accused of Emilia's murder. The second was when the case had been solved and he had taken Rose with him, despite her lack of years. The third time had been now, drawn back by Elizabeth's dark ugly beauty which still exerted a fascination for him, to say nothing of his daughter's enthusiasm for the West Country. It had been the Marchesa who had originally suggested John return to Gunnersbury and try to discover the identity of the true murderer. And so he had, eventually unmasking a person dangerously crazed in his view. But now all that lay in the past. It was April, 1767, and here he was feeling the first stirring of spring, not only in the land but also within himself. Impatiently, the Apothecary laid down his napkin and went outside in the direction of the stables, determined to ride out and find Rose and her intriguing instructress wherever they might be.

As he mounted the large, skittish, black stallion which Elizabeth had chosen for him when he first arrived, John found that today particularly he could not get the Marchesa out of his thoughts. Even though several years had elapsed since he first set eyes on her she had still refused to share his bed, telling him that he was merely seeking Emilia and that she was no substitute for his dead wife. With that he had been forced to content himself and in the sixteen months since Emilia's death had led a blameless and celibate life. But now, with spring's awakening – not only in the land but within himself – he was going to find this situation difficult to contend with.

Digging his heels into Jet, the dark horse's sides, the Apothecary set off rather faster than he had anticipated. Though he kept his seat well enough, he was not the world's best horseman and it had seemed to be his fate that wherever he went he was given some mettlesome mount, either that or one painfully slow. The compromise, the kindly, gentle horse who could go at a pace, constantly eluded him.

Reaching the edge of the high plateau on which Abbotswood Place – Elizabeth's fine house – was built, John looked down into the valley below. There, trotting along, were Rose and the woman with whom he was preoccupied. The Apothecary waved but they did not see him.

'Rose,' he shouted, for some reason not wanting to call to the Marchesa.

She looked up. 'Hello, Papa. Come down and be with us.'

The Apothecary motioned his horse downwards, leaning back in the saddle, wishing that he cut a more dashing figure, horribly aware of Elizabeth's amused stare following every move he made. Praying that he wouldn't fall off, he finally reached the bottom and gave Jet a thankful pat on the neck. Rose came forward to meet him and John looked at her, at her fine colour enhanced by the tumbling red of her hair.

'Hello, gypsy girl,' he said.

She smiled at him. 'Why do you call me that?'

He put out his hand and ruffled her curls. 'Because of your hair.'

'Don't you like it?'

'You know I love it. What do you think, Madam?'

Elizabeth had come to join them, sitting easily on her mount which today she rode side-saddle. She looked at Rose critically, treating her, as always, as a small adult.

'I would say that it is your finest feature. And when you grow up I believe it will break hearts.'

'What do you mean?' asked Rose, fractionally anxious.

'I do not speak literally. I mean that when you are seventeen there will be a queue of admirers which your father will have to send away.'

'What? Every one of them?' John's daughter burst out, and the two adults could not help but laugh at her earnestness.

'I promise I'll let the best of them stay,' the Apothecary answered. He changed the subject. 'Where are you two off to?' He addressed Elizabeth.

'I thought we might ride over in the direction of Wildtor.'

'Won't it be a bit rough for the pony?'

He actually meant for Rose but was too kind to say so in front of her. Fortunately the Marchesa understood, as she understood much about the Rawlings family.

'I didn't mean to the Grange itself. I shall turn back as soon as the going gets heavy.'

'Good. Then I'll come with you. You know I'm not much of a rider.'

'I think you are improving greatly. Another few months here and you would be as good as anyone in the county.'

'Ah yes, I need to talk to you about that,' John answered in an undertone.

The Marchesa shot him a look from her brilliant dark eyes. 'This afternoon perhaps. While Rose is resting.'

'Very good, Madam.' He trotted forward, catching up with his daughter who had pulled slightly ahead of them.

Everywhere he looked there were signs of the newly arrived season. The banks of the river glowed green as mint and randomly growing in the valley were clumps of wild daffodils, while primroses cascaded in abundance down the sides of the craggy pathway. Above him, grazing on the steep escarpment, were mild-mannered sheep, lambs suckling beneath them or running or leaping and generally behaving as all young, carefree creatures do. John thought of Rose and how happy she was in this habitat, letting the loss of her mother slip from her mind, enjoying the freedom of her life, the riding and walking and playing. He felt he could hardly bear to take her back to London, though he knew that that time was drawing near. For soon he would tire of being idle and want to pick up the threads of his life once more.

Again he caught up with Rose. 'My darling, do you miss London at all?'

'I miss Grandpapa, of course. But I don't miss Nassau Street.'

'We shall have to return soon, I fear.'

'Must we really?'

'Yes, my sweetheart. I'm afraid we must. Papa must see to his shop.'

'But Pa, could you not open a shop down here?'

'One day perhaps.'

'Oh please…'

But the Marchesa, who had been busy inspecting the swans on the Exe, had come to join them and the Apothecary, knowing that Rose would understand, had motioned the child to be silent.

Elizabeth looked at the two of them. 'Are you ready?' she asked.

John could not resist it. 'For what?' he answered.

The sensational glance swept him. 'That depends.'

He caught her eye. 'On what?'

'Who knows,' came the reply as she wheeled her mount and went off at a thundering pace across the valley.

John rode along beside Rose, thinking what a beautiful daughter he had, of how Emilia had been in the early stages of pregnancy when she had been killed, robbing him of both his wife and his second child. He had a sudden longing to see her grave again, to kneel beside it and talk to her. He knew then that only a change in Elizabeth's feeling towards him could make him stay in Devon much longer.

He turned to Rose. 'You love being in the country, don't you my darling?'

'Yes, Papa. But I like it where Grandpapa lives too.'

'Do you want to go and stay with him for a while when we get back?'

His daughter looked at him solemnly. 'Best I'd like it if we came to live in Devon.'

'I don't think that is going to be possible.'

'Then Grandpapa's would be nice.'

How easily pleased she was and how amenable; characteristics inherited from her mother, no doubt. He looked at Rose and she at him, and suddenly he saw Emilia peeping out at him, and was glad and sorry simultaneously. Glad that in a way his wife was still alive, that she had passed on her looks and her character to her daughter; sorry that he was going to be constantly reminded of how much he had loved her.

He slowed his horse. 'Shall we go back now?'

'Let's have a race first.'

'Very well.'

He held his wayward mount back so that Rose won easily, laughing and tossing her hair about and smiling at him.

'That was lovely, Papa.'

'Come along, sweetheart. It's time to go.'

'What about Mrs Elizabeth? Should we wait for her?'

John gave a wry smile. 'I don't think so. She'll probably be some hours yet.'

They made their way upwards through the height of the morning, past trees burgeoning with heavy buds, and bluebells not yet out but already showing their colour. Once more John felt uplifted by the essence of spring, and breathing in the scented air, relished every second. It would indeed be difficult to return to London but he knew that it was an inevitability that he had to face.

Later that evening, after he had seen Rose safely tucked into bed, he broached the subject with Elizabeth. As with all spring nights it had grown a little cold and she had ordered a fire lit in the parlour where they sat after dinner, both reading. He, looking at her covertly, thought how comfortable he was with her, how at ease, and knew that he was falling in love all over again. Which, given the loneliness he had felt since the death of his wife, was understandable. He fell to thinking where it was all going to lead, trying to imagine her living in London and not really succeeding.

She looked up suddenly. 'What did you say?'

'Nothing. I didn't speak.'

'Yes you did. You muttered something under your breath.'

'I'm sorry. I didn't realise.'

'John, what is it that's bothering you?' she asked in that frank way of hers.

He decided to be honest. 'Elizabeth, I feel that I ought to get back to London. I've been away long enough. I've a life to lead there. Do you understand?'

'Of course I do,' she answered. 'A man of your character could only stay inactive for so long. When do you plan to go?'

'In about two weeks.'

'Not before?'

'No. As you know it's Rose's birthday on the 28th of April and I am certain she would enjoy spending it here.'

'And so she shall. I shall give a party for her and invite some other children. And John…'

'Yes?'

'I've a mind to go to Cornwall shortly and I would consider it an honour if you would come with me.'

'How could I refuse an invitation put like that?'

Elizabeth's scarred face smiled, making her suddenly beautiful. 'Very easily I imagine. But I have a motive in going.'

'Which is?'

'I want to visit Helstone and see some ancient dances they perform there.'

'Dances?' asked John curiously.

'Yes. They're both as old as time; in fact one is certainly pagan. That one is called the Furry and the other Hal-an-Tow.'

'How do you spell that?'

Elizabeth did so, pronouncing Tow to rhyme with No. John listened carefully.

'Probably originally Heel-and-Toe, don't you think?'

'You're likely right. But it is the primitiveness of the occasion that appeals to me. The dance has its roots in pre-Christianity. Though the church wisely embraced it, it was originally to welcome spring. Don't you find that exciting, John?'

Not as exciting as I find you, the Apothecary thought, though he nodded and smiled enthusiastically.

'The Furry celebrates an expression of joy at the triumph of Life over Death. It is one of the oldest customs preserved in the country and I have always promised myself that I would go and see it on some occasion. And to watch it with you can only enhance the pleasure.'

What a way she had with her, John considered, taking in her coil of dark hair and the glance of her eyes. But he kept his voice quite even as he answered, 'Then I will accompany you gladly, Madam. I am sure that London can wait another three weeks or so.'

She smiled. 'Good. The dance is always held on the 8th of May. So we'll leave on the third if that is convenient.'

'And what about Rose? Should we take her?'

'Of course. It may be the only chance she ever gets to see the Furry.'

'Who knows?' John answered, and spread his hands.

Chapter Two

The Marchesa's coach was drawn up outside the front door and several servants were hurrying backwards and forwards loading the top with luggage. John, who normally would have lent them an unconventional helping hand, was on this occasion fussing over his daughter who was standing, large-eyed, wrapped in a travelling cloak, a hat on her head, a favourite toy clutched in her hand.

'Are we going to Helstone, Papa?' she asked for the twentieth time.

'Yes, darling. We are going to see the Furry Dance.'

'Does everyone dress in furs?' She giggled, laughing a child's noisy laugh at her own joke.

John smiled obediently. 'It's also known as the Floral Dance. But Furry is its proper name.'

He turned, as at that moment Elizabeth swept out, looking dramatic in an enormous feathered hat, the rest of her ensemble a mysterious shade of green, very elaborately finished. John felt that she was dressing in accordance with the seasons, preparing herself, no doubt, for the primitive pleasures of the dances they were going to see.

She smiled at the Apothecary and his child. 'We leave in ten minutes so make your final preparations.'

'How long is the journey going to take us?' he asked.

'About eight hours if we stop for dinner. The coachman says there is a reasonable track as far as Falmouth but it still means crossing Bodmin Moor.'

'What about Dartmoor?'

'He says the road, or what laughingly passes for one, circumnavigates that.'

'And what do we do after Falmouth?'

'Pick our way across country.'

John pulled a face. 'I hope Rose is going to be all right.'

Elizabeth gave him a rather disapproving stare. 'My dear friend, you are not attempting to mollycoddle the child, are you?'

'No, of course not.'

'Then consider that she will have your pistol and mine to protect her, to say nothing of the coachman and Rufus the guard. She will be utterly safe I assure you.'

'And as I remember you are rather a deadly shot, Madam.' Elizabeth raised a dark eyebrow. 'You recall that, do you?'

'I recall every detail,' he answered solemnly.

Just for a moment the Marchesa looked disconcerted and John knew that she was remembering, amongst other things, the one occasion when they had so nearly made love. Then she blanked her features, even though just for a second she had smiled a secret smile.

'Most retentive of you, Sir.'

'I am famous for my sharp memory, Madam.'

'How fortunate,' she said, and went back into the house.

Rose, who had remained silent throughout this exchange, looked at her father. 'Is Mrs Elizabeth cross, Papa?'

'No, my darling,' John answered, and he too smiled. He turned to his daughter. 'Would you like to use the water closet before we go?'

'Yes, please.'

'Right.' And he led her away to the somewhat smelly cubicle into which she insisted on going alone.

A few minutes later she emerged and she and John boarded the coach, sitting expectantly side-by-side, awaiting the arrival of the woman known to Rose as Mrs Elizabeth. With a servant accompanying her, the Marchesa appeared and, kissing her hand to the retainers who had gathered to bid her farewell, she, too, got on board.

'You're not taking a lady's maid?' asked John surprised.

'No, I shall have to care for myself,' she answered.

The coachman gave a crack of his whip and started the team and they went down the drive at a good pace, then turned towards Okehampton and the mysterious county of Cornwall that lay beyond.

Elizabeth had changed drivers since John had last travelled

with her to Gunnersbury, her new man being young and extremely handsome.

'What's his name?' he asked, indicating the fellow with a pointing finger.

'Jed Ryall. Why?'

'I was just wondering what happened to your other chap.'

'He took a post with Lady Cadogan, who called on me one day and coveted him. I believe he was required for both driving duties and other things.'

John looked at her quizzically, saying 'Ah.'

Elizabeth burst out laughing. 'Lady Cadogan is a widow and on her own. Does that answer your question?'

'Perfectly. If I were you I'd keep young Ryall under lock and key though.'

'Oh I will, don't you worry,' Elizabeth said airily.

They stopped at Okehampton for refreshment and comfort, then made their way to Launceston, where they crossed the border into the brooding county of Cornwall. Now the terrain grew rough and wild.

'Is this Bodmin Moor?' John asked the Marchesa.

'Indeed it is and a bleak and lonely place. They say a wild beast wanders about, slaying cattle and sheep. That's why I brought an extra shotgun.' And she indicated the tough-looking individual whom John had noticed clambering up to sit beside Jed.

'Are there any inns?'

'One or two. Do you want to stop?'

'Yes, for a short while. I could do with a drink.'

Elizabeth put her head out of the window. 'Jed, can you draw up at the next inn?'

'That would be Jamaica Inn, Ma'am. I wouldn't recommend it,' John heard him shout back.

'Why not?'

'It's a haunt of smugglers, Ma'am.'

'Then I insist on seeing it. John, are you game?'

'What about Rose? Will she be safe there?'

'We can leave her in the coach under the protection of Jed and Rufus.'

'Rose, would you mind that?' John asked, but the child made no answer and, looking closely, the Apothecary could see that she had fallen fast asleep.

A few minutes later the coach rattled over the cobbles outside a wayside hostelry. Looking round John saw a two-storey slate-tiled building with another construction at right-angles to the main part. It had a sinister, sombre air as if it could well hold the secret to dark deeds. The Apothecary hesitated but Elizabeth was already at the carriage door.

'Well, are we going in?'

He was about to ask if she thought it safe but could vividly imagine her snort of derision. Instead he opened the door and, getting out, handed the Marchesa down.

They entered a long low room, a fire burning in an inglenook to their right. Round this were huddled various figures, all appearing to be in a somnolent state. Yet despite this, John noticed that eyes appeared to open momentarily and a cough rang out, as did a prolonged fart. Automatically, he took Elizabeth's arm and tucked it through his.

'Can I help you?' growled a rough voice from a dark recess on the left.

Peering, John perceived a wisp of a fellow standing behind a bar, looking as out of place as it was possible to be. In fact so slight was the man that it seemed as if even Elizabeth could have thrown him with ease. Never the less, he was the owner of the voice from hell.

Somewhat startled, John replied, 'A glass of Bordeaux and a glass of...' He turned to Elizabeth.

'Claret, if you please.'

'Claret.'

He was half expecting the wisp to say that they didn't have such things in stock but the gravel voice answered, 'Take a seat and I'll bring you your order.'

Elizabeth and John sat in a dark corner and, exchanging

glances, absorbed the extraordinary atmosphere. And then, most unexpectedly, one of the figures snoozing by the fire stood up and, producing a fiddle, started to play. Instantly everything changed. His fellow sleepers shook themselves awake and from hidden recesses more instruments appeared. Suddenly the air was full of sound as the fiddle joined with a flute, a drum and a tambourine.

'Dance, Madam and Sir,' suggested the gruff-voiced barman as he brought their drinks. And the next second Elizabeth was on her feet and cavorting wildly. John, unable to resist the music's insistent beat, got up and seizing her round the waist, began to improvise great leaps and bounds.

Jamaica Inn was transformed; transformed by the sound of that curious band of musicians who had so suddenly started to play. It was as if they possessed some kind of magic, so irresistible were the tunes they produced. Eventually both Elizabeth and John ran out of breath and collapsed into their chairs laughing, drinking their wine, flushed and feeling strangely happy.

Then a curious thing happened. The fiddle player came tap-tap-tapping in their direction and John realised that the man was blind. Of medium height and build, his long dark hair tied back with a bit of greasy ribbon, his clothes, which had clearly once been of quality stuff, now stained and disreputable. He wore a pair of spectacles, the lenses painted black.

'Penny for the band, Sir,' he said.

It was an unusual voice, heavily Cornish in its intonation.

John reached into his pocket and produced a shilling. 'Thank you,' he said, giving the fellow the coin.

The man felt it, realised its worth, and gave a bow in John's general direction. 'Very kind of you, Sir. I do thank 'ee.'

He tapped his way back to his companions and they struck up once more. Elizabeth looked at John.

'I wonder where they're heading. Do you think it could be to Helstone?'

'I don't know. I hadn't really thought about it. But yes, I suppose you're right. They're certainly not resident here.'

Elizabeth laughed; a warm sound. 'I can hardly imagine Jamaica Inn boasting its own orchestra.'

John smiled as well. 'No, I think not.' He stood up. 'Come, we've tarried long enough. Rose will be waking up.'

'You love that child more than anything, don't you.'

'Yes.' He was suddenly serious. 'Could you love her as well?'

Elizabeth gave him an enigmatic smile. 'I already do,' she answered.

The bleakness of Bodmin Moor, in contrast to the warm valleys of Devon, brought an involuntary shiver to the Apothecary. He sat, one arm round Rose, who by now was fully awake, gazing out of the window, wondering about the beast that Elizabeth had described and whether it was reality or a creature of legend. In this gaunt countryside – where there was little or no sign of the coming of spring – it was possible to imagine anything.

Bad weather lay ahead for the sky was growing dark and sporadic drops of rain had started to fall. John and Elizabeth exchanged a glance.

'Why don't we stop somewhere and make the rest of the journey in daylight?' he asked.

Elizabeth nodded. 'A good idea. As soon as we're off this accursed moor we can make for St Austell and spend the night there.'

'Shall I tell Jed?'

'No, I'll do it.'

And once again Elizabeth put her head out of the window and shouted instructions. Back came Jed's call.

'I'm glad you said that, Ma'am. This moor is terrible hard going.'

And John thought, as they bounced their way across cart tracks, that he had never known anything so uncomfortable and wondered at the bodily endurance of Rose, although until now she was clearly finding the whole thing a great adventure and had hardly noticed the rigours of the journey.

As the day darkened even further their ordeal finally came to an end. Leaving Bodmin behind them they picked up the old coaching road and journeyed to St Austell in relative comfort. Once there they made their way to The White Hart, a goodly sized inn, and booked three rooms for the night.

An hour later they dined in the parlour reserved for travellers of quality, Rose yawning and tired-eyed throughout. At the end of the meal, John excused himself temporarily and carried the child upstairs, where she went straightaway to bed. As he left the room, however, she spoke in a sleepy voice.

'Papa.'

He turned. 'Yes, sweetheart.'

'Are you staying close by?'

'I have the room next door. Now, go to sleep like a good child.'

'Will you come and see me later?'

'You know I will.'

'Goodnight, then.'

'Goodnight.'

He went downstairs and found Elizabeth where he had left her, staring into the fire, a glass of wine untouched before her on the table.

'Tell me your thoughts,' he said, smiling at her.

She looked up. 'I was thinking about my son,' she answered.

John did not know what to say so remained silent.

'Rose reminded me of him. He was so sweet when he was young, such a lovely child. I loved him with all my heart, you know.'

John merely nodded, not interrupting her flow.

'Dear Frederico, how they ruined my beautiful boy.'

The Apothecary thought then about the Society of Angels, who had once prowled the streets of Exeter and who had welcomed the Marchesa's son into their ranks and introduced him to the delights of opium smoking.

'He was so changed in the end,' Elizabeth said, and for the first time John heard a catch in her voice, 'that even I hardly recognised him.'

'You must put it behind you, Elizabeth. We all of us have tragedies to contend with. You really must let the memory go.'

She looked up at him and gave a bitter little smile. 'Yes, my friend, you have had your share of grief as I well know. Tell me, how are you coping. Really.'

'I carry on for the sake of my daughter. No, that isn't quite true. I carry on for my own sake as well. Because I still want to taste life, to know its peaks and troughs. And there's another thing as well.'

'Which is?'

'I carry on to see how we are going to end, Marchesa.'

She covered his hand with her own. 'What do you mean?'

'You know perfectly well. Every day I am drawn a little closer to you.'

'Do I? Do I know that?'

'Well, if you don't you should by now. Emilia has been dead for well over a year and…'

He broke off, not quite certain how much more he should say.

'You miss her both mentally and physically?'

'I find it lonely, yes.'

Elizabeth leant towards him. 'I long to kiss you,' she said with a smile, repeating something she had said to him a long while ago.

'And I you,' he answered, and bending his head took her in his arms.

Chapter Three

At long last she was ready for him, though why the capricious woman's mood had finally changed John was far from sure. But he did not question it, gladly accepting her eagerness to consummate their long association. Going up the stairs she leant against him and, opening her bedroom door, led him inside. Once within, with the door securely locked, they kissed long and deep. And in this kiss was all the Apothecary's pent-up loneliness and longing, together with his desire for Elizabeth which had been there from the moment he first saw her.

An unhappy memory came then, of the depths of his feelings for Emilia. Involuntarily, John sighed. Elizabeth must have heard for she put her hands on either side of his face.

'Don't be sad.'

'I'm not. In fact I am extremely happy.'

For answer she lay down on the bed and, reaching up, pulled John down beside her. For a minute they remained like that, looking intently into each other's face, then the waters of the dam broke as love finally came to them both and together they entered a world of magic.

He woke in the middle of the night, thinking he had had the most wonderful dream. Then, reaching out, he felt her, sleeping deeply but still warm and soft from loving. Lighting a candle which lay beside the bed, he took in every detail of her. The black hair was spread out like a dark veil, curling and tumbling round her head; her cheek was swept by long thick lashes; the scar which made her at once both ugly and arrestingly beautiful, was softened by the light. Silently, John wept. He wept for Emilia and the fact that his heart had moved on; he wept for Elizabeth that she had had such a hard and difficult life. Eventually though, when he had stared at her for what seemed like an age, he blew out the candle and, holding her close to him, slept better than he had for months.

He awoke early next morning and crept along the corridor

to his own room where he got into bed. But he couldn't sleep, his mind a strange mixture of peace and guilt. He knew that he had loved Emilia truly, yet now he felt completely absorbed by Elizabeth. And this gave rise to terrible feelings of regret. Yet at the same time he knew that he had fallen deeply in love with the Marchesa and that nothing could stop that passion from growing. And then, suddenly, he remembered something that he had once heard; that love was like a river that flowed into tributaries, and he knew that that was what was taking place within him. Though he would never stop loving Emilia, his flood of feeling had moved inexorably on.

He was just closing his eyes to sleep again when there was a tiny knock low down on his door.

'Come in, sweetheart,' he called, expecting Rose, and was astonished to see a very small chambermaid bearing a jug of hot water.

The Apothecary wondered whether to beg her pardon but decided to ignore it. Instead he asked, 'Have you seen my daughter? She has the room next door.'

'Oh yes, Sir. She's up and washing herself.'

John smiled. 'I'll go and help her.'

The girl bobbed a curtsey. 'If you please, Sir, I can do that. It would be more suitable.'

'She has no mother,' John said by way of explanation. 'My wife died some while ago.'

The maid looked stricken. 'Oh, I'm so sorry, Sir. I'll go to the little girl immediately.'

The Apothecary, who had been trying to clarify why it was he and not a woman who looked after his daughter, bowed to the inevitable, said, 'Thank you,' and ruefully shook his head as the maid left the room.

Half an hour later he and Rose sat at breakfast awaiting the arrival of Elizabeth. His daughter, the Apothecary was amused to see, had inherited his liking for a large repast in the mornings and was currently tucking into a sliver of ham. John was ravenously hungry and was just ordering more bread when the Marchesa swept up to the table. This morning – in his eyes at least – she looked radiant and his heart gave a disconcerting lurch at the sight of her.

He could not resist asking how she had slept.

'Very well, thank you,' she answered, and ordered tea and toast. She turned to Rose. 'Are you looking forward to seeing the Furry?'

The child nodded, her mouth being too full to speak. When she had swallowed she said, 'Tell me about it, Mrs Elizabeth.'

'Well, it's very old, probably the survival of a pagan ritual dance to do with the rite of spring. It's always danced on the 8th of May, except when that date falls on a Sunday or Monday when they change the day.'

'Go on,' said Rose.

'Couples dress up and dance in and out of people's houses and the whole town is decorated with flowers and greenery. Then as well as the Furry – or Floral Dance as it is also known – they do another strange ceremony called the Hal-an-Tow.'

Rose looked enthusiastic.

'To start off with, the youths taking part go into the neighbouring woods and gather branches of sycamore. Then they perambulate the town, waving the branches over their heads and singing the Hal-an-Tow song at various places of vantage. I don't know the words but apparently they are the survivors of a mediaeval sea shanty.'

'I told you it was Heel-and-Toe,' interrupted John.

'You're probably right.' Elizabeth gave him a look in which lay a certain fondness.

He returned the glance equally then turned to his daughter. 'So now you know some more.'

'It sounds very interesting,' she said in her advanced way, and returned to her breakfast.

An hour later they left The White Hart behind them and took the coaching road to Falmouth. From there Jed turned inland and they picked their way over rough lanes and cart tracks to Helstone.

Looking through the window, John studied the place with interest. There was one large main street with several houses and a building standing out into the thoroughfare. The other streets that he could glimpse were narrow and winding. The whole village was surrounded by pleasant hills and trees, and there was a fine church standing out to the right, while a river ran at the bottom of the town. He thought it rather enchanting and quaint.

'It's a magic place,' said Rose suddenly.

John shivered, he had no idea why. 'What makes you say that, sweetheart?'

'Because it is,' she answered, and refused to elaborate further.

They went downhill into the town, through the small streets, then turned left and found themselves in the broad thoroughfare. Elizabeth looked to her left.

'There's an inn,' she said. 'And it's called The Angel.'

'That's where we'll stay, then.'

And John put his head out of the window and called up to Jed, who pulled the coach to a halt before the main front door. Rufus jumped down and pulled down the step for John to dismount. Having handed Elizabeth out, the Apothecary turned back to lift down Rose. She came willingly enough but he felt as he picked her up that she was trembling.

'What's the matter, darling?'

'I don't know, Papa. I feel a bit frightened.'

'Of what?'

Once again she answered, 'I don't know.'

But he could pay her no more attention for the landlord was coming forward to greet them. 'Good day, Sir and Madam. How may I help you?'

'We would like some rooms,' Elizabeth answered promptly. 'We have come down for Flora Day.'

'Very good you'll find it too, Mam. Would that be two rooms you require?'

John was hoping she would say yes but she said, 'No, three.

This is my companion, Mr Rawlings. The little girl is his daughter, Rose. We also require a room for the servants, so four in total.'

Jed and Rufus appeared, bearing the luggage between them. 'As you say, Mam. Now, if you'd like to follow me.' The landlord led the way up a staircase and turned left. 'How will this be, Mam?'

He threw open the door to reveal a pleasant room that overlooked the street.

'It will suit me perfectly,' Elizabeth answered, smiling at the man, who was, John thought, quite handsome in a dark, saturnine way.

'And I thought this for the young lady.' He showed them a much smaller, darker room next door.

'Rose?'

'Where is Papa going to sleep.'

'I have a room vacant on the next floor, if that is agreeable, Sir?'

John was about to open his mouth to refuse, when Rose spoke up. 'I'd like to be up there, then I'll be close to you Papa.'

The Apothecary bowed to the inevitable. 'Very well. Do you have two rooms above, landlord?'

'I do, Sir.'

'Then kindly show us.'

Elizabeth spoke. 'I shall refresh myself after the journey. I will see you downstairs in half-an-hour, John.' And with that she disappeared into her chamber.

The Apothecary was left with no alternative but to climb another flight.

Thirty minutes later everything had been sorted out and John descended the staircase, his daughter holding his hand. He found Elizabeth in the parlour talking to a very unusual-looking woman. Small and extremely thin, she wore a big pair of spectacles which magnified her eyes to an enormous size, giving the impression that she had no other features in her face. She jumped as John entered, shooting him a nervous glance.

'Ah, my dear,' said the Marchesa, giving him a rapid kiss on the cheek. 'Are you all settled?'

'Yes, perfectly, thank you.'

'Mrs Legassick, may I present my travelling companion, John Rawlings. And this is his daughter, Rose.'

Mrs Legassick twittered nervously. 'Oh yes, how do you do? How do you do, indeed?'

She gave a sudden smile baring rather small, sharp teeth. Rose, meanwhile, made a polite bob.

'Oh, what a sweet child. How delightful.' She patted Rose's red curls with enthusiasm, her victim pulling something of a face. 'I, alas, have not had any little ones. Are we going to be friends, my dear?'

Rose remained silent, staring at the floor, and it was John who spoke up.

'She suffers with shyness from time to time. Please forgive her.'

Nothing could have been further from the truth but he felt obliged to make some kind of excuse for his daughter's unusual quietness.

'Perfectly all right,' gushed Mrs Legassick. 'Such a dear little soul. Not like the other little girl who is staying here. But, hush, I mustn't speak out of turn.'

Elizabeth asked, 'Have several people arrived to see the Floral Dance?'

'One or two. I am here with my companion, Mrs Bligh. We both originally came from Cornwall so we have returned to see the Dance. No, the child I spoke of is little Isobel, here with her mother, a Mrs Pill.'

'Isobel Pill,' said John under his breath, and catching Rose's eye, his mobile brows rose in amusement.

'They are accompanied by a Mr Painter, would you believe?' Mrs Legassick giggled nervously.

'Good gracious,' said Elizabeth. 'I can hardly wait to meet them. Who else do we have here?'

'A lady travelling alone. I believe she might well be an actress or something of that nature. She is a Miss Warwick. That about makes up the number, I think.'

'Most interesting,' said John. He turned to Elizabeth. 'Shall we stroll before we dine?'

'By all means.'

She took his arm and they stepped forth, the child holding his hand on the other side.

They found themselves in an unusually wide street down the side of which flowed a tumbling brook. To ensure that people could step over it, leats had been built which did not hide the rapid torrent that passed beneath. Rose stopped, fascinated.

'Oh look, Father. It's a stream.'

'I think it's a river, Rose. But I don't know which. Do you, Elizabeth?'

'No, but we'll find out. What an amazing thing.'

'Isn't it.'

But the Apothecary's next remarks were suddenly stilled by the sight of the three people coming towards them who could only, if their descriptions were anything to go by, be Painter and Pill, accompanied by little Isobel.

It was to the man that his eyes were drawn, as were those of Elizabeth, he noticed. Tall, just under six feet in height, with black hair tied back in a bow, he was devastatingly handsome and well aware of it. The woman, by contrast, was plain as a poppy seed, and had made no attempt at all to enhance her looks by the use of powder and paint. Shorter than her companion, she was slim but that was about all that could be said in her favour. She wore a small pair of spectacles perched on an unexceptional nose, while the mouth beneath was thin and closed like a trap. Her eyes were so nondescript as to be almost colourless, and she gazed at the world unsmilingly.

Her child, on the other hand, was quite pretty but spoilt by the most ferocious scowl. Aged about seven, or so John reckoned, she peered out belligerently at the passers-by from a rather attractive pair of eyes beneath a mop of dark hair. The Apothecary stole another glance at Painter to see if he was the father but felt fairly certain that the man was not responsible.

Isobel, aware that she was being observed, grasped Painter's hand and hid her face in his breeches, an indelicate move to say the least. Rose simply gaped, open-mouthed, at the performance.

'Mr Painter, Mr Painter,' came the muffled voice. 'Stop them staring at me.'

Painter made a bow as best he could with the child burrowing into him, and flashed his green eyes in Elizabeth's direction.

'Forgive me, Ma'am. Fact is the child's highly strung. Do apologise.'

He had a simply stunning voice, well modulated and pleasant to listen to. He was obviously a product of a first-class education, John considered.

Elizabeth laughed. 'Makes her sound like a fiddle.'

At this Mrs Pill entered the conversation.

'There's no need to be personal, Ma'am.'

'I had no intention of so being. I apologise if my remark caused offence.'

'Not at all,' said Painter, eyeing the Marchesa up. 'Apology accepted. Kathryn meant no harm, did you dear? Where are you staying?'

'At The Angel. We've just arrived.'

'Splendid, so are we – staying there I mean. Allow me to present myself. I am Timothy Painter.'

'How do you do? My name is John Rawlings.'

The men bowed. Then Tim went on, 'And this is my fiancée, Mrs Pill, and her daughter Isobel.'

Kathryn Pill bobbed a somewhat grumpy curtsey.

Elizabeth spoke up. 'I am Elizabeth di Lorenzi. I am delighted to make your acquaintance.'

Tim looked at her with a sparkle in his eye. 'You are Italian, Madam?'

'No, I am English, Sir. My late husband was a Venetian.'

'I see,' he said, and put a wealth of meaning into the two words.

Mrs Pill, clearly noticing that her companion was more than a little distracted by the exquisite Elizabeth, said, 'We must continue our promenade, I fear. Good day to you both. No doubt we shall meet again.'

'We certainly will,' said Tim Painter pointedly.

John gave him an amused look. 'It has been most interesting, Sir, Until next time.' And with that he and his party made their way up the street.

Rose turned to look at him. 'I didn't like that girl, Papa.'

'Why, darling? She didn't do anything to you.'

'Nonsense,' said the Marchesa briskly. 'She was a horrible child and there's an end to it. All that hiding her face and burying herself in the young man's leg. She's far too old for such a caper.'

John burst out laughing. 'I see that I am hopelessly out-numbered and I concede victory immediately. From now on little Isobel shall be held up as an example of what not to be.'

Rose suddenly took Elizabeth's hand. 'I am glad we came here. It is going to be unusual.'

'Why do you say that?' the Marchesa asked curiously.

'Because I believe it is,' Rose answered, and releasing her fingers, went skipping up the street.

Chapter Four

That evening, quite late, while John Rawlings embraced Elizabeth di Lorenzi before making his way back to his own room, a sound of music came from the streets below. Raising his head, John listened, then he looked at the Marchesa, who lay propped up against the pillow.

'Does that seem familiar or am I imagining it?'

'But there's an extra instrument – or two even.'

And she was up off the bed and had gone to the window, throwing open the casement in order to peer out. John followed, rather more lazily, and stood beside her.

Below them, gathered outside The Angel, were the band of musicians they had encountered in Jamaica Inn. And, sure enough, they had acquired a mandora and a fagotto player – a somewhat unusual instrument – on their journey to Helstone. Leading them was the blind fiddler, who stood in their midst, foot tapping, body swaying, giving his all. A group of people had already gathered round them and were clapping to the persistent beat. John turned to Elizabeth.

'Shall we join them? Rose is asleep so we can step outside for a while.'

But Elizabeth was already pulling on her male garb, not bothering to squeeze into her stays. John, turning from the window, admiringly watched her dress. Her figure was the same as when he had first seen it, long and lean, almost masculine had it not been for the swell of her beautiful breasts.

'You're lovely,' he said sincerely.

'You think so?' she answered with a half smile.

'You know I do.'

'Thank you.' And she turned away to complete her toilette.

Five minutes later they were ready and went down into the street to join the small crowd gathered round the musicians. There were now six instrumentalists in all: the blind fiddler himself, the man with a pair of kettledrums strapped round his waist, the flautist – a wee pixie of a person – together with the tambourine, the mandora and the fagotto players. They had also acquired along the way a monkey with a tragic face. Dressed in a jacket and a small hat, both of which had seen better days, the wretched creature had attached itself to the tambourinist. He was a spry young fellow with curly brown hair and eyes almost the same colour. But for all that he was painfully thin and looked as if he could do with a good meal or three. The mandora player, on the other hand, although also thin, had the look of an aesthete, being long of hair and nose, and with a cultivated manner which added to the languid way he plucked the instrument's strings. The fagotto blower, on the other hand, was fat and friendly, puffing his cheeks out as he played and generally looking round him with an amusing twinkle in his eye, making the crowd laugh. While the man with the kettledrums appeared a regular rogue, having a craggy face and periwinkle eyes which he fastened on the Marchesa with a very naughty gaze.

'What a motley crew,' she said laughing.

'But they make a good sound,' John answered. He bowed to her. 'Shall we dance?'

'Why not?'

And the couple whirled off, only to be joined by others, so that in the end everyone – with the exception of one or two elderly people – was prancing away to the music. Eventually, though, it came to an end and the blind fiddler, assisted by the young tambourine player, sent the monkey round with a hat. As the creature approached, its two keepers not far behind, the Apothecary spoke.

'Well done. Your music is most enjoyable.' The monkey rattled the hat which had a few coins in the bottom. 'Now, I'd better pay you, young fellow.' John put out a tentative finger towards the creature but it backed away nervously. 'Where did you get him?' he enquired of the tambourine man who had joined the group.

The young chap bowed low. 'Hello, Sir. I'm Gideon. I remember playing for you in Jamaica Inn. We actually bought him at a market. He had been with a band before apparently but for some reason was put up for sale. I think his previous owner died.'

'He seems very nervous. Do you think he was badly treated?'

'More than likely. We picked him up for very little money.'

Elizabeth said in her straightforward way, 'Well, I expect he'll be well fed with you – and loved as best you can.'

The young man answered simply, 'It's hard to love a monkey but I must admit to having certain feelings of fondness for it.'

'Then that's as well.' The Marchesa put a shilling in the hat, as did John. The sad monkey's face contorted into something resembling a grin before it scampered away to its next customers. The fiddler shuffled up to them. 'Thank'ee, Sir. I'll play again.'

He picked up his bow once more and the Apothecary, at close quarters now, studied the man. He was unkempt, that much was certain. A great tangle of black hair, streaked here and there with grey, was visible beneath the battered hat he always wore, which was an amazing creation, sporting a selection of dilapidated feathers at one side. It reminded the Apothecary of drawings of Robin Hood he had seen from time to time, and he could not help wondering whether the fiddler ever removed it.

Beneath this fantastic head of hair were a pair of black spectacles, worn no doubt to hide his sightless eyes from the world, which sat atop a hawkish nose. His face, stained a deep brown by constant exposure to the elements, was pitted with the scars of smallpox, and indeed one could have declared him to be a regular vagabond had it not been for his mouth. For this was passionate and well-formed, the mouth of a sensualist. It was, the Apothecary concluded, the one thing that betrayed him to be a musician, speaking as it did of finer feelings.

Apart from this unusual quality the fiddler was thin, reasonably tall, and despite his lack of flesh, strong and wiry. Yet again, his hands were exquisite; small and beautifully shaped as well as being nimble, one running over the strings like a bird in flight, the other guiding the bow to produce beautiful sounds. John, watching him, felt drawn to the man despite his strange appearance.

Elizabeth meanwhile was stamping her feet and clapping, and when a strange young man bowed before her and led her off to dance, John could only smile half-heartedly as he watched them whirl down the street. It was then that he felt a tug at his hand and, looking down, saw Rose.

'What are you doing up?' he asked, somewhat crossly.

'Isobel woke me,' she answered, her great eyes awash with tears.

John crouched down. 'What do you mean?'

'She came into my room and stood staring at me. Don't be cross, Papa.'

He was filled with tenderness. 'I'm not, sweetheart. I just want to know what happened.'

'I told you. Isobel entered my room and stared at me.'

'Did you speak to her?'

'No. But, oh Papa, it was the expression on her face. It was as if she wanted to kill me.'

'Well, stay up for a bit then I'll go back and sit with you. And tomorrow morning I'll speak to her mother.'

'What will you say?'

'I shall tell her what occurred and ask for an explanation. Don't worry, darling, it won't happen again I promise you.'

Elizabeth, breathless and laughing, was brought back by the young man, who was in very much the same condition. Seeing Rose's unhappy face she stopped short but at a silent signal from John, said nothing. His daughter, meanwhile, having cried a little, was being cheered by the atmosphere in the crowd.

'It's exciting, Papa.'

'Isn't it. Now, listen carefully. The blind fiddler is just about to start again. And, see, he's got a tame monkey with him.'

They stood enthralled while the tatterdemalion band struck

up once more and played their music to the ever-growing group of people. Rose, John noticed, could not take her eyes from the small simian, which walked round and round with the hat, collecting quite a goodly sum in the process. Eventually, though, they played their final chord, took a bow, and wandered off in the direction of The Blue Anchor. Elizabeth smiled at Rose.

'Are you tired?'

'Yes. But Papa said he would sit with me while I go to sleep.'

'Well then, so he shall.'

They went back into The Angel and John carried the half-asleep child upstairs and put her to bed.

'Rose, do you want me to lock you in?'

'No, I wouldn't like that. Just sit beside me.'

But something made him stay even when Rose's breathing deepened until he, too, dozed off in the chair beside the bed. How long he remained like that he couldn't say but he woke suddenly to find that all was dark, the candle which had been burning having guttered out while he slept. John froze in the darkness, aware of a sound over by the door. There could be no doubt of it. Someone was entering the room.

He stood up silently, crossing the small space as quietly as he could, but a floorboard creaked beneath his weight. Realising that the other person would now be aware of his presence, he sprinted to the door and threw it open. There was nobody there but hurling himself up the corridor he spied a small figure clad in a nightgown. It would appear that Isobel had decided to torment his daughter once more.

The next morning at breakfast John once again signalled to Elizabeth not to ask any questions, though he could see that she was longing to know exactly what was happening. He did say, however, that he was anxious to talk to Mrs Pill and her daughter.

'I don't believe they are down yet. The only people I have seen so far are the two ladies, Mrs Legassick and Mrs Bligh. They went out early to perambulate.'

'Wait a minute. I can hear someone coming now.'

They turned their heads to the door but the vision that entered was nobody that either the Apothecary or the Marchesa had seen before. However, this did not stop either of them staring round-eyed. For the woman was indeed a sight to behold.

Dressed to the inch in the very latest fashion, her head covered by a superb hat, her jewels glittering in the morning light, she waved at them nonchalantly before drifting across the dining parlour to take a seat. John frankly could not take his eyes off her.

He guessed her to be in her forties but she had that timeless quality of all great beauties. The setting of her face was stunning – or had once been so – though the Apothecary could see a certain hardness about her visage which made him wonder exactly what her antecedents were. Her hair, though vividly blonde, was beautifully arranged beneath her hat, and the rest of her features were perfect, everything from her great, luminous eyes to her sweet little mouth which was superbly placed. Feeling John's gaze, she turned politely.

'Good morning to you, Sir. A nice day, is it not?'

He was thoroughly nonplussed. Rising from his chair he made his very best bow. 'Indeed it is, Madam. May I present myself? My name is John Rawlings.' He bowed again.

She returned the salute graciously, bowing from the waist. 'And I am Diana Warwick. How do you do.' Her gaze swept down and took in Elizabeth. 'And this is Mrs Rawlings?'

'No, Madam. I am Elizabeth di Lorenzi, widow of the Marchese di Lorenzi of Venice.'

'I am honoured to make your acquaintance, Ma'am.'

'As I am yours.'

'This is my daughter, Rose Rawlings,' John added somewhat lamely, frankly daunted by the combined power of these two extraordinary women.

Diana Warwick's glance took in Rose as if she were preparing to sketch her. Eventually, she said, 'You have very beautiful hair, child.'

John's daughter smiled dutifully. 'Thank you, Ma'am.'

It was at this juncture that Mrs Pill and Isobel entered the room, Tim, a lazy grin on his face, bringing up the rear. He cast his eyes round, saw Elizabeth, and gave a magnificent bow.

The Apothecary fixed Isobel with a meaningful glance to which she responded by pulling a face. Furious, he was about to go over and have it out there and then, but Elizabeth laid a restraining hand on his arm.

But more was happening. Diana Warwick had noticed the handsome man bowing to Elizabeth and was making little movements at her table in order to attract attention, which, after a few moments, she succeeded in doing. Tim Painter, on the point of sitting down, saw the dazzling woman in the corner and was frankly making a banquet of her with his eyes. Kathryn Pill's momentary look of annoyance was rapidly overtaken by a somewhat phoney smile. She gave a small curtsey in Miss Warwick's direction, then sat down and took to ordering her breakfast in a business-like manner. Tim, after bowing fulsomely once more, also took his seat.

'It would appear that the lady has made an impression,' murmured John.

Elizabeth gave a cat-like smile. 'Mrs Pill covers her anger well,' she whispered back.

The Apothecary dropped his voice even lower. 'How old do you think Miss Warwick is?'

The Marchesa ran her eye over the woman who was by now glancing at a newspaper as she sipped her tea. 'Same as me. In her late forties.'

John stared at her. 'I never think of you as that age. To me you will always be young and alluring.'

Elizabeth laughed aloud. 'Maybe, but how does the rest of the world see me, that is the question?'

'Well, if our Mr Painter is anything to go by I would imagine very much as I do.'

She did not reply but instead stretched out her hand and

laid it on John's arm. For a moment there was silence, then Rose spoke.

'That horrible Isobel is looking at me.'

'Well stare at her, do. You've nothing to be afraid of Rose. She can't hurt you.'

His daughter looked up at him. 'I'm not so sure of that, Papa.'

Breakfast over, John went to tackle Mrs Pill. Crossing to her table he gave a formal bow and said, 'I wonder if I might have a word, Madam?'

Kathryn regarded him icily. 'Pray do.'

'I would rather it was in private.'

Tim Painter looked up, the expression in his eyes one of amused laziness. 'I'll leave you then.'

'I feel you should be present, Sir. But I really meant could we speak somewhere else, not in so public a place.'

Isobel spoke in a whining tone. 'What does he want, Mama?'

Mrs Pill looked at her lovingly. 'Nothing, my sweetheart. But I think it best if you go for a walk with Mr Painter.'

'I don't want to.'

'Neither do I,' added Tim.

Mrs Pill pursed her plain lips together but instantly gave in. 'Then in that case you must both remain. Shall we step into the other parlour?'

'Certainly,' said John.

Once inside the other room, deserted except for an elderly gentleman scanning a paper, he came directly to the point.

'Mrs Pill, your daughter is terrorising mine. She came into Rose's room, waking her up, and stood there silently staring at her.'

The unprepossessing features worked, then she said, 'That is not possible, Sir. I think your child is fabricating the whole story. Isobel sleeps in my room and was with me the entire night.'

'But I saw her with my own eyes. After Rose told me what

had happened I waited in her room and heard the intruder for myself. I rushed to the door and witnessed your daughter disappearing up the corridor.'

Mrs Pill's mouth tightened to a trap. 'I cannot credit what you are saying, Sir. You must have seen someone else. Isobel did not leave my side.'

It was hopeless and John knew it. In the face of such a staunch denial he had no option other than to make a stiff bow, bid the trio an abrupt good morning, and angrily withdraw.

Chapter Five

To say that John was angry was understating the case. He fumed his way back to the breakfast room, banging the parlour door loudly behind him. Starting to speak to Elizabeth before he could even see her, he discovered to his chagrin that the room was empty. Standing for a moment or two, feeling utterly foolish, shuffling from one foot to the other, he eventually made his way out of The Angel and into the street.

To the right of the inn stood an open courtyard beyond which were the stables and coach house. In the distance the Apothecary could see the Marchesa, holding Rose's hand, talking to Jed the coachman, together with their guard, Rufus. He started to make his way towards them, then stopped, intrigued by a well which stood in the stable yard. Its outer wall was about three feet in height, not nearly high enough in view of the well's enormous depth which, when he peered down into the darkness, seemed to him to be about forty feet. Indeed it was so deep that it was impossible to glimpse the bottom. Above the well was a device for lowering buckets on a rope, at present hanging idly. Intrigued, John leant over once again, but even though he allowed time for his eyes to adjust to the darkness he caught but the merest glint of the water below.

'Trying to see the bottom, Sir?' It was one of the inn's hostlers who spoke.

'Yes. It seems very far down.'

'That's because the water level is low. It rises and falls according to the weather, y'see.'

'Well, well,' John answered, then realised what he had said and grimaced.

The hostler chuckled. 'Ah, the old ones are always the best, Sir.'

'Indeed.' The Apothecary straightened up from leaning on the wall. 'Nice to speak with you, my friend.'

'I'm always around the yard, Sir, if you need to know

anything about the old place. Worked here since I was a lad, like.'

'We'll have a chat about it some time but presently I can see my friend and my daughter. Good day to you.'

'Good day, Sir.'

They parted company, John joining Elizabeth. Rose immediately turned to her father.

'What did she say, Papa?'

'Nothing very much.' He decided to be honest with the child. 'Actually they denied everything. Said that Isobel did not stir all night.'

Rose went as red as the flower after which she was named. 'But you saw her.'

'I know I did. I can't think why her mother is being so duplicitous.'

'Because she probably wasn't there with her. She was probably out with Mr Painter.'

'You know I think you're right,' John answered. He smoothed Rose's curls which in her agitation had started flying wild. 'Anyway I believe it best we forget it now. Let us speak of other things. Elizabeth?'

'You are utterly right. We are here on holiday, after all. So sweetheart, what would you like to do today?'

'Go in search of the monkey,' John's daughter answered promptly, then looked puzzled when both her father and the Marchesa burst out laughing.

They did see the blind fiddler's band, complete with its simian pet, quite frequently during the next three days. In fact, John thought, it was hard to avoid them. Wherever they went, either in the town or the surrounding countryside, they seemed to come across them, much to the delight of Rose.

On the day before the Furry Dance they set forth in the carriage to see the sea. It was only a short ride to the nearest point, Porthleven, and fortunately the day was fine. Rose was brimming with joy throughout the journey. John, watching her, felt a tug at his heartstrings that his late wife, Emilia, was not there to observe the child as she first glimpsed the vastness of the ocean. But he firmly thrust such ideas away, knowing that to dwell on the past would do neither him nor Rose any good. Instead he shared his daughter's pleasure, hanging out of the carriage window beside her as the sea appeared in all its tumbling glory.

'It's wonderful,' breathed Rose. She pulled John's sleeve. 'Why haven't I seen it before?'

'Because we live in London. That's a long way from the sea.'

They abandoned the coach and made their way on foot to a wide cove where all three removed their shoes and paddled in the waves. Poignantly reminded of his honeymoon, which he and Emilia had spent in Devon, John remained somewhat quiet and withdrawn. But if Elizabeth noticed this she said nothing, while Rose was too preoccupied with the sand and the shells and the snow-capped waves to be even aware of his silence. After a while the two adults sat side-by-side on the damp shingle while John's daughter played by herself. The Apothecary sighed.

'Poor Rose. She could do with a companion.'

Elizabeth's black hair caught on the wind and a big strand of it blew loose. 'Well, no doubt you will provide her with one in time.'

'What do you mean?'

'My dear, you are bound to remarry and have more children. You will meet somebody, have no fear.'

'I have already met her,' John answered, leaning back on his elbows and watching Elizabeth through eyes narrowed against the sun.

She turned to him, the expression on her face serious. 'But, John, I have no wish to marry again. Oh, it's not because I still yearn for my husband. I have put those memories behind me years since. No, it is because now I am independent and have been for such a long time that I could no longer bear the thought of sharing my life with another. Do you understand?'

'No.'

'I have explained the situation to the best of my ability,' the Marchesa said coldly.

'I find what you say incomprehensible. Surely everyone wants to find a mate.'

'You do, most certainly. But I would prefer to have you as a lover.'

'Then there is no chance of you following me to London when I go?'

Elizabeth gazed out to sea, pulling the remaining strands of hair loose so that it blew round her face. 'I will visit you for a season but that is as far as the mood will take me.'

'Do I mean nothing to you?' asked the Apothecary petulantly.

She turned swiftly and kissed him full on the lips. 'As much if not more than my husband. But it is I who have changed. Besides, I am older than you. You must find a young woman, John. A woman who can give you a family.'

Why, thought the Apothecary, do I have to fall in love with such difficult women? First Coralie Clive, the actress, wedded to the theatre and not to a husband. Then Emilia Alleyn, who had loved another man until the time she met John. And now the most confusing of them all; Elizabeth di Lorenzi who was determined to follow her own path – and follow it alone.

He sighed aloud and the Marchesa laughed and tickled him under the chin. 'There, John. Be of stout heart. You are young yet.'

He got to his feet, rather inelegantly. 'Come along. Time we went back.'

But Elizabeth was not paying attention, instead gazing out to sea. 'What's that ship making for the beach?'

John stared. 'I'm not sure. But there's something about it I don't like the look of.'

'I wouldn't be surprised if it was smugglers.'

'Not landing goods in daylight, surely?'

Elizabeth gave him a loving look. 'Oh, my sweet London boy. How innocent you are. The blackguards round this coastline are in charge of events. The number of law enforcers is pitiful compared with the smuggling gangs, which can number up to a hundred strong. But I think you're right about that vessel. Let us be off.'

They called Rose, who came reluctantly, the pockets of her dress full of shells. Rapidly John dried off her feet and put on her shoes and stockings.

'We're going to explore, my darling. So please to hurry.'

'But I want to watch the ship that's coming in.'

'We can see that from further away. Now come along.'

Eventually they dragged her away from the beach and made their way to the place where the fishermen's boats were moored. There were several boats tied up within its embrace including a somewhat larger vessel than was customary. Elizabeth looked it over with a seasoned eye.

'As I thought. I feel certain the fisherfolk have another, more lucrative, way of making a living. Do you agree?'

'I do, Madam. I spy a low-life ale house further down the path. Would you be seen dead in such a place?'

'I would certainly. And to make my point, I reckon they serve some goodly spirits within.'

John chuckled, his good temper returning. 'Then let us go and sample them.'

It was indeed a rough establishment. The place was thick with tobacco smoke which had discoloured both walls and ceiling, further it was packed with disreputable characters who mixed freely with honest fishermen. From the beams were hanging various bottles and herbs, and for a minute John was reminded of his Apothecary's shop and felt a moment's pang of nostalgia. Every eye turned to look at Elizabeth – probably the first woman ever to enter the place – and there were several growls and whistles of a lewd kind. John fixed the perpetrators with as dark as look as he dared, and bowed the Marchesa to a ramshackle stool, the only seat available.

Just as she had predicted, the cognac was of the finest and was clearly an illegal import, probably coming from Guernsey where English taxes did not apply. However, after one glass John grew anxious about Rose, who had been left in the carriage under the watchful eye of Jed, and he and Elizabeth made their way back. But they stopped short as they rounded the bend and the coach came into their line of sight, for Rose was standing outside talking to a woman. The Apothecary began to increase his stride but Elizabeth laid her hand on his arm.

'Don't John. She's talking to a Charmer.'

'A what?'

'A wise woman. This one is a Romany, a gypsy. She won't do her any harm.'

John stared at the owner of tanned skin and black hair which had been plaited, long and thick, hanging to the gypsy's waist. Into the plait she had woven flowers, while on her hip the woman carried a basket full of pegs, lace mats, lucky charms, and heather tied up in little bunches. Even while he watched he saw her hand Rose something, in response to which the child gave a polite bob. He would have called out but yet again Elizabeth silenced him.

'John, I told you, the woman is harmless. Rose is lucky to have been blessed by her.'

The sound of their voices must have carried on the breeze because both the gypsy and John's daughter turned their heads in the direction of the newcomers. John caught a flash from eyes clear and fresh, then the woman heaved up her basket and walked away, leaving Rose gazing at the object in her fist.

'What did the Charmer give you, sweetheart?' asked Elizabeth as they approached.

'A good luck charm. See.' And she held out her hand.

John stared at a tiny little doll, about two inches in length and made of old bits of material sewn together.

'That looks interesting,' was all he could think of saying.

'She said it was very powerful and would protect me. That I must carry it always.'

'Well then you must do so,' John answered seriously.

'I shall, Papa.' She slid her hand into his. 'She was nice, you know.'

'I'm sure she was. Did she tell you her name?'

'Yes. It's Gypsy Orchard. She's on her way to Helstone to sell her wares.'

'We shall probably pass her on the way back.'

And they did. As the coach left Porthleven and headed for the Angel Inn they saw the woman, strolling down the lane, quite solitary, but singing to herself as she went. Rose leaned out and waved, and again John had a flash of those clear wide eyes as Gypsy Orchard returned the salute.

Chapter Six

It was the night before the Floral Dance and the whole of the evening the town had been filling up with people, while the residents were busy decorating their houses with greenery and flowers. John, having put Rose to bed, had entrusted her into the care of Jed and Rufus, who were downstairs in the taproom consuming ale, and had walked round Helstone with Elizabeth, who had linked her arm through his in a familiar manner he had found extremely pleasing. Everywhere they looked, the citizens had been leaning from windows or shinning up ladders adorning their dwelling places with boughs, floral tributes, or a proliferation of both. The effect of this was to fill the town with a fresh smell which he had found quite delicious.

As they had promenaded they had met several of The Angel's other guests. First they had seen Mrs Legassick accompanied by Mrs Bligh. John, who had not met the other woman before, was amused to observe that she was much younger than her companion. Quite petite, with a very good figure and reasonably pretty hair, she clearly fancied herself as being extremely attractive to the opposite sex, and made much of curtseying, simultaneously casting her eyes upwards then over the Apothecary. He could not resist kissing her hand and enquiring how she fared.

'I am extremely well, Sir. What fine company we have staying in our hotel to be sure. Why with you and Mr Painter I declare we hold the monopoly on the most handsome men in town.'

Mrs Legassick had fluttered about. 'Oh, Cousin, how forward of you. Shame on you. Shame I say.'

Mrs Bligh had given her an amused glance. 'Come now, Muriel, you have the same thoughts but are too nervous to voice them.'

'Oh la, Tabitha, I should die of mortification to speak as freely as you do.'

'Oh stuff.'

All this was said in a light-hearted bantering way, much to John's relief, and Elizabeth saved any potential embarrassment by laughing, though John suspected it was politeness which made her do so. However at that moment the two ladies were joined by two men, who hastened up to them through the crowd.

'Ah, my dears, we are so glad we have found you. We asked for you at The Angel but they said you were strolling through the streets.'

'Strolling the streets,' echoed the other man.

'Oh Cousins, we're delighted to meet up with you.' Mrs Legassick turned to Elizabeth. 'My dear Marchesa, may I present my cousins Geoffrey and Gregory Colquite?'

'Indeed you may.'

'Cousins, this is the Marchesa di Lorenzi.'

Mrs Legassick said this with an awed sound in her voice and John wondered that Elizabeth did not use her more important title of Lady Elizabeth. But she was a mettlesome woman and probably would have taken any suggestion of that as foolish.

The two male cousins bowed, then straightened simultaneously, giving the impression that they were marionettes. But other than their similarities of speech and movement, they could not have been more unalike. One was extremely tall, well over six foot and with not a spare ounce of flesh on him anywhere. He was also, the Apothecary thought, totally bald beneath his wig, which bestrode his dome uneasily being somewhat on the tight side. The other man was quite short, not much over five foot, and inclined to be tubby. The tall man had a pair of spectacles which flashed over pale blue eyes; the short man had vivid brown eyes which sparkled as he spoke, which he now did.

'My dear Madam, it is a pleasure to be presented to you.'

'A pleasure,' echoed the other one.

They both bowed again and Elizabeth swept a curtsey. 'Gentlemen, the delight is mine.'

Mrs Legassick spoke. 'Let me explain our family. We are all Cornishmen – and women of course.' She tittered noisily. 'But both Mrs Bligh and I married Englishmen, who, alas, predeceased us. Consequently we decided to pool our resources and share a home. The brothers Colquite are the sons of our uncle Josiah and we often see them when we come visiting Cornwall.'

'Where do you live?' asked John, curious.

'In Wiltshire,' Tabitha Bligh replied, twinkling her eyes and tossing her blonde head.

'It's an awful journey for them,' said the short plump one, whom the Apothecary had identified as Geoffrey. 'In fact we are determined for you both to move back here.'

'Move back,' repeated Gregory.

Mrs Legassick neighed. 'We shall have to wait and see about that.'

Elizabeth curtseyed again. 'If you will forgive us. We have to meet someone.'

There was a good deal of bobbing and bowing but eventually the four moved off down the street.

'Neatly done,' said John appreciatively.

'I was afraid that we might find ourselves too long in their company.'

But they got no further in their walk, both of them stopping in their tracks to stare. For coming towards them was the exquisite Diana Warwick in company with Tim Painter, who was doing his very best in the way of being charming.

'And where is Mrs Pill?' said Elizabeth under her breath.

'Stuck with horrible little Isobel, I'll warrant,' answered John, and burst out laughing.

Seeing them, the couple stopped and Tim gave the most elegant of bows.

'Greetings, Sir and Madam. A fine night is it not.'

'Very fine, Sir.'

'It should be good weather for the Floral Dance tomorrow,' Diana ventured.

'Certainly. And how is Mrs Pill?' asked Elizabeth in that direct way of hers.

Tim gave a careless laugh. 'It seems little Isobel is unwell and she is ministering to the invalid.'

John couldn't help but laugh in return. 'Too much wandering round the corridors at night, I expect.'

'Indubitably. The child is an accomplished liar by the way.'

Diana Warwick gave Tim a surprised glance. 'How can you say that about your own daughter?'

'She's nothing to do with me, Madam. She is the offspring of old man Pill. She was six years old when I met her mother. But, believe me, she grows nastier with each passing year.'

'Is Mrs Pill then a widow?' This from Elizabeth.

'Yes. Her husband was considerably older than she. He died when the child was four.'

Leaving Mrs Pill on the lookout for someone to take care of her, thought the Apothecary. Not that he considered Tim Painter a good choice by any manner of means.

Diana Warwick gave a truly delightful smile. 'My, it's getting late. I suggest we cross the road, Sir,' she said, quite inconsequentially.

Tim looked slightly startled as the beauty dropped a hasty curtsey and literally fled to the other side of the street. Bowing, he mumbled an apology and joined her. John stared at Elizabeth.

'Well, I've seen some odd exits in my time and that was certainly one of them.'

'It was almost as if she had seen someone she was trying to get away from,' the Marchesa answered thoughtfully. She stared up the street but there was no one except a middle-aged man with a long wig and a great stick, somewhat old-fashioned in his garb, walking along, quite alone.

'Very strange,' the Apothecary replied. He offered Elizabeth his arm and they continued on their way.

After having wandered around for a while strains of music filled their ears, and at the bottom of the town, where Coinage

Hall Street sloped steeply away, they could see a crowd dancing. Elizabeth smiled.

'I'll wager the monkey will do well tonight.'

'And not only he.'

For sitting on a barrel outside The Blue Anchor, Gypsy Orchard was telling fortunes.

'I must go and hear mine.'

'No,' John answered, for ever since an old woman had foretold the death of Emilia he had had a dread of such things.

Elizabeth had given him a direct look. 'If I didn't know you better I would say you were afraid.'

'Frankly, I fear what they will say. I'd rather you didn't go.'

'But, my dear, I am determined. Go into the hostelry and drink some ale. I will cross the woman's palm with silver.'

John had no option but to comply and went into The Blue Anchor determined to belittle whatever it was that the gypsy foretold. Inside, somewhat to his surprise, he found Tim Painter, who had obviously abandoned Miss Warwick and gone in search of his own pleasures, sitting on a settle with a slim young man of about twenty years of age, who was squeezed up next to a fat man. They were both, judging by the look of them, well in their cups, and the Apothecary thought that Mr Painter must have downed several pints fast since being in the company of Diana Warwick.

'How do,' said Tim companionably. He edged up on the wooden bench so that John had room to sit, somewhat uncomfortably. 'What would you like to drink, Sir?'

John, feeling suddenly reckless, said, 'A pint of ale, if you please.'

'Good choice, my friend. Good choice. It's brewed on the premises, don't you know. Strong and powerful.' He stood up and went in pursuit of a serving wench.

The Apothecary turned to the other man. 'Good evening, Sir. I'm afraid we haven't been introduced.'

'Nicholas Kitto, Sir. A native of Helstone.' He attempted to rise in order to bow but found himself incapable of movement, partly because the man on his right was so huge that had Nicholas relinquinshed the seat he would never have been able to squeeze back in.

John smiled sympathetically. 'Rawlings, Sir. John Rawlings. Of London.'

'A pleasure to meet you, Sir. You've travelled a long way to see the Furry Dance. Were you already in the area?'

'I've been staying in Devon but must soon head back for town, alas. But my companion insisted that I see this ancient tradition before I go.'

'How wise of him.'

'Her, actually.'

'Ah,' Nicholas answered.

John wondered momentarily whether he should say that Elizabeth was merely a friend but decided that such a statement would appear gauche, as well as being totally untrue. He let the moment pass.

Tim appeared with a wench bearing their order and requesting the Apothecary to move up, forced his way back onto the settle.

'A health to all,' he said, raising his glass.

John, liking the man for all his obvious faults, did likewise. While he drank he studied Nick, who had a certain indefinable air about him, though of what the Apothecary was not certain.

He was a good-looking young fellow and had made an out-of-town effort with his clothes, which were reasonably cut though of a hideous plum shade which clashed horribly with his red hair. In fact he was pretty highly coloured, having bright pink cheeks and a great mass of freckles. Yet despite these handicaps he had an air of refinement, his features being clean cut and rather becoming. John, watching him, wondered about the young man's parentage. But Tim was speaking.

'Here's to both you good fellows. I've never met either of you before but I feel as if we have always known one another.'

The Apothecary, forcing his mind back to the present moment, gave a somewhat sickly grin, but Nicholas, who clearly lacked friends of his own age, responded with enthusiasm.

'I'll drink to that and gladly, Sir.'

It was at that particular instant that John felt rather than witnessed the entire ale house become quiet and somehow tense. Turning, he saw that Elizabeth had walked in alone – enough to frighten the local population – and rising he went immediately to her side to show that she was not unescorted.

'Well?' he said.

'Well what?'

'What did the gypsy have to say? Anything of interest?'

He was looking directly into her face, treating the whole thing as a joke – or attempting to. And just for a split second he saw the expression in her eyes, dreamy yet alarmed, before the shutters came down and she answered, 'My dear, the usual stuff, that is all. But she amused me so it was worth the money.'

He knew by her intonation that he would get no more out of her, so decided to play the game accordingly. 'Did you buy any good luck charms?'

'No, but she gave me this.'

Elizabeth held out her hand and he saw a small hare, this one made of metal unlike Rose's little doll.

'The golden hare,' said the Apothecary, picking it up.

'Yes, she said to be careful of it,' answered the Marchesa. She smiled. 'Here, you have it.'

'No, no. I'll buy one myself,' John answered.

'I insist. It's a present for you.'

'Very well. I accept. Thank you very much.' And he tucked the hare away, deep in a pocket.

Bidding good night to Tim and Nicholas, who blushed a violent shade of red on seeing the Marchesa, they made their way out into Coinage Hall Street. But Gypsy Orchard had gone and the crowds were beginning to thin out. Thinking to himself that Elizabeth was in an odd mood, brought on no doubt by having her fortune told, the Apothecary walked quietly back to The Angel where he wished her good evening and went to his own room.

Chapter Seven

He was awoken at first light by the noise of drums beating out a strange and exotic rhythm, and for a moment or two John Rawlings lay quite still, thinking how pagan was the sound and imagining primitive man worshipping the sun to such an insistent beat. The music struck a chord with some odd emotion within himself, and getting out of bed, dressed only in his nightshirt, he crossed to the window and threw back the shutters. Below him in the street he could make out the forms of several young men, each one carrying branches of red and white may blossom. They were chanting the words of a strange song and John threw up the window and put his head out, the better to listen.

> *'Robin Hood and Little John,*
> *They both are gone to the fair O!*
> *And we will go to the merry green wood,*
> *To see what they do there O!*
> *And for to chase O!*
> *To chase the buck and doe O!*
> *With Hal-an-Tow,*
> *Jolly rumble O!'*

So this was the famous Hal-an-Tow song. Surely its similarity to a sea shanty and the title itself, so reminiscent of Heel-and-Toe, were indicative of its origin. But the men were singing the chorus and the Apothecary craned his ears once more.

> *'And we were up as soon as any day O!*
> *And for to fetch the Summer home,*
> *The Summer and the May O!*
> *For Summer is a come O!*
> *And Winter is a gone O!'*

John stepped back into the room, wondering about the origins of both the Furry and Hal-an-Tow. One was a survivor of paganism, that much was certain. But exactly how and when it had started neither he nor anyone else could be certain. He had heard several versions of the origin of the dance. One that Saint Michael had been engaged in an airborne battle with the Devil for the possession of Helstone. Needless to say the Archangel won, gaining his victory by throwing a stone at Satan which caused him to fall, beaten, into Loe Pool. The inhabitants, who were watching from below, danced with joy at this angelic triumph. Another version of this story told how the battle took place in France, causing Saint Michael to retreat from his Mount on that side of the Channel to St Michael's Mount in Cornwall. Satan, afraid of crossing the water, lifted off the lid of Hell and hurled it at his adversary. Once again the missile missed but fell right in the centre of Helstone. Where, or so John had been reliably informed, it was to this day built into the wall of The Angel. There was even a third version in which a fiery dragon passed over the town, slain, of course, by Saint Michael.

Washing in cold water and shaving as best he could, the Apothecary dressed in workaday clothes, afraid of anything better getting damaged by the general high spirits of the crowd. Then he went next door to wake his daughter.

She was not only up but struggling into her clothes, a sight that touched him to the heart. He stood in silence for a moment, she unaware of his presence, and watched her wrestling with her dress. Then he coughed politely. Rose spun round and saw him.

'Oh, Papa. Did you hear the music? It is so exciting. I can't wait to go and see them.'

'Come here then, sweetheart. You are trying to get your arm through the neck opening. Let me help you.'

She stood still but he could tell that she was seething with excitement and as soon as he had fastened up the last button and put on her shoes, Rose headed for the door.

'Wait a minute, child. Have you cleaned your teeth?'

'No,' she answered reluctantly.

'Then kindly do so.' And he handed her a little pot containing a mixture he had prepared himself, one of the main constituents of which was Portugal snuff and another gum myrrh.

Rose hurried through the proceedings then turned to the Apothecary, breathing enthusiastically into his face. He waved a hand in front of his nose.

'Very powerful. Now come along.'

As they passed the Marchesa's door, Rose asked, 'Should we wake Mrs Elizabeth?'

'No, it's a little early. She'll come down when she's ready.'

So saying they went into the street outside and looked around.

A goodly collection of men and boys, the youngest being about fourteen years of age, were heading up Coinage Hall Street, banging drums and various other noisy instruments. As well as bearing May blossom they also had greenery in their hats, together with great smiles and a deal of noisy laughter. John, again struck by the primitive sight, listened to another verse of the song.

'Where are those Spaniards
That make so great a boast O!
They shall eat the grey goose feather
And we will eat the roast O!
In every land O!
The land where'er we go
With Hal-an-tow O!
Jolly Rumble O!'

So there was a line in it that spoke of the Spanish Armada, while the grey goose feathers referred to the arrows of English archers.

Like the bowmen of Agincourt, thought John, and felt patriotic and proud.

On the opposite side of the street he could see Kathryn Pill and Isobel, clapping their hands noisily and making much of waving at the group of singers. Standing a little further down from them were the four cousins, Muriel Legassick, Tabitha Bligh, together with Gregory and Geoffrey Colquite. They seemed to have gathered several friends with them, including one large lady with a sweep of white hair beneath a huge hat, and very large, very sensual eyes. She caught the Apothecary gazing at her and gave him a slow secretive smile. Slightly disconcerted, John looked away.

Isobel was making the usual fuss, refusing to hold her mother's hand and stamping her foot. Even while he watched her the child twisted out of Mrs Pill's grip and ran into the crowd of singers, joining in their song with a 'la la', sung hopelessly out of tune.

'Isobel, come here,' shouted the mother, but to no avail. The child continued to dance along with the men, some of whom were annoyed, one or two smiling with embarrassment, but the majority frankly angry.

'Trust *her*,' said John.

A big lad, tall and well built, leant down to the girl and said, 'Move along, little lady. This be a man's dance.' And he put his hand on her shoulder.

What happened next was unbelievable. Isobel turned on him like a savage dog and sunk her teeth into his flesh, drawing blood. The man let out a howl of pain and moved rapidly away, at which several of the other band of singers turned on the child.

'Out you little witch. Be off with you before we call the Constable.'

Isobel stood there looking defiant, then she poked out her tongue to its full length and ran as fast as her legs could carry her down the hill, out of Coinage Hall Street, and off in the general direction of Loe Pool. Kathryn, after a moment's hesitation, followed in pursuit, shrieking, 'Come here, Isobel. Come here!'

John, glad that he had Rose with him and a valid excuse not to join in the chase, said, 'What a perfectly horrible child.'

'I'm not like that am I, Papa?'

'Not in the least I'm delighted to say.'

He picked Rose up and swung her onto his shoulders, 'There. Can you see better?'

'Yes. Shall we follow the singers?'

'We certainly shall.'

'Won't Mrs Elizabeth wonder where we are?'

'We'll go back soon and have breakfast with her.'

'Oh good. Do you like her, Papa?'

How to explain to a young child that he had fallen in love with the Marchesa and was determined to somehow or other persuade her to marry him. Impossible, thought John, and simply answered 'Yes, very much.'

'I like her too.'

But John was no longer concentrating, having just caught sight of Tim Painter making his way up the street at a strolling pace. So he had been down at the far end all along, unless he had joined Kathryn when she had gone running down in pursuit of Isobel. But if that were the case why had he come back alone? And where were the other two? Had he been on his own the Apothecary would have investigated further but a pressure on his shoulders told him that Rose was desperate to follow the singers. So, with one final look in Tim's direction, John complied and went marching off up the street towards the school.

Breakfast was a hasty affair because Elizabeth was anxious to join the festivities. And she was not to be disappointed. As soon as they got into the street the notes of a solitary fiddle were heard clearly on the morning air, and who should come into their line of vision but the blind fiddler himself, leading a long line of dancers making their way through the narrow alleyways, hand-in-hand. The dance itself was graceful and dignified, the dancers walking forward, then the men changing places and turning the female partner of the other man before they changed places once again and turned their original partner. But it was to the curious habit of dancing in and out of houses, which stood open and welcoming, that John's eyes were drawn. The dancers entered by one door and left by another, never wavering in their steps. And all the while the fiddler, assisted by Gideon, the thin young tambourine player, and the monkey, drew them on through the town.

'Who leads the dancers?' John asked a local fellow who was watching the line of swirling people.

'Helstone folk, born and bred. The lady is always the most recent bride. There's a deal of jealousy about the man though. It's supposed to be the most important person, but everyone thinks that role applies to him. I've known men fight over the honour.'

The Apothecary grinned. 'I can imagine.'

'I'll wager that some get married the day before the festivities in order to fit the bill,' Elizabeth put in.

'Aye, that and all,' the man answered.

John ran his eye over the spectators, who had been growing steadily in number. He could see Mrs Legassick and Mrs Bligh together with the Colquites and their other friends, including the large lady with the white hair and soulful eyes, all standing together and cheering everyone on. There was no sign of Mrs Pill or Tim, or little Isobel come to that, but the beautiful Diana Warwick, dressed finely and causing quite a stir, had sallied forth alone and stood quietly viewing the passing parade.

And it was at that moment that John had the strangest feeling that all was not well. That something, somewhere was amiss.

He had had these premonitions before, several times, and knew how dangerous it was to ignore them. He turned to Elizabeth.

'My dear, will you look after Rose for me? I just want to go and have a look round.'

She shot him a questioning glance but said nothing. 'All right. Of course I will. Will you be long?'

'About thirty minutes; an hour at the most. I just feel I should. Do you understand?'

'No, but Rose and I will be all right. Won't we?' She bent down to the child who, for answer, planted a kiss on her cheek and went on watching the dance.

'Allow me to do the same,' John said, and briefly embraced the Marchesa. Then, turning, he hurried down Coinage Hall Street towards the fields that lay at the end.

As he went he tried to rationalise his thoughts. Why should he have had that unwelcome but familiar feeling that all was not well? And what was it that made his footsteps lead him out of town towards the fields that lay at the bottom? He had no answers but only a determination to discover all that he could. He walked on for another ten to fifteen minutes, then stopped, amazed. He was looking at one of the largest lakes he had ever seen in the West Country.

The Loe Pool – a misnomer if ever there was one – glinted serenely in the sun, but John had been told that at times the mountainous seas broke over Loe Bar and into the Pool, flooding the Cober Valley as far as Helstone. It was easy to see at those times that the town had once had its own port, but this had silted up long ago and now the nearest point to the sea was Porthleven.

The place, as far as he could see, was utterly deserted, not a soul about. Wondering how the search for Isobel had concluded, the Apothecary walked slowly round the Pool – a very goodly stretch – wishing that this strange feeling of dread would dissipate. Eventually, though, he tired of wandering aimlessly and set direction for Coinage Hall Street once more. He had reached the bottom of it when he heard the sound of running feet and Tim Painter, sweating slightly and not looking as calm and collected as usual, came panting down.

'Have you seen Isobel?' he asked abruptly.

The Apothecary's fears returned. 'Not since this morning, no.'

'Well the little bitch has vanished and her mother is in a

high hysteric. I tell you I'll wring that child's neck when I catch up with her.'

John cast his mind back to the earlier scene, seeing again the look of anguished surprise on the face of the young male dancer and the spiteful expression on that of little Isobel.

'She went running away towards the meadows and beyond. But I've just come from there and there's nobody around. The place is deserted.'

'Don't worry we've searched the area high and low and she's not there. Her mother is even suggesting that some brave chap dives in the Pool and looks for a body.'

John frowned, thinking to himself that the lake was vast and wondering where a diver would begin.

Tim looked at the town, which had filled up with even more people since John had left it. 'And who are we going to get to do it on a day like this? You can see for yourself that it's a public holiday,' he said.

'Have you informed the Constable?'

'No, not yet. I doubt that he's on duty either.'

'Constables are always on duty,' John answered severely.

'Well, will you go and find him? I'm too busy searching.'

Everything inside the Apothecary rebelled at the very idea but his sense of responsibility battled with the emotion until he eventually said, 'Oh all right.'

'Thanks old chap. I'll continue the hunt for the horror and she'll feel the back of my hand when I catch up with her.'

'A good plan,' said John with feeling, and continued up the road.

Chapter Eight

It seemed that there was to be no let up in the festivities. The dancers continued on, the fiddler now being joined by the rest of his musicians who played the rousing tune with great enthusiasm. The monkey, sent round once more with the hat, returned with it full and, realising it had done well, chattered enthusiastically. John, fighting his way through the crowd, which was building up to enormous proportions, eventually managed to find Elizabeth and Rose.

'I'm sorry I was so long but something fairly annoying has happened.'

'What?'

'I met Tim Painter and Isobel has vanished.'

'Dreadful child! When was she last seen?'

'Apparently it was this morning. In fact I witnessed her departure. She flew off down the street towards the meadows and possibly Loe Pool, and has disappeared without trace.'

'What caused her to go?'

'She bit one of the Hal-an-Tow men on the hand and I think she was afraid that someone was going to punish her. So she fled, with her mother in hot pursuit I might add.'

'And now nobody can find her?'

'Correct. Anyway, I promised Tim that I would tell the Constable for him.'

Elizabeth pulled a face. 'Who is he, do you know?'

'I'm afraid I haven't an idea. That's another bit of research I must undertake.'

'Well, Rose and I were going off to get refreshment. We can ask along the way.'

They all set off in the direction John had just come from and by the time they had reached The Angel had discovered that the Constable was a local blacksmith named William Trethowan. They were further informed that he would no doubt be in The Blue Anchor at this hour. John looked apologetic.

'It's not really a suitable place for a child. Do you mind if I go alone?'

'As long as you promise to catch up with me later.'

'What are you plans?'

'Rose and I are going to wander through the town and watch the Faddy.'

'What's that?'

'It's what they call the line of dancers. I should imagine it comes from old English, when fade meant to go.'

Rose spoke for the first time. 'Well, I'm glad Isobel has faddied. She won't come and stare at me at night now.'

'She'll probably be back before bedtime, but I will make sure she leaves you alone.'

'She'll be too tired by then anyway, Papa.'

'Very true,' said John. He bent down and kissed his daughter. 'Look after Mrs Elizabeth for me.' And he was off, heading purposefully for The Blue Anchor. Somewhat to his surprise, he found the Constable straight away. The chap was in the taproom holding forth about something or other and was clearly as drunk as a lord already. Having bought himself a pint of ale to steady his nerves, John approached with certain trepidation. The Constable, who was enormously tall and broad, a veritable giant of a fellow, bent his head down and said, 'What do you want, little man?'

'To speak to you if I may, Sir.'

Trethowan roared with laughter. 'Well, of course you can speak. The question is, will I listen?'

This brought a chorus of belly laughs from the other occupants of the bar, all of whom were well the worse for drink. John decided that the only thing to do was to act mysteriously.

'I've a tale to tell, Sir. A tale of a terrible child and what might have befallen her.'

'Taken off by a bad man, was she?' said somebody.

'Shush,' demanded Trethowan. 'I want to hear.'

Well at least he'd caught his attention, thought John.

'This girl is a stranger to these parts and went to see the Hal-an-Tow this morning. Anyway, little monster that she is, she insisted on joining in and when the men remonstrated with her she bit one of them on the hand. Then, when they turned on her, she ran down the street in the direction of the fields, possibly towards Loe Pool and hasn't been seen since. So I thought, Sir, as you are the Constable, you ought to be told.'

There was silence in the room for a second and then the blacksmith burst out laughing.

'So a child has gone missing, has she. I'd like a sovereign for every young 'un that gets lost on Flora Day, so I would.' He paused, drank half a tankard of ale in a swallow, then bent down to the Apothecary once more. 'Tell you what, my friend, if she's still lost tomorrow morning then come and see me and I'll organise a search. Meanwhile, may I suggest that you go and enjoy the rest of the day as I intend to do. Goodbye.' And he turned his large back.

John felt utterly deflated. His mysterious ploy had failed dismally and now he was left with no alternative but to limp back to The Angel with his tail between his legs. He bought himself another pint of ale for consolation and went to sit in a dark corner to think about the situation. But he had no time to get very far for the door to the taproom opened and there were the brothers Colquite with the two other men the Apothecary had noticed earlier. Snatches of their conversation drifted towards him.

'…there's enough to form a…' This last word said very low so that it was impossible to hear.

'…but what about th…' John could not catch the rest.

'Nonsense.' This from Geoffrey Colquite. 'Let us proceed as planned.'

'Oh, well you always were…'

At that moment they were disturbed by the arrival of a potboy and that particular conversation ceased, though one voice continued talking loud and enthusiastic rubbish. John drank up and walked out past the quartet. They greeted him as if he were a long-lost brother, calling him over and bowing most politely.

'My dear Sir, how very nice to see you.'

'Nice to see you,' echoed Gregory.

'May I present even more cousins, Eustace Sayce and Herbert Reece?'

A couple of males rose and bowed. One was short and round with a face like a grinning red melon. He was the one who had been conversing noisily and now he winked at the Apothecary and rolled his eyes. He obviously considered himself a character and wanted everyone else to do so as well. The other was very small, almost dainty, with tiny little hands and feet. They were, all things considered, a very ill matched duo. John bowed politely and made small talk but eventually extricated himself and headed off for The Angel, thinking deeply.

His main thought was about the actual role of Constable. It was generally a detested occupation, compulsory and unpaid, so much so that several citizens appointed a deputy to do the job for them. This had resulted in the formation of a class of men, mostly illiterate and existing on the pittance paid them by their employers, who had become professional deputies. Some, indeed, held the office for many years, going from one employer to the next as the obligatory year came to an end. And it seemed to the Apothecary that Helstone's Constable resented the job tremendously. Indeed it may well be true that children were lost during the Floral Dance. Considering the crowds who watched, it seemed more than likely. But for all that, John had found his attitude patronising and pretentious, at the very least he could have organised a search for the missing Isobel.

John believed that she was probably hiding in the woods near Loe Pool and that she would come out when things got quiet and she grew hungry. The best idea was to enjoy the rest of the day. With this thought uppermost in his mind, he whistled his way into The Angel to discover a scene taking place in the dining parlour. Mrs Pill was in floods of tears and refusing to be comforted by anybody. One look was enough to send John up to his room to fetch his medical bag.

He returned and studied the situation. Tim Painter had given up and was taking the opportunity to give Diana Warwick, who sat serene and lovely and a little bit remote, the eye. Meanwhile, Elizabeth and Rose watched fascinated but did not attempt to interfere. This was being done by Mrs Legassick, who held the semi-swooning woman in a tight embrace. The female whom John had noticed earlier, namely she of the large frame and succulent eyes, was also comforting Mrs Pill. Indeed she looked up as the Apothecary entered the room, attempting to appear professional.

'Shush, my dear. I think this gentleman is a doctor,' said Mrs Legassick.

'I am an apothecary actually, Madam. Now, Mrs Pill, let me have a look at you.'

He knelt beside the fainting woman, acutely aware that the large lady was watching him with a positively lecherous expression on her face.

Fortunately Isobel's mother was too far gone to put up much resistance and swallowed a measure of physic that the Apothecary guided towards her mouth.

'There, that should calm her.'

'One of your magic potions?' It was the big woman speaking. 'But excuse me Sir, allow me to present myself. I am Anne Anstey. I am so interested in the apothecary's art. My late husband was one of your brotherhood, you know.'

'Charmed, Madam. My name is John Rawlings,' John answered briefly, peering intently into Mrs Pill's face which was utterly drained of colour. Suddenly, and rather shockingly, her eyes flew open and stared into his.

'She's drowned,' she hissed in a thrilling sibilant. 'My girl's drowned and I know it.'

The thought that the Apothecary had resolutely been

pushing away ever since he had seen Loe Pool now came surging back.

'Nonsense, my dear,' said Mrs Anstey, 'she'll be home soon. As soon as it gets dark. They don't like being out after dusk, do little girls.'

But John, thinking of the size of Loe Pool and guessing at its depth, thought of little Isobel and knew that whatever faults the child might have had, she did not deserve a fate like that.

'Tell me,' he said gently, 'exactly what happened today. Explain to me what you saw.'

The physic was obviously starting to take effect because Mrs Pill was visibly starting to relax. The weeping had stopped and along with it the high hysterical voice. Indeed her speech was now quite quiet and slow.

'As I think you saw, Mr Rawlings, Isobel ran away from me down the street. I followed but being older I can't run as fast as she, further my clothes impeded me. In any case I saw her sprint into the fields at the street's end. Then I briefly lost sight of her as she disappeared into some trees. But then I saw her again as she hurried on. To cut to the heart of the matter I had some difficulty getting to the Pond because of the marshy land surrounding the Cober but I managed to make my way round it and there lay this enormous lake.'

'Tell me, did you see Isobel there?'

'No, no. I feel that she had already fallen in by the time I got there.'

'But you have nothing to prove that. It's only what you suspect.'

'Come now, Kathryn. We walked right round the lake – a distance of about five miles, I might add – and nowhere was there a sign of anyone having fallen in. It is all in your imagination. I swear it.' Tim Painter had joined them and was doing his best to cheer up his light-of-love.

Mrs Pill shook her head. 'I know that she has gone. You cannot deny a mother's instinct.'

'I'm not denying it but I think you're wrong,' Tim answered impatiently, and John caught himself thinking that the man was hardly sympathetic.

He cleared his throat. 'Madam, if I might suggest you retire and have a rest. I have informed the Constable of the turn of events and he has agreed to organise a search tomorrow. But it is his contention that Isobel will return before nightfall. And I think there is a good chance that he might be right.'

Kathryn made signs that she wanted to rise and Anne Anstey heaved her to her feet. 'Now you get some sleep, Mrs Pill, my dear. I promise to be here when you wake up again.'

John asked, 'Would you like me to accompany you to your room?'

'No, I shall be perfectly all right. I'll just go down for an hour or two.'

And with that she staggered out, accompanied by the ever-present Mrs Anstey.

Elizabeth looked directly at John. 'What are the chances of the child having fallen in?'

He raised his shoulders. 'How would I know? The Pool is certainly large and deep but without any evidence one could not possibly say.'

'But what do you really think?'

'I shall wait and see if she returns before I say anything further.'

Tim Painter spoke up. 'Well, now that she's gone I think Kathryn might well be right. I mean where did the child disappear to? She hasn't been seen since this morning and that is a long time ago now.'

The three of them stared at each other helplessly and it was at this moment that there was a movement in the doorway. Turning they saw the Constable, breathing hard and somewhat red in the face.

'Ah, Sir,' he said, advancing on John, 'wasn't it you who came to report a missing child earlier?'

'Yes, that's right. Why, do you have news of her?'

'Yes, Sir, I do. She, or a child answering her description, has been seen.'

'But I didn't give you her description,' the Apothecary answered.

'Never the less, she's been spotted.'

'Where?' asked Tim Painter.

'Up in the town, beyond the school and close to the church.'

'What was she doing?' asked Elizabeth.

The Constable roared with laughter. 'Why, bless you all, she was dancing of course.'

John was not sure who ran the faster, him or Tim Painter. Panting up the street to where the Guildhall stood, they turned left into the steeply sloping lane that led to the church. They pounded down this, going as fast as they could, at the same time calling out, 'Isobel? Where are you?'

There was no answer but they did not let that deter them. Instead they ran towards the holy building and, only slowing their steps slightly, sprinted the last few yards over open country to where the church stood serenely in its own grounds.

'Do we go in?' asked Tim.

'Of course. She might well be hiding inside.'

Removing their headgear, which both men had thrust on before they started to run, they proceeded in through the door in the porch. Immediately the atmosphere of the church made them walk quietly and speak in subdued voices. There was no one in sight but a step behind them had them spinning round hopefully.

An elderly cleric stood there, sweet-faced and very kindly in appearance. He seemed astonished to see anyone and John realised that after the morning service very few people must visit the church on Flora Day. He made a formal bow.

'Good day to you, Sir.'

'Good day, young man.'

Tim Painter gave a lazy bow. 'How do?' he said.

'Have you by any chance seen a young girl, aged about

seven? She has a mop of dark hair and was heading for the church when last observed.'

'Yes,' said the vicar surprisingly. 'A child answering that description was hiding in here but ran out when she saw me.'

'How long ago was that?' This from Tim Painter.

'About fifteen minutes or so. She can't have got far.'

'Thank you a thousand times,' said John. 'If you don't mind we'll go in pursuit.'

'I'm glad I was of service. I hope to see you in church some time.'

'Oh, you will,' the Apothecary called over his departing shoulder.

Tim Painter, on the other hand, raised his hat but said nothing.

Chapter Nine

They ran out and back to the Guildhall as quickly as they had come. John, panting somewhat, looked at Tim and thought to himself that the fellow was in the peak of condition, lean and fit and not in the least out of breath. Painter, aware that he was being stared at, gave the Apothecary the familiar idle smile and said, 'When I get my hands on that little bitch I'll give her a lesson she won't forget in a hurry.'

John slowed his pace. 'You don't like the child, do you?'

Tim chuckled, sounding quite human. 'I can't stand her. In fact I've disliked her ever since I first saw her.'

'Then why…?'

'Money, old boy. Mrs Pill is damnable rich. Old man Pill was a wealthy merchant and when he shuffled off, his widow gained the lot. Now I'm quite happy to admit I am delighted to be a kept man. It seems to me that work is something to be avoided if at all possible. By the way, you surprised me today. I had no idea you were an apothecary.'

'Really? Well I have been since I was sixteen.'

'What do you mean?'

'That's how old I was when I began my indentures.' John allowed a small smile to cross his features as he thought of his old Master. But Tim was continuing to talk.

'Anyhow that wily old bird Pill left a clause in his will that means his widow loses all her money should she remarry. So I have to remain the perpetual lover, which is wretchedly tiring let me assure you.'

John could not help but grin by the frankness with which it was all said. Then he thought of Elizabeth, of her strangely beautiful face with its ugly scar, of her strong, almost masculine, body, of the thrall she held him in, and determined to regularise their situation.

As if reading his thoughts, Painter said, 'That's a handsome piece you're involved with. What exactly is your relationship?'

John gave him an amused glance. 'We're close friends – that is all.'

'All?'

'Yes,' the Apothecary answered shortly, and let the matter drop.

They had been searching while they spoke, going up to the top of the town until it vanished into trees and countryside. There was no sign of Isobel but undeterred, knowing that she could not be far away, they came back and searched the length of Meneage Street. The crowd had now thinned and the dancing had ceased in this particular spot. John, looking at his watch, saw that it was three o'clock and realised that the gentry folk had all gone to tea. Distantly he could hear the sound of the Cornish fiddler – as he had come to think of the man – but all was quiet elsewhere.

'Where *is* the wretched girl?' Tim asked in exasperation.

'Probably back in the bosom of her mother by now.'

'Well I suggest we return to The Angel and have some ale. I'm sick to infirmity of looking for the child.'

'So am I,' answered John, feeling tired and longing to sit with Elizabeth and just talk.

They exchanged a glance and then went into the hostelry. There was no sign of the Marchesa but the three ladies, namely Mrs Legassick, Mrs Bligh, and the omnipresent Anne Anstey, were partaking of afternoon tea. They made much of the arrival of the two men, inviting them to join them. Tim Painter refused, quite abruptly John thought.

'Thank you, but no. Mr Rawlings and I are bound for the taproom.'

Anne Anstey made a moue and smiled widely. 'How tired you gentlemen must be. Did you find little Isobel?'

'No. Isn't she here?' asked Tim, surprised out of his lethargy.

'We haven't seen her,' said Mrs Bligh.

'God's life. Perhaps she's gone directly upstairs.' He turned to John. 'Rawlings, old chap, go and check the situation for me. I can't abide any more of Mrs P's hysterics.' And with that

that most handsome of creatures strode off in the direction of the bar.

John, only too aware of Anne Anstey's warm glances, bowed and left them equally quickly, climbing the stairs to where he knew Kathryn was lying, hopefully unconscious. The physic he had given her had been a combination of mistletoe, valerian root and vervain in equal parts. This was a well-known remedy for nervous disorders and should also have had a certain sedative effect. Hoping for the best, the Apothecary knocked extremely gently on the door.

Somewhat to his dismay a voice immediately answered, 'Come in.'

She was sleepy, there was no doubt about that, but had not actually gone to sleep. Instead Mrs Pill lay in a darkened room, her eyes closed but for all that still conscious.

'Isobel? Have you found her?'

'She was in the vicinity of the church, Mrs Pill. She is perfectly safe and has not fallen into the Loe Pool.'

Kathryn reared up in the bed, looking far from attractive. 'Where is she? Is she downstairs?'

'No, not exactly.'

'Then where have you hidden her? What's happening? Oh God, spare me from further misery.'

She started to weep again and John's hand automatically reached for the salts which he always carried about his person.

'Mrs Pill, please don't distress yourself. Take a deep breath from this bottle.'

'I don't want your horrid sniffs. Take them away. What have you done with my girl? Where have you hidden her? What game are you playing with me, Apothecary?'

'None at all, I assure you, Madam. The fact is that Mr Painter and I must have missed her by ten minutes or so. We then searched the town high and low but I'm afraid that Isobel eluded us.'

'So she's still not been found?'

'No,' John answered flatly, 'I'm sorry but those are the facts.'

Mrs Pill let out a terrible gurgle and fell back on the bed with a thud. Realising that the shock had been too great and she had fainted, the Apothecary hurried to her side.

His medical bag was downstairs where he had left it earlier and now he ran down to retrieve it. Thankfully all the ladies had gone about their business and the parlour was empty. Snatching the bag up, John hurried back to his patient, and while she was unconscious took the opportunity of administering some more of the sedative he had given her previously. Then by holding his salts beneath her nose he brought her round once more.

She wept quietly and the Apothecary felt so sorry for her that he put his arms round her.

'She will come back,' he said, but even as he uttered the words he wondered to himself whether he was speaking the truth.

Tim Painter was well away by the time John caught up with him. He had also been joined by young Nicholas Kitto, this evening looking like a sleek and happy ginger cat, wearing an emerald green suit cut by a tailor from Redruth, or so he informed the Apothecary. This particular garment enhanced his naturally red hair and freckles so that with his strangely fine features the fellow looked positively handsome.

'Are you coming to the ball tonight?' he enquired of the other two men.

'No, I shall remain here and see what's what,' Tim answered, slanting his eyes.

'I would like to go. How does one get hold of tickets?' said John.

'From the landlord of The Angel. The ballroom is here. But hurry, it may well be sold out.'

At that moment from the street outside there came the familiar strains of music and Elizabeth appeared bearing Rose, large-eyed, in her wake. There was the usual stirring of male disapproval but the Marchesa ignored it and walked up to the group fearlessly.

'Gentlemen, good evening. As you can hear the dancers are returning. Tell me, did you find the child?'

'Little beast eluded captivity once more,' answered Tim in his beautiful voice, never taking his eyes off the Marchesa, who returned look for look.

Nicholas turned to John. 'Sir, will you present me to the lady?'

The Apothecary, feeling somewhat put out, performed the introductions, remarking as he did so how charmingly Elizabeth curtsied and how well Nicholas conducted himself while the formalities were obeyed.

Rose, meanwhile, took refuge behind her father's legs, staring out at all that was taking place with all-seeing eyes. John, suddenly aware of her presence, bent down to her.

'Shall we go outside and watch the dancers, sweetheart?'

'Yes, Papa. I would like that.'

He straightened up and looked at Elizabeth. 'Rose and I are going to see what is going on. Would you care to join us?'

'Very much. Excuse me, gentlemen.'

Both Nicholas and Tim made disapproving noises but accepted the Marchesa's departure with reasonable grace. Once outside, she turned to John with a brilliant look.

'I have bought two tickets for the ball tonight. Do you want to come or should I ask Tim Painter to accompany me?'

'Are you serious?' John asked severely.

'Of course not. I would prefer to dance with you.'

'Then nothing would give me greater pleasure than to be your partner.'

Elizabeth looked business-like. 'What is happening about Isobel? Had she been seen or was it just a false rumour?'

'No, the Vicar saw her near the church. It's the damnedest thing but the child is definitely avoiding capture.'

'Why? Nobody is cruel to her. In fact her mother dotes on her, I would say.'

'Yes, but Tim might be handy with his fists. He openly admits that he dislikes the child.'

The Marchesa shook her head. 'No, he hasn't got it in him to beat anyone. He's too indolent; too relaxed. The only thing that would arouse him from his torpor is the pursuit of a pretty woman.'

'He is involved with Mrs Pill because she has been left a considerable amount of cash apparently.'

'I thought it would be something like that.'

Rose, whom they had temporarily forgotten, suddenly piped up, 'Oh see the ladies. Don't they look strange.'

John followed the line of her pointing finger and saw Mrs Legassick, Mrs Bligh and Mrs Anstey cavorting down the street in what appeared to be an odd form of morris dance. Partnering them were the two brothers, Geoffrey and Gregory Colquite, and their cousins Eustace Sayce and Herbert Reece. What it was about the dance that was unusual the Apothecary could not possibly have said. But it seemed as if all seven of them were abandoning themselves to the music, dancing wildly and as if their very lives depended on it. Even respectable Muriel Legassick appeared to be quite worked up, her little mouth in a tight line, her eyes glistening. John smiled to himself, glad to see such a decent bunch of people enjoying themselves in so uninhibited a manner.

'Odds my life,' said Elizabeth, laughing to herself, 'I'm sure they rival the Furry Dancers themselves.'

But she had spoken too soon, for down the street in a great and colourful line were coming the gentry folk, refreshed and ready to dance the night away. Watching them, the Apothecary thought them almost magical; the women dressed finely in vivid colours, hats and bonnets upon their heads, the men in their turn in their best clothes, glittering buckles winking upon their shoes as they whirled their partners in the brilliant sunlight. And it was then that he caught a glimpse – and glimpse only it was – of little Isobel. Just for a second the crowd of onlookers across the street parted and he distinctly saw her, dancing along, parodying the adults. He caught her eye, gestured to her, called her name. She heard him, stared at him, then she vanished once more, and it was with that one brief sighting he had to be content. Even if he hadn't caught her he knew she was safe and would no doubt return when she finally grew tired.

By the end of the evening he was deeply in love. The sight of Elizabeth in white muslin, her black hair cascading round her shoulders, worn loose and unconventional, had driven him practically mad. As he had partnered her through the dances for six or eight couples he resented the moments when he had to leave her and dance with the other women in the set, glad when she put her gloved hand back in his and gave him an unreadable glance. That she was deliberately playing with him the Apothecary had no doubt, but he had no power to prevent it.

Emilia was starting to fade into memory, yet she would still come in the night to haunt his dreams. Had he loved her as much as he loved Elizabeth he asked himself? Yet there could be no comparison of the depth of his feelings. He felt that his marriage and all the many memories that were attached to it had assumed an almost unreal quality and that Emilia herself was beginning to slip away.

Yet even in thinking of the future the Apothecary knew that difficulties lay ahead. As soon as his visit to Cornwell was ended he must return to London. And he felt certain that Elizabeth would refuse to accompany him. Therefore his principal challenge lay in persuading her to give up her country seat and to dwell with him in town. Yet how he was going to do it he had no idea. With a determined effort, John tried to put the whole problem out of his mind and concentrate instead on having a thoroughly good time.

Elizabeth looked up at him. 'What are you thinking?'

'About Emilia,' he answered truthfully.

'You loved her very much,' she replied, not as a question but a statement of fact.

'Yes I did.' He held her close. 'But now I have fallen in love with you, Elizabeth. In fact with each passing day it grows a little more.'

She smiled at him quizzically. 'You're certain of this?'

'Positive.'

The Marchesa gave him an inscrutable glance. 'And you are contemplating proposing to me, no doubt?'

'Well, I...'

'My sweetest Apothecary, I love you too. Who wouldn't? But I will never marry you. Of that you may rest assured.'

And so saying she whirled him off his feet in a lively jig.

Chapter Ten

That night he made love to her with a feeling he had never experienced before, for combined with his passion was a kind of neediness, a longing for her that in some way he knew could never be satisfied. And perhaps, he thought, when he eventually returned to the loneliness of his room, it never should be. For didn't marriage bring with it a necessity of boredom, a familiarity which did not sit easily with the high emotions he felt? The Apothecary, undressing then getting into bed, knew then that whatever fate Elizabeth was going to hand out to him, he would continue to love her despite all.

Exhausted, he fell asleep at once only to dream of little Isobel. In the dream she was standing in the doorway of his room, a mocking smile on her face as she stared at him.

'Isobel,' he said. 'You must stop hiding.'

'But I've found the perfect place,' she answered, and in the way of dreams vanished from his sight.

He woke late the next morning to discover Rose standing in exactly the same spot, looking at him in much the same manner.

'Come on, Pa. You're very late.'

'Pass me my watch, sweetheart.'

Rose retrieved the handsome piece, a twenty-first birthday present from John's father, Sir Gabriel Kent, and handed it to the Apothecary.

'Good God, it's ten o'clock. Why didn't you wake me before?'

'I did come in but you were in a deep sleep.'

John sat up, feeling somewhat guilty, and saw that Rose was fully dressed. 'Who helped you get ready?' he asked.

'Mrs Elizabeth.'

'Is she up as well?'

'She has joined the hunt for Isobel.'

'Isn't the little toad back yet?'

'No, Papa. She stayed out all night.'

Rose's face took on a slightly virtuous expression which John found highly amusing. He threw a pillow at her.

'And there's no point in trying to look pious,' he said.

Rose answered, 'What does pious mean?'

'It means... Oh, never mind. Go downstairs and wait for me. I'll be about quarter of an hour.'

His daughter duly trotted off and it was left to the Apothecary to wash and shave to the best of his ability, then to hurry into his clothes. Having dressed himself in his travelling suit, prepared for a search, he went down to find Mrs Pill, white-faced and silent, sitting in the parlour with Tim Painter, who was trying to comfort her in an off-handed sort of way. Diana Warwick was also sitting quietly in a corner, taking in everything that was going on but saying little. The rest of the guests, including the Marchesa and Rose, were absent.

John approached Kathryn Pill. 'My dear Madam, I hear that your daughter has not returned.'

She turned on him a terrible look. 'No, Sir. And now I know for certain that something is grievously wrong. The child would have come back as soon as it got dark. I am positive of that.'

Yet again the Apothecary felt a clutch of fear and took himself to task for not crossing the road and grabbing the girl, even if it had meant disturbing the Furry.

'When was the last time she was seen?' he asked.

'At about five. Miss Warwick saw Isobel in the street. She called out to her but the child ran away. Oh, Mr Rawlings, I blame myself totally for not going to find her.'

'We could all do that,' drawled Tim Painter.

Kathryn rounded on him. 'Yes, and so you should take the blame. I was ill yesterday afternoon and was in no fit state to search. But there was nothing the matter with you.'

'I'll remind you that I ran all the way to the church, accompanied by Rawlings here, when I heard the girl had been sighted nearby.'

She looked slightly mollified but continued in the same

vein. 'That was good of you but there was no reason to abandon your duty and go to the taproom. You should have sought her high and low.'

Tim looked askance. 'I did. So did John. Then we decided that enough was enough and we'd earned a drink. And that's all I've got to say on the matter.'

John could not help but admire the man for the way in which he handled the angry female. He felt certain that he personally would have cringed with apology and emerged in disarray. Now Tim said airily, 'The rest are out looking. Should we join them, Rawlings?'

'Yes, let's.'

Miss Warwick called from her corner, 'May I search with you, gentlemen?'

'Oh please do,' Tim oozed.

Mrs Pill shot him a black look. 'And I shall come too,' she announced. 'After all, Isobel is my daughter.'

They went out into the street where they divided into groups. Tim and Mrs Pill, who took Painter's arm in a most determined fashion, would search the top part of the town; John and Miss Warwick the bottom end. Looking round for Elizabeth and being unable to see her, the Apothecary, out of politeness, offered the beautiful Diana, who this morning looked radiant, his arm. She curtseyed, dimpled a smile at him, and took it.

Deciding that they should search every alleyway leading off the main road, John plunged into the first. Most of them were stable yards but in one he discovered a blacksmith at work. Straightening up at the sound of approaching footsteps, John saw that it was none other than William Trethowan.

'Found your little girl, have 'ee?' the Constable asked, wiping a huge and dirty hand across his forehead.

'No, Sir, we haven't,' the Apothecary replied forthrightly. 'In fact I am searching for her at this very moment. Now I believe you said something yesterday about organising a proper look. Have you done anything about it?'

The Constable straightened up looking slightly shamefaced. 'If truth be told, Sir, I haven't as yet.'

'Why not?' John asked, feeling somewhat annoyed.

'Because yesterday was Flora Day and I've only just got back to work.'

'That's as may be. But the fact remains that a child has gone missing and has now been absent all night. So I suggest that a proper search is organised swiftly.'

At last he seemed to be making headway, for the Constable laid down his tools, calling out to another chap, 'Rob, I'm off to organise a seeking party. Take over my duties for a while.'

'Meanwhile,' John continued crisply, 'the lady and I will continue with our look around.'

They poked about the yard, Mrs Warwick standing well clear of anything messy, until they were certain that Isobel was not concealed anywhere. Then they moved on, Diana declaring that the girl was a little wretch to be sure.

'Do you have children?' John enquired of her tactlessly.

Miss Warwick sighed, a pretty sound. 'Alas, Sir, I am not married.'

'Tell me,' said the Apothecary, to cover his confusion, 'why did you travel to Helstone on your own and without a lady companion? What I mean is, of what interest is this pagan dance to you?'

She tapped him gently on the face with her fan. 'You're very forward, Sir, to ask such questions.'

'Forgive me. I'm just naturally curious.'

'Well, I came to meet someone if you must know.'

John brimmed with curiosity. 'Really? And who might that be?'

She laughed, her voice the sound of a waterfall. 'Now that would be betraying a confidence, would it not. Let it suffice that I tell you I have a friend hereabouts.'

A male, thought John. He smiled and said, 'Madam, I will intrude no further on your privacy. After all, it makes you all the more intriguing that you have a little secret.'

She smiled up at him and John thought that she really was one of the most ravishing creatures he had ever seen. Yet again he caught himself wondering how old she was.

Returning to Coinage Hall Street they walked briskly down to where the meadows began. Miss Warwick stared at her elegant dress.

'I think, Sir, that I should change my clothes if I am to go searching any further.'

He was most intrigued by her and more than a little amused. So much so that despite the power of his feelings for the Marchesa he could not resist giving Diana's hand a little squeeze.

'My dear Madam,' he said, his eyes very lively, 'I would not dream of dragging you over such rough terrain. I shall continue on my own.'

'But that would be a great pity,' she responded, quite definitely flirting with him, 'could we not just tell Mrs Pill that we got this far but could not proceed further? Besides where is the Constable going to look? Surely at Loe Pool.'

John stood for a moment thinking, then decided that he had searched round the Pool once and was damned if he was going to do so again. In fact, he considered, he was not over-keen on little Isobel and was assisting with the search only out of a sense of duty. He turned to Miss Warwick.

'Then if I may escort you back to town?'

'Certainly, Sir.' And she swept a deep curtsey.

They did not hurry about their walk back and consequently were the last to arrive at The Angel, where, they discovered, Mrs Pill was holding a council of war. Pale but determined, she was finally managing to instil a sense of worry into her listeners.

'I admit,' she said, 'that Isobel tends to be disobedient and not come when she is called. But for her to stay out all night is unheard of. I tell you in all seriousness that something is amiss.'

'I have seen the Constable and he is organising a proper search some time today.'

'What do you mean by that?' came Tim's beautifully educated voice. 'Haven't we looked properly then?'

'There's no need for those remarks,' answered Mrs Pill testily. 'It is my opinion that my daughter has been abducted.'

'But by whom?' asked Mrs Legassick, who had joined the party with her friends, all of whom had been out looking. 'And for what purpose?'

Kathryn went dangerously white. 'Who knows why? Probably for some unlawful design.'

'Oh surely not,' said a Mr Colquite, and the other echoed, 'Surely not.'

Anne Anstey put in tactlessly, 'Oh yes, I have heard of young girls being abducted. They take them to work in brothels or to send overseas to tend the plantations.'

Mrs Pill made a terrible retching sound and Tim said, 'Steady on!'

Tabitha Bligh, who clearly regarded Mrs Anstey as some kind of rival, answered, 'How cruel of you to say such things. Why, you could send the poor woman into an hysteric.'

John, who had been thinking much the same thing, glanced at Mrs Pill but saw that with great determination she was remaining in control of herself.

'So what are we going to do?' she asked, her face set and rigid.

Everybody stared at everybody else but nobody said a word. The Apothecary broke the silence.

'We can do nothing until the Constable has searched the place. Then, I believe, we must follow his advice.'

But even as he spoke he recognised the futility of his words. William Trethowan was at heart a fairly simple man and would probably be as puzzled by Isobel's disappearance as everybody else. He addressed Mrs Pill.

'Madam, we have just searched the town. There is nothing we can do further until the Constable reports to you.'

'You're right, of course. But I have such a sense of futility. A longing to see my child again. Just sitting here makes me feel quite sickened.'

'I don't know what to suggest.'

Elizabeth spoke. 'I believe we should pass the time as pleasantly as possible. Why don't we look round the local shops?'

Mrs Pill shook her head. 'You go by all means. Personally, I would rather wait here for the Constable.'

'Do you mind if I take a stroll round?' Tim Painter asked, fixing Diana Warwick with such a meaningful glance that it shot through John's mind that he might be the man she had come to meet.

'No, no, you go,' Kathryn answered, not noticing.

'Thank you.' And he made a hasty exit accompanied by most of the other men, only too glad to get away from the depressing atmosphere.

John caught Elizabeth's eye and bowed. 'May I accompany you?'

'Provided Rose wants to go, yes.'

The child stood up, nodding enthusiastically. 'Yes please, Papa.'

'Then it's settled. We'll go and shop.'

As he passed Miss Warwick she gave another deep curtsey. John paused. 'Madam, will you be all right on your own?'

'I shall find company, don't worry, Sir.'

'Then I'll bid you good day.'

'Good day, Sir.' And under her breath she added the words, 'Dearest Mr Rawlings.'

They delayed their return to the hostelry, relishing the time alone together. During their perambulations they passed the seven friends, Mrs Legassick and Mrs Bligh, together with the hot-eyed Anne Anstey, the brothers Colquite and the other two cousins walking dutifully behind.

John, somewhat amused by them, said, 'I wonder if they ever separate.'

'You know very well they do. Didn't you come across the men in The Blue Anchor?'

'Yes, but only once. Do you think they sleep together and take turn and turn about?'

She laughed that deep laugh of hers. 'What an amazing thought.'

'Isn't it though?'

But the more he considered it, the more the Apothecary began to wonder just what was the nature of the cousins' inseparable relationship.

Chapter Eleven

The Constable's search was over and the news was not good. He had gone to see Mrs Pill, finding her sitting in the parlour of The Angel, and had solemnly announced that they could not find her child anywhere in Helstone.

She had gone stiff with grief, her plain face taking on a mask-like expression. 'Are you saying that my girl has gone?' she croaked, out of drawn, white lips.

William Trethowan, looking acutely miserable, shuffled from foot to foot. 'Yes, Mam, I'm afraid that is so.'

'Then she has been abducted?'

'Unless there's been an accident at Loe Pool.'

'An accident? What do you mean?'

Totally lacking tact Trethowan blundered on, 'They do say round these parts that every seven years or so the Pool claims a victim.'

Kathryn let out a low cry. 'So that's where she is. Oh God help me.'

'I'm not saying she is there Mam. It's just a possibility.'

'Then you must send down a good swimmer. Someone who can look for her body.'

'Mam, have you see the size of the Pool? It would take a strong man several hours to walk round.'

'But surely you can organise something? We are talking about my child. My only child.'

With these words she started to weep copiously and unattractively while the wretched Constable shifted his weight from one side to the next, looking as if he would rather be anywhere in the world but here. His agony was relieved by the arrival of Tim Painter, who strolled in nonchalantly, smelling of ale.

'Found her?' he asked cheerfully. Then he stole a glance at the loudly weeping Kathryn and added, 'Probably not then.'

'No, Sir,' put in Trethowan. 'The child is nowhere to be seen.'

'Well, that's a blow to be sure. What do you suggest, my good man?'

The Constable shook his head. 'I don't know what to say, Sir. I must confess I'm in a spot.'

Tim turned to Kathryn, who was emitting low convulsive sobs. 'Come on now, old girl. There's no need to upset yourself.'

'There's every need,' she answered in the grimmest tones. 'My daughter, my Isobel, is probably dead and all you can do is make inane remarks. How can you be so unfeeling?'

It was at that moment that the Apothecary walked in, having left Elizabeth and Rose slowly walking round the shops. He took one glance at Mrs Pill and went straight to fetch his medical bag, returning with it a few minutes later and immediately giving her some physic. While he poured he spoke to William Trethowan.

'I presume your search was in vain?'

'You presume correctly, Sir.'

'Um. Wait outside for me a moment. I want to have a chat with you. I'll just attend to Mrs Pill first.'

'Are you a doctor?'

'An apothecary.'

'Good as,' answered Trethowan, and went out.

Painter meanwhile was standing beside Kathryn looking and being totally ineffectual and as if he couldn't wait to get back to the ale pot. John shot him a severe glance.

'Look after her for a moment or two. I just want to have a word with the Constable.'

'Very well. I'll do my best.'

John, feeling uncertain about leaving his patient, stepped outside with a certain reluctance to where Constable Trethowan awaited him. Looking at the man, whose attitude had changed completely since the first time they had met, the Apothecary came straight to the point.

'Do you think Isobel is dead, because you know I saw her last evening, as did Miss Warwick.'

William looked grim. 'I'm aware of that fact, Sir. Mr Painter told me. But I can assure you that she's not hiding. She's either been abducted or that's what's happened to her.'

'But surely she's not been murdered? If she's dead it must be accidental.' But the Constable's unswerving stare made him add the words, 'I imagine.'

'Truth to tell I don't know what to think, Sir. The child is a stranger hereabouts so you can't say she made any enemies. I've a mind to ask the gypsy woman what she reckons.'

John stared at him incredulously. 'You don't believe in all that rubbish, do you?'

The minute he had spoken he regretted it, for Trethowan frowned darkly and said, 'I be Cornish, Sir. So don't mock me about my beliefs.'

'I'm sorry. I meant nothing personal.'

'Don't you want to come with me? Aren't you the least bit curious?'

And John had to admit that part of him was intrigued as to what Gypsy Orchard would say, though his sane sensible self refused to have anything to do with it.

He assumed a nonchalant air. 'I'll wait for you to report back to me. I must go in search of my companion and my daughter.'

Trethowan lowered his voice. 'I'd keep a close guard on your maiden, Sir.'

'Why? What do you mean?'

'There could be funny people about.'

John's stomach lurched. 'Are you referring to those strange individuals who love children above all other?'

'I am indeed. If Isobel has been abducted then like as not there may be one working down here.'

'Come to watch the lads and lasses who gather round on Flora Day.'

'Precisely.' The Constable pulled out a watch. 'I'm off to try and find Gypsy Orchard, Sir. Goodbye.'

And John was left staring at his departing back, half wishing that he were going with him. He returned to the parlour to find Mrs Pill deserted by Tim, sitting on her own, gazing vacantly at the wall.

'Would you like to lie down?' he asked.

She stared at him listlessly. 'I don't care,' she answered. 'I won't sleep if I do.'

'I can give you a pill that will soothe you.'

'But I want to stay awake in case…just in case…there is any news.'

The Apothecary felt unable to answer her so merely cleared his throat. Mrs Pill put out a bony hand and seized his arm.

'Mr Rawlings, do you think Isobel is dead?' she asked, repeating his earlier question to the Constable.

John shook his head. 'I don't know what to say. It is possible I suppose.'

'But if she is not I tremble to think what might be her fate.'

Determined not to go down that road, the Apothecary stood up. 'I shall go and find Mr Painter for you.'

Mrs Pill sighed. 'That wastrel. Don't bother yourself. I think I am better off on my own.'

John, who was rapidly feeling that Tim was a total waste of everyone's time, said nothing and was saved any further embarrassment by the entry of Rose and Elizabeth. His daughter, he noticed at once, looked tired and somewhat red about the eyes. He raised a mobile brow at the Marchesa, who said quietly, 'She has been upset by Isobel's disappearance.'

'But she didn't like the girl,' he answered in an undertone.

'I know but that hasn't stopped her feeling sorry.'

John, shaking his head with sad amusement, bent down and picked his daughter up into his arms. 'You funny little thing,' he said.

'Oh Papa,' she said, and burying her head in his neck, Rose started to cry.

Mrs Pill sat motionless and Elizabeth, sitting down beside her, took her hands. John, seizing the moment, carried Rose out into the yard where they were uninterrupted except for the stamp and whinny of horses and the occasional plodding of an hostler. Sitting down on the wall by the well, John snuggled the child onto his lap.

'What's the matter, darling?'

'Oh, Pa, what has happened to Isobel?'

He sighed. 'I wish I knew.'

'I didn't like her but I do feel sorry for her.'

'I experience the same emotion.'

'You're sure she's not hiding?'

John looked at his child very seriously. 'I don't see how she can be. The Constable is a local man and he would have found her if anyone could.'

Rose wept afresh and some of her tears fell on John's hands, moving him profoundly. He held his daughter very close, thankful with all his heart that she had not gone missing, loving her as the last vestige on earth of Emilia, wondering what sex his unborn child, the child that perished with its mother, would have been.

His reverie was disturbed by the sound of someone approaching and, looking up, he saw that Diana Warwick was coming towards him. Putting Rose down carefully, he stood up and bowed.

'Mr Rawlings, I was thinking how sweet you looked holding your child. You are a most unusual and loving father.'

'I am all that Rose has got,' he replied honestly.

She looked at him with a bright smile. 'But you will remarry, surely.'

John's thoughts flew to Elizabeth and again he answered truthfully. 'I am not sure about that.'

Diana smiled beautifully. 'There's many a woman who would like you for a partner, Sir.'

'It's kind of you to say so.'

'I only speak the truth.'

And with that she curtsied and went on to the stables, enquiring audibly about hiring a horse. This put an idea into John's mind and he turned to Rose.

'Would you like to go for a ride?'

'Oh, yes please Papa.'

'Then we'll ask Mrs Elizabeth to join us.'

Half an hour later it was all done. The livery stables which worked in conjunction with The Angel had provided them with two stout mounts and a pony for the young person. Then the three of them clattered out of the stable yard and set off to the right in the direction of Loe Pool. Elizabeth, as was usual with her, led off at some speed, particularly when they reached the open country beyond the town. John and Rose followed at a sedate pace, suitable for the child, good rider though she was. So it was that they reached the Pool and stopped to marvel at its size and splendour. In the distance to the right, standing on high ground overlooking the lake, was a great house. But it was not to this that the Apothecary's eyes were drawn. He looked instead at the horse that Diana had hired, grazing beneath a tree, its reins looped loosely over a branch. Beside it stood another horse, also cropping the turf.

John knew instantly that the lady in question was with her mystery man and felt his natural curiosity reach overwhelming proportions. Thinking to himself that it couldn't possibly be Tim Painter – unless the man had moved very fast – he longed to get a glimpse of who it was. Yet his natural revulsion against Peeping Toms held sway. He said to Rose, 'Shall we dismount or do you want to search for Mrs Elizabeth?'

Rose turned on him a stricken face. 'She isn't lost too, is she?'

John laughed. 'Not she. She's probably just ridden on a little. She'll be back, don't worry.'

'Then I'll get off.' And she slid to the ground in quite an expert fashion before John could catch her.

He dismounted and stood beside her, looking at the enchanting vista. Then the thought came that if Isobel had vanished into the Pool it would be almost impossible to find the girl. He had seen many lakes but this one was particularly wooded on its shore line and would be almost impossible to search.

A low laugh coming from the group of trees to his right made him glance over, and there, to his great astonishment he saw Diana Warwick emerging accompanied by the red-headed aristocratic-looking Nicholas Kitto. So that was it! She must have met Kitto somewhere and they had formed a liaison, a liaison which was still continuing.

But why the secrecy? the Apothecary wondered. What was it that prevented them from announcing to the world that they were sweethearts? Then it occurred to him that Diana might be married despite her claiming otherwise, and with it came the certainty that she was a good deal older than young Kitto, possibly even as much as twenty years.

Rose, quite unabashed, waved enthusiastically in the manner of children and called out, 'Good day, Miss Warwick.'

'Good day,' she called back, obviously extremely embarrassed.

John meanwhile was muttering at his daughter, 'Just leave it, Rose. Don't say any more.'

But she either didn't hear him or was just being wilful because she called out, 'The Constable couldn't find Isobel.'

'I know, my dear. Isn't it a shame.'

Meanwhile Kitto, who had been surveying the scene, decided to make the best of it and came forward with a grin.

'Hello, Rawlings. We meet again.'

'Yes, indeed,' said John over-heartily, attempting to appear nonchalant.

'Miss Warwick and I are old friends,' continued the young man, flushing despite his brave approach.

'Oh, excellent,' the Apothecary answered in the same vein.

'I must be getting back,' said Diana.

'Oh, really? Well I'll see you as arranged then.'

And Nicholas bent down to assist his ladylove to mount, cupping his hands together to receive her foot as she climbed into the side saddle.

John was partly amused by the incident yet greatly puzzled. It seemed to him that there was something odd about the pair of them, but what it was totally eluded him. He felt certain, though, that he would discover it eventually.

Elizabeth rode up as Nicholas left, having given Diana several minutes start. John, observing the Marchesa closely, thought he had never seen anyone as beautiful. Her black hair was loose, flying out as she cantered along, and the colour was fresh in her cheeks. Today she rode side saddle, something she did not often do, but it suited her well. Only the ugly scar, the flaw in the diamond, detracted from her being totally lovely.

She stared at Nicholas's departing back. 'I see you had company.'

'More than that. A little bit of a mystery. I'll tell you about it later.'

Elizabeth turned her mount so that she was once more surveying the Loe.

'It's a vast area. Heaven help the child if she's fallen in. She'll never be found,' she added under her breath, conscious of Rose's presence.

'I agree,' John answered heavily as the three of them set off for home.

Something made him stop at The Blue Anchor, something other than the smell of their home brewed ale. Telling Elizabeth and Rose to continue on to the inn, John walked in, fairly certain that he would find William Trethowan, and sure enough the chap was seated in the bar. But this time he wore a serious expression and was only with one crony, talking quietly. He looked up as John entered and beckoned the Apothecary over.

'Now, Sir,' he began, 'I know you don't hold with fortune telling and the like but you must remember that Gypsy Orchard is a Charmer, and that means she is highly respected round these parts.'

John sat down. 'Tell me about Charmers. What do they do?'

'They are magic people. They can cure all kinds of illnesses and ailments; warts, wounds, adder bites. They can stop bleeding in both people and animals. Gypsy Orchard was born with the gift and that's why I trust what she says.'

'And what does she say about Isobel?'

'I'd rather you heard that for yourself, Sir.'

Once again John was seized with a terrible fear, remembering that time so long ago when an old woman had foretold Emilia's death. At the time he had thought it all trickery and fakery but events were to prove him wrong.

'I don't think…'

''Twill be for your benefit, Sir.'

But he could say nothing further. There was a rustle in the doorway and there she stood, dark and tanned, her basket on her hip, her eyes staring straight into John's soul. And what eyes they were. Clear as a Cornish river, with all the light and shade attached thereto, dancing and glistening in the candlelight. Indeed, as she turned to the Constable, John could have sworn that they glinted like emeralds in the gathering shadows.

He stood up and bowed. 'Madam.'

She laughed, lightly and musically. 'Just call me Gypsy Orchard if you would, Sir. I'm more used to it than anything else.' And she put out her hand.

John took it and the second he had done so felt something of her power. It coursed through him like a flash of lightning.

'You're a healer, too,' she said. 'In fact that is what you do all the time. And you're very good at it. But you do something else as well. Now what is it?'

She closed those remarkable eyes for a few moments, then they flew open again. 'I know,' she said. 'You hunt down villains and killers. That is the other part of your life.'

The gypsy motioned John to sit and, taking a seat beside him, took his hands and turned them palms uppermost. Despite himself, despite his fear of what she might be about to say, he was enthralled.

'A complicated man,' she said after a few moments, 'who has known much joy and much sadness.' She lowered her voice so that the Constable would not be able to hear her. 'You are blessed with the power of healing and will continue with this work until the day you die.' Gypsy Orchard smiled then gave him an amused look. 'You have a daughter and will also have a son.'

'My wife is dead,' John answered bitterly.

'I am aware of that.' She grinned at him and he saw the flash of strong white teeth. 'You don't need a wife to get a boy, Apothecary.'

He couldn't help but smile in return. 'Then who will be my son's mother?'

'As to that I am going to keep you guessing.'

'You don't know, do you.'

'You may accuse me of spinning a yarn but I tell you what I see. It is not wise to mock a Charmer, Sir.'

'I'm sorry. I spoke out of turn. Please continue.'

But she had turned his hands over and given them back to him. 'Let's talk about the missing child instead.'

John, reluctantly realising that he had spoilt his chance of learning more, said, 'Oh very well. Tell me what you see regarding her.'

'She's dead, Sir. Dead and gone.'

'You're certain?'

'Convinced.'

'Then how did she die?'

'She was drowned, poor little mite. Gone back to the water from which she came.'

John shivered, despite himself. 'Is she in Loe Pool?'

Gypsy Orchard shook her head slowly. 'I'm not sure, to be

honest with 'ee. I felt the waters close round my head but I was not certain from where they were coming.'

'And this is what you told the Constable?'

'Just as I tell it to you now.'

'Then may God rest her soul.'

'Amen.'

They sat in total silence, neither William Trethowan nor his companion saying a word, and into this quiet there stole the distant sounds of music which grew louder and louder until eventually it came through the doors of the inn in a great clamorous cacophony. John looked up and found himself peering into a small anxious face wearing a hat, its body thrust into a jacket, its little hands held out in a piteous gesture.

'Hello, little fellow,' said John.

It was the monkey, for once not carrying the collecting hat and bearing its usual sad cast of features. Gypsy Orchard said, 'It has known suffering, that creature.'

'What do you mean?' asked John.

'It has had a cruel master. But now it is free of him and with a reasonable crew. Particularly the blind man.' And she laughed as if at some joke of her own.

John stood up. 'Can I cross your palm with silver, milady?'

She rose also so that yet again he was looking into those freshwater eyes of hers. 'No, that is my gift to 'ee,' she said.

Trethowan spoke up. 'I reckon we'll have to search the Loe best we can.'

John nodded. 'Looks like it. I'll try and round up a few strong swimmers.'

'Aye, do that. Well, goodbye Sir. I'm home to my dinner.'

Picking up the monkey, John went into the next door bar to discover the band playing for all they were worth. They stood in the midst of a small crowd, entertaining one and all, and there was a roar of approval when the Apothecary entered with their simian pet.

'He wandered off, did he?' said the tambourine player, laughing.

Taking the creature from John's arms he handed him his instrument which the monkey began to play haphazardly.

'Well, now, Wilkes, be taking my place, will 'ee?'

John laughed. 'Is that his name? Wilkes?'

'Yes, after that evil politician. But we meet again, Sir. As you know, I'm Gideon.'

'Yes, I remember.'

'The rest of the mob have names too. The mandora player is Zachariah, and the fagotto, Giles. The kettledrums man is George and the flautist is John.'

'And your leader, the blind fiddler? What is he called?'

Gideon chuckled softly. 'He's just known as the Gaffer.'

'Doesn't he have a name?'

'Reckon he did years ago. But he's probably forgot it.'

'Good gracious. Anyway, allow me to introduce myself. I'm John Rawlings.'

'Nice to make your acquaintance.'

'Let me buy you all a pint of ale before I go.'

'Obliged to you, Sir. We'd like that, wouldn't we boys?'

The members of the band nodded and winked to show their approval, not missing a note of the music as they did so. The Gaffer, meanwhile, was jigging about in time to his own playing, thoroughly enjoying himself. John stared at him, thinking him a jolly good fellow but wondering what it was about the chap that seemed somehow familiar. It was probably, he concluded, because the blind fiddler was a type, an unusual one but for all that a type. The sort that one associated with country fairs and gatherings, and dances organised by farming folk.

Reluctantly, because he was enjoying the music and the general atmosphere, John made to go but was stopped in the doorway by Gypsy Orchard. Her white teeth flashed disconcertingly.

'Take care of your son when he comes, Sir,' she said, then laughed, and hurried off down the street, her hips swinging, her basket still balanced on one of them, her doorknocker plait woven with flowers from the hedgerows.

John stood, shaking his head, and at that moment William Trethowan, the Constable, who had been delayed within, came out of the hostelry. He had changed since their first meeting, the Apothecary thought, now having an air of humility where first he had appeared overbearing. He approached John and cleared his throat.

'Should I tell Mrs Pill what Gypsy Orchard said, do you think, Sir?'

'I think best not. Though she'll probably find out from someone.'

'Poor soul. I pity her. Tell me, is Mr Painter the child's father?'

'Not he. I think he drifts through life trying to have a good time and he considered little Isobel a hindrance.'

'Um.' The Constable rubbed his chin. 'Sufficient to murder her maybe?'

'Do you know,' John answered thoughtfully, 'you could well be right.'

When he got back to The Angel it was to find that dinner was being served in the dining parlour. Hastily going to his room to change into something more fanciful, a black and silver ensemble somewhat reminiscent of his father's mode of dress, John joined Elizabeth downstairs only to discover that Rose was missing.

'Where is she?' he asked, suddenly panicking.

The Marchesa smiled reassuringly. 'She was tired out, poor little thing. I put her to bed and she fell asleep immediately.'

'But she hasn't dined,' said John, genuinely worried, unaware of how amusing he looked in his fine fancy rig with such a perturbed face.

'Oh my dear, look at you! You possess all the qualities of a fine mother hen. A missed meal won't kill the child. Lack of sleep is far more dangerous.'

The Apothecary grinned sheepishly. 'You're right. Being a sole parent is very difficult.'

'I've told you before – you will remarry.'

'Not until the day you say yes, Elizabeth.'

She gave no answer but tapped him lightly with her fan, then she took his arm and went in to dine.

Mrs Pill was absent and so were Mrs Legassick and Mrs Bligh. Anne Anstey, however, was present, sitting alone. She gave him a rapturous smile as he entered but turned her nose up at the sight of Elizabeth. The four male cousins, who were not staying at The Angel, had come in anyway and were tucking in heartily to their vittals, particularly the melon-faced man who considered himself a sure card and was, as usual, holding forth between chews. Diana Warwick, looking ravishing in a gown of palest blue, also sat alone, wistfully sipping soup. John made much of bowing to her but gave only the smallest salutation to Mrs Anstey. Elizabeth, inclining her head graciously to the assembled company, allowed John to help her into her chair, then sat serenely while he ordered wine.

'Mrs Pill must be resting,' she said in an undertone.

'Clearly, yes.'

But they were not able to pursue this topic of conversation for at that moment the door of the dining parlour was flung open to reveal Tim Painter, looking for all the world as if he had stepped straight out of a fashion plate, his dark hair tied back in an exquisite bow, his lilac suit glittering with embroidery in deep blue. He bowed to the entire room.

'Good evening,' he said, his delicious voice filling the empty corners. Then he saw Miss Warwick and in one stride had arrived at her table. 'Madam, may I join you?'

Nicholas Kitto or no Nicholas Kitto, Diana was clearly attracted to the gorgeous man standing before her.

'Mrs Pill is not with you, Sir?'

'No, she's taken to her bed.'

'I'm sorry to hear that. Yes, of course you may. I shall be pleased with the company.'

'Then I will gladly oblige.'

And snatching up her hand which had been resting on the table top, Tim kissed it long and lingeringly.

The entire room, which had gone silent during this exchange, now burst into conversation.

'Well, I reckon he's onto a winner,' said Sayce, the melon man, and burst into guffaws of laughter despite the fact that he still had food in his mouth.

'Shush,' whispered one of the Colquites.

'Damned if I will,' Sayce roared, and wiped his eyes with his napkin, meanwhile stealing a glance round the room to see if others were watching him.

Elizabeth raised a brow at John. 'Tim wasted no time I see,' she whispered.

'He's a randy lad for sure,' the Apothecary murmured back.

'I wonder how far he will get.'

John raised a suave eyebrow back at her. 'Her heart is supposedly taken by another.'

Elizabeth leant forward. 'Really? Who?'

'A young local blade called Nicholas Kitto. You saw him depart – at least I think you did – from Loe Pool this afternoon.'

The Marchesa's eyes glistened. 'Tell me all that you know.'

'Not much really. Simply that Miss Warwick – who I would estimate is several years his senior – met the young fellow somewhere or other and they have set up a clandestine affair.'

'Does one or other of them have disapproving parents?'

'Nicholas I would imagine. I can't quite imagine Diana having parents.'

Elizabeth pealed with laughter and John silently drew breath. At that moment he felt that he stood outside himself and looked on the scene, knowing that all his life, come what may between him and the dark-haired scar-faced woman with whom he would like to throw in his lot, this would be something he would remember always. The sable loveliness of her, throwing her head back in the candlelight, appreciating his humour, at ease with him in every way.

It was at this juncture that Sayce belched loudly and said, 'By Gad, that was damnable good food.' He stood up, his little eyes taking in the entire room, who stared at him, some friendly, others wishing the man would be silent and sit down again. 'Ladies and gentlemen, allow me to give you a toast. I raise my glass to those master chefs who have laboured behind the scenes to prepare tonight's feast. I ask you all to rise and drink to them.'

John, finding the fellow a total bore, none the less got to his feet, as did Elizabeth.

'The cooks, God bless 'em,' said Sayce.

Everyone drank, including Tim Painter and Diana Warwick, then sat down again, rather hurriedly John thought. But Sayce wasn't done with them yet. He remained standing and launched into an anecdote.

'Forgive me one and all if I may crave your attention a moment more. I want to tell you a yarn of my boyhood…'

His voice rambled on, punctuated with a great many wheezing laughs and thigh slaps, and all the time his tiny mean eyes were seeking out the company, looking for approbation, demanding attention, playing to his audience of would-be admirers.

Tim had long since stopped paying the man any heed and was concentrating all his charm on Diana. Leaning across the table, he covered one of her hands with his, and muttered something inaudible.

John said with asperity, 'I would have thought he might have paid some small consideration to Mrs Pill.'

'Not he,' Elizabeth answered. 'Mr Painter is a man with an eye to the main chance in life. As long as his next drink is guaranteed, as long as his next mistress – be she only for a night or two – is provided, then he is happy. He is an opportunist and the pangs of conscience that might allay the rest of us for things done or not done, simply don't apply to him.'

'Then he is brutal,' John answered softly.

'I don't think he would agree. In his mind he cares about people, worries about them. But in reality he doesn't give a straw.' Mutually they looked over at the subject of their conversation and saw that he now held both Diana's hands and was gazing at her with a steadfast expression on his face.

Mr Sayce stopped his discourse at this juncture and sat down amidst half-hearted applause. Everyone started to concentrate on their food once more with the notable exception of Anne Anstey, who suddenly began to choke, gazing piteously over a white napkin which she held tightly to her mouth.

'Oh dear,' John murmured to Elizabeth. 'I have a feeling I am about to be summoned.'

Digging in to her game pie, the Marchesa merely rolled her eyes at him in silent agreement.

Mrs Anstey continued to make alarming noises to the point that John stood up and crossed over to her table.

'Can I assist you, Madam? Perhaps a glass of water might help.'

For answer Mrs Anstey heaved violently, though thankfully not productively. John side stepped.

'I must get out,' she gasped, and practically threw herself into his arms. Throwing a desperate glance at Elizabeth, who most unsympathetically just grinned, the Apothecary began to lead her from the room.

Sayce stood up. 'Can I do anything?' he asked, glancing round the diners to make sure he had been noticed.

'Yes, accompany us if you would,' John answered desperately, struggling under Anne's not inconsiderable weight.

'Certainly, old boy. Keep a cool head in a crisis, Sayce, my old mama always used to say.'

Together, staggering slightly, the two men took Mrs Anstey outside the dining parlour and into the hallway, where she stood gasping and clutching her abdomen. John took the opportunity to race upstairs for his bag of medicines. On his return, however, he found both Sayce and the woman concerned had vanished. Feeling annoyed, he marched back into the dining parlour to discover Anne Anstey fully recovered, drinking a glass of wine and toasting Eustace Sayce, who, in return, was glowing in her fulsome compliments, together with the rest of his party.

Angrily, John sat down. 'Well, I must say...'

Elizabeth whispered, 'Oh come now. Surely you're glad to be rid of her? I'll swear she has designs on you.'

'Yes, you're right.' He looked round and saw to his astonishment that Tim and Diana were also absent.

'And where did they go?'

'Only one place I can think of,' Elizabeth answered, and slowly winked her eye.

Chapter Thirteen

In the eerie light of dawning Loe Pool had taken on a dark and sinister air, very different from the warm and pleasant aspect of the previous afternoon. Seeing it, the rising sun striking the sheet of water and burnishing it to gold, John felt that it had a mysterious quality, a quality of things unseen and unspoken, and for a moment felt his imagination run wild, wondering whether a merry-maid splashed in its depths.

He had gathered together three strong swimmers; himself, Jed and Rufus, the coachman and the guard, who had been having an excellent time of it in Helstone, spending every day at leisure and every night in the taproom. The only restriction to their total freedom had been the Apothecary's insistence that they remain at The Angel in the evenings, keeping an ear out for Rose and occasionally checking her welfare. Other than for that small duty they had had a complete rest from work. But now they had been called in to help look for the body of Isobel Pill.

John had hoped to bring Tim Painter in to assist but there had been no sign of him last night after his sudden disappearance with Diana. And to call him this morning would have been bad manners indeed. So the Apothecary and his small contingent had presented themselves to the Constable before first light and declared themselves willing to undertake the grisly task that lay ahead.

William Trethowan, in company with three other powerful men, had met them at the bottom of Coinage Hall Street, and then the little troop had walked the rest of the way to the Loe and arrived just as the sun was glinting over the horizon.

'If she's there she'll be in the shallows. But if she *was* murdered, then her killer might have had had a boat and weighted her down.'

John shook his head. 'If she was killed, then whoever did it acted on the spur of the moment, I feel certain of it.'

'Then she should be somewhere where we can get at her. So let's to it.'

He positioned his men at quarter of a mile intervals and told them to dive in and look around, then, having covered the delegated area, to keep moving on. But even as he set them the task the Constable had a hopeless air about him, as if he knew that however hard they searched they would come up with nothing.

John, diving into the green water, found it depressing and rather horrible and not a task that he would wish on anyone. And when he surfaced, having ploughed his way through weeds, he could see in the distance that Rufus and Jed were equally miserable at the task which it had been their duty to perform. Eventually, though, after four hours searching, the Constable called the wretched business off.

'It's useless, lads. There's nothing down there but dead dogs. If the maiden's in the Loe then she's sunk to where we can't get her.'

'What'll us do, Willum?'

'Leave it be. There's naught else. I'll have to see her mother and tell her straightly what's transpired.'

'I'll come with you if you like,' the Apothecary offered.

'No, Sir, it's a grim task but I'll do it on my own,' the Constable replied with dignity, earning himself even more credit in John's eyes.

It was by now seven o'clock and the weary men, having towelled and dressed themselves, started the walk back into town. As they did so William beckoned John to one side.

'Excuse me asking, Sir, but have you any experience of this kind of thing? I mean through your apothecarying or such-like?'

John decided to admit everything. 'Yes, as a matter of fact I work from time to time with Sir John Fielding, the Principal Magistrate of London. Years ago I was briefly suspected of committing a murder but fortunately when he questioned me, Mr Fielding, as he then was, realised I was telling the truth. I assisted him to find that murderer and I have been doing so ever since, off and on.'

'London is a long, long way from here, Sir, of course. But I reckon you must be thought something of to work with Sir John.'

'Have you heard of him?'

'No, Sir, to be honest I haven't.'

'He's blind you know. He's known to the mob as the Blind Beak.'

'You don't say.'

'And talking of that, what do you know about the blind fiddler?'

The Constable chuckled. 'The Gaffer? Not very much really. He first appeared on Flora Day about five years ago. He organises the music, as you've heard for yourself. None of them, not he nor his band, want paying for the privilege. Instead they send a boy round – this year it was a monkey – with a hat. Then they move on. I reckon they'll be going in a day or two.'

'And what about the rest of the people?' John asked. 'Will they be off soon?'

'Oh yes. In the next few days the town will return to normal.'

'And Isobel's murderer – if he exists – will walk away with the others. That is if she *is* dead.'

Trethowan stopped in his tracks, forcing the Apothecary to do likewise. 'You may believe me a superstitious fool, Mr Rawlings. And I suppose that in many ways I am. But I have great faith in Gypsy Orchard. She's been around Helstone ever since she was a thin little girl fending for herself. And I've asked her things in the past and what she has told me has always come about. So if she says to me that Isobel is drowned, then drowned the child is.'

It was a great testament of belief and in the face of such blazing sincerity John would have felt cheapened and somehow shabby if he had argued. Instead he said, 'Then you face a difficult situation, Constable.'

'I've a plan for that, Sir.'

'And what is it?'

'To ask everyone staying at The Angel Inn to remain a few more days while I continue to search.'

'And if they refuse?'

'Then I shall regard them as mighty suspicious and question them hard.'

'And if that doesn't work?'

'Then I shall reluctantly be forced to let them go.'

John was silent, resuming his walk back to Helstone, thinking that both he and the Constable were going to have a great deal to do before people left the town for good. He was still contemplating where it would be best to start when he reached the front door steps of the hostelry and turned in, meeting Muriel Legassick and Tabitha Bligh on their way out.

'Good morning, ladies,' he said pleasantly.

They both bobbed curtsies. 'Good morning, Mr Rawlings, and a very fine one too.'

'When are you thinking of leaving, may I ask?' he enquired politely, getting straight down to business.

Mrs Legassick smiled and her eyes behind her spectacles loomed suddenly large. 'Well, it rather depends on the Colquites. They are all for us remaining at The Angel for a few days more but then they live close by and do not have the tedious journey back to Wiltshire to contend with. But we shall make up our minds today, you may depend on it.'

Tabitha, who had been running her eyes over the Apothecary, said, 'And what about you, Mr Rawlings? What are your plans?'

'I shall probably remain for another few days,' he said airily. 'It rather depends on the Marchesa's wishes.'

'Oh yes, of course, your travelling companion.' Tabitha robustly stressed the last two words. 'How delightful it must be for you, to be sure, to have such a charming lady to escort.'

'Oh yes it is. Very. Good day, ladies.' And bowing once more, the Apothecary made his way inside.

It was shortly after seven in the morning and the general

flow of people were coming down to breakfast. John, realising that he looked a scallywag but not really caring, decided to join them, hoping that Elizabeth and Rose would soon put in an appearance. The early morning exercise had given him a ravenous appetite and he ordered ham, eggs, herrings and various other delicacies that the bill of fare was offering. He was just through his third slice of gammon when Rose entered the room alone. He stood up and kissed her.

'Good day to you, my darling. Did you sleep well?'

'Yes thank you, Papa.'

'And where is Mrs Elizabeth?'

'I knocked on her door, Papa, but she didn't answer.'

John looked up from his food.

'Strange. I hope she's alright.'

'Perhaps she didn't hear me.'

'None the less I think I'll go and check. Now you stay here like a good girl and eat your breakfast. I shall only be a few minutes. Wait for me, Rose.'

Leaving the table, the Apothecary hurried up the stairs and gave a loud knock on the Marchesa's door. There was no reply, and acting on instinct he went to Mrs Pill's room and knocked there.

'Come in,' said Tim Painter's voice.

Opening the door he found Kathryn, Tim and Elizabeth talking together earnestly.

'I'm sorry. Am I intruding?'

They looked up and John took in the fact that Mrs Pill was not only up and dressed but had a most determined expression on her face.

The Marchesa got to her feet. 'I've taken up enough of your time.'

Kathryn spoke. 'No, my dear, you have been most kind.' She turned to John. 'Mr Rawlings, I have decided to return home and fetch what few male servants I have. They, together with my brother, will then return and search Helstone high and low for Isobel. You see, I will never believe she is dead until I see her body for myself. I think she is being held captive in someone's house. That is what I reckon.'

John would like to have agreed with her but Gypsy Orchard's face as she described water coming over her head, returned to haunt him.

'I hope you're right,' he said feebly.

Tim spoke up. 'I shall stay and continue the search in the meantime.'

Surreptitiously Elizabeth and John exchanged a look, remembering his performance on the previous evening with Diana Warwick. Then they chorused, 'Yes.'

Mrs Pill put on her travelling cloak and arranged a hat on her head.

'My coachman waits below,' she announced and proceeded from the room, Tim Painter at her heels. John and Elizabeth descended the staircase more slowly.

The Marchesa turned to look at him. 'Did you find anything this morning?'

He shook his head. 'No, I'm afraid not.'

'The child is dead, isn't she?'

'According to Gypsy Orchard, yes.'

'And that woman is a Charmer which means she has an ancient gift.'

'Really.' Remembering the gypsy's prophecy about his son, John suddenly gave a broad grin.

'And what are you smiling about?' asked Elizabeth, giving him a sideways glance.

'Wouldn't you like to know,' John answered.

They entered the dining parlour together and the Apothecary looked across at his table. His daughter, whom he had left sitting there, promising her father that she would wait for him, was missing. He turned to Elizabeth.

'Rose? Where is she?'

She stared at him blankly. 'When did you last see her?'

'She was down here, eating breakfast with me. I told her to stay but...' John hastened to the serving girl. 'My daughter was sitting at that table.' He pointed. 'Did you see where she went?'

'She went away with a lady, Sir.'

'Who? Do you know her?'

'Yes, Sir. She's staying here but I'm not sure of her name.'

'Thank you.'

He and Elizabeth were off, flying down the street in different directions, calling Rose's name loudly. Inside himself, John felt physically sick, the horrible thought going through his mind that there could be a gang of child abductors at work in Helstone and that Rose was their latest victim. Having run the length of Coinage Hall Street and back on the opposite side, he saw Elizabeth hurrying down on the other part of the road. Calling her name, he ran rapidly across and joined her. Too out of breath to speak, she merely shook her head.

John gasped, 'Let's look in the stable yard.'

They passed under the lamp-hung arch and then stopped dead. Sitting on the wall by the well was Anne Anstey, clearly recovered from her choking fit of the previous night. Next to her was Mrs Legassick, and wedged in between them, clearly hanging on every word Anne was saying to her, was Rose.

'Don't be angry,' said Elizabeth quietly. 'Remember she's young yet.'

John put on as pleasant a countenance as he was capable of, and walked forward, calling his child's name. She looked up startled, then scrambled off the wall. But it was at Mrs Anstey that he was actually staring, so that her expression made a sharp impression on him. Just for a second he saw guilt, followed by a conscious effort to mask that emotion. Then her usual lecherous expression returned as she ran her eyes over the Apothecary, standing there in his rough-and-tumble state.

'What a delightful daughter you have, Mr Rawlings. She and I have just been getting better acquainted.'

'So I see,' John replied unpleasantly.

'Run along to your father, dear.'

But Rose had already crossed the short distance between them and had wound herself round the Apothecary's legs. And it was at that moment, with the air full of tension and John wondering how to handle the situation, that a first floor window flew ajar and a maid's frantic face appeared in the opening.

'Help!' she screamed. 'Somebody please come!'

Every head craned back as they all looked upward.

'What's the matter?' called John.

'Oh Sir. It's Miss Warwick. Oh come at once. I think she's been murdered.'

She was lying on the bed, quite naked, and just for a moment John caught himself admiring the perfect figure topped by a pair of exquisite shapely breasts. Then he remembered where he was and took himself to task. Crossing to Diana Warwick's side, he bent over and applied his fingers to the pulse in her neck. There was nothing. It was as the chambermaid had suspected. Miss Warwick was dead.

The Apothecary straightened up. 'I think, my girl, that you had better send for a physician.'

'Oh yes, Sir. I'll go at once.' And the frightened creature left the room in a hurry.

Alone with the corpse, John began the task he loathed, examining the dead woman to see if there was any indication as to what had caused her death. Gritting his teeth, he started with the head, gently feeling her neck for signs of anything broken. There was nothing. Neither was the face marked in any way. Nor did her breath smell of any poison and there was no swelling of the lips or tongue. Indeed, other than for a startled expression in the staring eyes, Diana Warwick could have just dropped off to sleep. After looking into them for a second or two, John drew down the lids.

Though he was loath to look, the vaginal area revealed recent sexual activity.

'Surprise indeed!' thought John, certain that Tim Painter was the man involved.

But as to the cause of her death, there was no outward sign. Puzzled, John stood up as the door opened to reveal a slim dark young man.

'And who might you be, Sir?' he asked John suspiciously.

John gave a brief bow. 'I'm an apothecary. I'm staying in the inn and was first on the scene to examine the body.'

The man nodded his head. 'I'm Dr Penhale. Well, Sir, what have you deduced?'

'Nothing at all, Sir. It would appear that the woman died of natural causes.'

'Have you any reason to think she should not?'

'None. Except for the fact that she was relatively young. That and…'

But how to put into words the uncomfortable feeling he had been left with since the disappearance of Isobel?

'Except what, Sir?' asked the doctor, who had started to examine the body.

'Nothing really. A child vanished the day before yesterday, that is all.'

Dr Penhale was examining Diana's privy parts. 'Seems this woman had had intercourse shortly before she died.'

'Yes, I gathered that.'

'Who was she, do you know? I mean, did she have a husband?'

'She used the title Miss Warwick and there was no sign of any such person. I rather imagine she was a woman of the world, if you take my meaning.'

'I do take it, Sir. But what do you think caused her to die?'

'Is it possible that a subtle poison has been used?'

'It would have to be something unknown because the wretched woman did not vomit or have laxes. But why do you think it might be murder, Mr Rawlings?'

'As I told you, Dr Penhale, the strange disappearance of a little girl has unsettled me. But it is probably quite coincidental and Miss Warwick has died naturally.'

The doctor looked at the corpse again. 'Do you think it possible that she was smothered?'

'By a pillow you mean?'

'That, or something similar.'

'In the act of ravishment?' John asked.

'Yes, I would have thought that could have happened.' Dr Penhale shook his dark head. 'But surely our imaginations are running riot. Here is a woman who died during – or very soon after – venery. That is all there is to it, unless…'

'Unless?'

'As I said earlier, perhaps her unknown lover took her life.' Dr Penhale gave a short laugh. 'Here am I, just taken over my father's practice, and a strange death occurs. Well, I will report the matter to the Constable.'

The two men prepared to leave the room but not before they had stood on either side of the bed, looking at the last mortal remains of Diana Warwick.

'She was very beautiful,' said the doctor.

'Yes, Sir, she was. How old do you reckon her to be?'

'I don't know. It is difficult to say.'

John gazed at the lovely face, now the colour of a snowdrop. 'I would think about forty,' he said.

The physician answered, 'You're probably right. Shall we cover her up?' And the two of them pulled a sheet up and hid that most delectable of women from the world.

As they left the room, John turned the key in the lock, and the physician turned on him a look of surprise.

'Just to make sure no one enters,' the Apothecary said by way of explanation.

Dr Penhale allowed the first smile of the day to cross his rather set features. 'You think of everything, Mr Rawlings. Have you any experience of these matters?'

'Yes,' said John shortly, and left it at that.

Downstairs everything was very quiet. Elizabeth sat with Rose, while Mrs Anstey and Mrs Legassick, together with Mrs Bligh, who had joined them, were pretending to read newspapers. They all looked up as John and the doctor came in.

'Is it true?' Elizabeth asked quietly.

'Yes, I'm afraid it is.'

She looked into his eyes and asked a silent question and John shrugged his shoulders, indicating the three other women who sat, silent as mice, listening to every word uttered.

'Come, my dears,' he said to the Marchesa and his daughter, 'let us step outside.'

Taking Rose's hand, Elizabeth moved rapidly out of the front door to the street. The Apothecary spoke in an urgent undertone.

'She's dead all right but with no outward signs of violence. Yet both the doctor and I agree that she could have been smothered. He is going to report the matter to the Constable.'

The Marchesa made a face. 'Tim Painter?' she said.

'Exactly what I thought.'

'John, what are you going to do?'

'I've got to speak to him and also to Nicholas Kitto. Urgently. Have you seen Tim at all?'

'No, not a sign since Mrs Pill went off in her carriage.'

'Well, I'm going to find him. God's life, I seem to do nothing but spend my time searching this benighted town.'

Elizabeth smiled. 'I can think of worse places to look.'

John grinned. 'So can I. Tell me one thing, did Kathryn know that we found nothing this early morning?'

'Yes, and it strengthened her determination to come back with reinforcements.'

'Good. Are you all right looking after Rose?'

'Rose and I are always all right.'

'Excellent. Then I'll be off.' And planting a swift kiss on the cheeks of the Marchesa and his daughter, John made his way to The Blue Anchor. Exactly as he had thought, he found Tim Painter in the taproom, downing ale at some speed. Without ado John went up to him.

'Good day to you, old boy…'

But Tim stopped short, seeing the expression on the other's face.

'How was Diana Warwick when you left her?' John asked abruptly.

A range of expressions, culminating in one of extreme innocence, raced over the handsome man's features.

'Well, thank you.'

'That won't do, Painter. The woman's dead and there is bound to be an enquiry as to how she died. So I'll ask you before the Constable does. When and where did you last see her?'

Tim swallowed the rest of his glass of ale and drawled, 'Well you could give as good an opinion of that as I, my friend.'

'How so?'

'Because when we left the dining parlour she complained of feeling a little faint. So I escorted her to her room and that was the last I saw of her. But you say she's dead? What a terrible thing. I can scarcely believe it.'

His expression during this speech was one of studied innocence mixed with shock, and John, watching him, decided that the chap would have made a first-rate actor.

'Well, you had better start believing it,' said the Apothecary, 'because you will have to tell your tale to the Constable.'

Tim looked mortified. 'Why? Why should I? I merely escorted the poor woman to her chamber. What have I to do with her death?'

His beautifully moderated voice had raised a little in anger and one or two other customers gave him a glance.

John thought carefully, then decided to be forthright. 'Look Tim,' he said, 'it would be better to make a clean breast of it to me rather than lie to those in authority. William Trethowan is far from stupid and you could be in serious trouble if you told him a falsehood.'

Painter turned away, banging his glass down on the counter. 'Another pint of your excellent ale, if you please,' was all he said.

The Apothecary had been dismissed and he knew it. But for all that he believed little of what had just been said to him. Tim Painter was hiding something, of that much he was absolutely positive.

Nicholas Kitto was the next person he should call on but he hadn't a notion where the fellow lived. However a few discreet enquiries at The Blue Anchor, plus the passing of a coin, provided him with the necessary information. It appeared that young Nick was studying to be a lawyer and currently had taken articles with the firm of Penaluna Brothers. Having received directions as to where this was situated, the

Apothecary walked to Meneage Street, wondering exactly how he was going to present himself. In the event, though, the situation was made easy for him. Nicholas was just being shown out, face pale as a cloud, with the firm direction to return home.

John bowed. 'My dear Sir, allow me to escort you. You are clearly unwell and need someone to walk with you.'

Nicholas, barely recognising him, gave a feeble nod. 'Kind of you, Sir.'

'Not at all. I am an apothecary and used to dealing with illness. Here, take my arm.'

'Gladly,' Nicholas replied, and they set off in sad procession, crossing the road and making their way up the street that led to the church. Somewhat to the Apothecary's surprise, they walked up to the last house in the lane, a rather large and grand affair, and here they stopped.

'Thank you so much,' the young man said weakly.

John, seizing the moment, answered, 'Oh I couldn't possibly leave you alone. I must hand you into the care of your parents.'

Nick pulled a face. 'I only have a mother and I believe she might be out.'

'Then I will come and sit with you until she returns. And I won't take no for an answer.'

Once inside, the Apothecary looked round. The house was simply but expensively furnished in tasteful colours. Indeed it was the best dwelling he had been in since his arrival in Helstone. But he had little time to take more than a cursory glance for no sooner were they within than Nicholas turned the colour of a blanched almond and collapsed into a chair, his head swinging down between his knees.

John, wishing he had his bag of physics and potions, looked round the room and saw several decanters standing on a tray. Rapidly he crossed to it and poured brandy into a glass. This he guided towards Nicholas's lips.

The young man sipped and looked up, then he burst into uncontrollable tears, weeping as loudly and mournfully as a child. Clutching at John's coat, he murmured, 'Oh my God, my God. How can I face the future without her?'

This was John's cue and he took it, the ruthless side of his nature dominant.

'You mean Diana?' he said softly.

'Yes, of course.'

'Then you know she's dead?'

'Yes, yes,' sobbed the wretched youth.

'How did you know?'

'Because I found her.'

'I see,' said the Apothecary, taking a seat beside him. 'Now perhaps you would like to tell me all about it.'

There was a silence broken only by the chiming of a long case clock and the sound of a carter proceeding down the lane. Finally Nicholas spoke, his voice punctuated by sobs.

'How far back do you want me to go?' he asked tremulously.

'To the very beginning,' John answered him.

'The first time I met Diana was with my father.'

'But I thought you said…'

'Yes, I did. I have a father but I always thought of him as my uncle, that is until recently.'

'Are you by any chance illegitimate?' John asked.

Nick looked at him, his eyes still pouring tears. 'Yes, of course I am.'

'Then who is your father?'

'I'd rather not say.'

John immediately leapt to the conclusion that the man was a local dignitary and that was why his identity was being protected.

'Very well. Please go on.'

'I first met Diana when I was twelve. She was a few years older than I was…'

Probably about twenty years, thought the Apothecary irreverently.

'Anyway she was a poor young girl from Truro and my father rescued her, brought her to Helstone and took her under his wing.'

Well aware of the meaning of that, John checked himself for being so flippant when the young fellow telling the tale was obviously in extremis.

'And where was your mother at this time?'

Nicholas made a strange noise. 'My mother has put it about that I am her nephew. She went away to give birth to me and returned, according to her, with her sister's child. My father has set her up very nicely as you can see.'

John looked about him. 'Yes, it is an elegant house indeed.'

A strange expression crossed Nick's face. 'My father is quite an important man, you see.'

'I imagined he must be someone of substance.'

Nicholas looked as if he was longing to go further but had come to the conclusion that discretion must rule. 'He is,' was all that he said.

John decided that he must return to the matter in hand. 'Tell me about yesterday.'

'I had arranged to meet Diana early in the morning. At six o'clock, before my mother rises. I was going to leave the house and hurry to The Angel.'

'Yes?'

'Well, I got there a little late; at about a quarter past. I rushed upstairs to Diana's room and knocked on the door. There was no reply so I tried the handle and it opened and I went inside. It was dark within but the curtains were not drawn and she was lying on the bed.'

Nicholas stopped speaking and his shoulders began to heave. John, terrified that the young man was going to be seized by another fit of weeping said, 'Finish your story, I beg you.'

'I…I bent over her, and then…'

'Go on.'

'One of her arms fell over the edge of the bed and swung.' He shot the Apothecary a piteous look. 'Oh, Mr Rawlings, she was dead.'

And the poor chap burst into tears once more.

Chapter Fifteen

About half an hour later the Apothecary left Nicholas's house and, being so near to the church, entered in order to think quietly. Taking a seat in one of the pews, he got his ideas in order. Firstly the disappearance of Isobel Pill had now taken on a decidedly sinister aspect. With no sign of the child or her body it was beginning to look more and more like a case of abduction, despite Gypsy Orchard's graphic description of her death by drowning. Yet, he supposed, that somewhere in the dark recesses of Loe Pool the body might still be lurking. An unpleasant thought.

His mind moved on to the death of Diana Warwick. He completely believed Nick who, it seemed to the Apothecary, would be incapable of weaving such a web of lies and deceit. Yet when asked why he hadn't reported the death to the Constable, the poor young man had admitted that he was slightly ashamed of the liaison and had been too afraid to go to the authorities. Tim, on the other hand, was patently lying. But had he murdered her? Indeed, had she been murdered at all? Or had she died of natural causes, due, perhaps, to over-exertion? John looked grim at the last thought, his mind dwelling on what exactly Diana had been. It seemed to him that she was working as a prostitute when Nicholas's father – whoever he might be – had picked her up in Truro and set her up in a little house somewhere. Then, at some stage, she had turned from father to son, presumably when the old man tired of her.

It suddenly seemed important to John to discover this unknown person's identity and enquire discreetly whether he had seen the lady recently. Perhaps he might be able to throw some light on the matter of her death. But in any event, the Apothecary felt extremely curious as to who the man could possibly be. But how he was going to find out was an entirely different matter.

Sighing, he rose from his pew, still thinking hard, and at

that moment the church door opened and the three women – Muriel Legassick, Tabitha Bligh and Anne Anstey – entered in a bunch, talking in whispers. Something made John sit down again and, occupying a back pew as he was, behind the entrance door, he knew he hadn't been seen. From this vantage point, he watched them with interest.

They were supposed to be cousins but he had to confess that there was no family resemblance that he could observe, as they came in wildly assorted sizes and shapes. Mrs Anstey was the largest, oozing out of the top of her gown with an amazing décolletage that made John's head swim. She had white hair, swept up under a vast hat, beneath which her lecherous eyes rolled as she cast them round the church, taking in all the artefacts. She was most like Mrs Bligh to look at, the Apothecary supposed, but even then the resemblance was not striking. Tabitha Bligh, who fancied her chance as greatly as Anne, was staring round to see if there were any men present and, not having noticed the Apothecary, had a bored expression on her face.

'A reasonable place,' said Anne Anstey loudly, 'for a church.'

'It certainly is,' responded Mrs Legassick, 'but then I have known it a while.' She turned to Tabitha. 'Do you remember when…' Here her voice dropped to an inaudible whisper.

Tabitha giggled and inexplicably raised the hem of her garment, revealing a short but shapely leg. Meanwhile Mrs Anstey had swept down the aisle as far as the altar rail where she paused before opening it and moving up to the altar itself.

John stared aghast. Though not a particularly religious man – not typical of his time – this behaviour was quite unacceptable. And then, quite unexpectedly, he coughed, not once but twice. Every head turned and each lady froze where she stood. There was nothing for it but to rise from his pew and make a bow. They all curtseyed in return and hurried towards him.

'Oh, Mr Rawlings, you naughty man. I'm afraid we didn't see you,' chirruped Mrs Legassick.

Dying to reply, 'That was obvious,' John manfully smiled and said, 'Truth to tell I dropped off to sleep,' thus covering his tracks.

Mrs Anstey had hastily retreated from the altar, leaving the rail undone. She now swept forward and curtseyed once more, revealing a great deal of cleavage in the process.

'Mr Rawlings,' she said in a deep voice, 'what are you doing here alone? You are usually surrounded by a horde of females.'

'How kind of you to say so,' he answered, clutching his hat to his heart.

She stared at him suspiciously, wondering whether he was being facetious. John kept a straight face.

'I was just admiring the beauties of this church,' she said, just a little uncertainly.

'It is indeed very fine. Now, ladies, will you give me the pleasure of escorting you back to the inn?'

John had the strangest feeling that he should not leave them alone in the place.

Mrs Bligh smiled up at him, her eyes vanishing as she did so in a horde of merry creases. 'We are quite capable of making our own way, Sir.'

'Then in that case,' John said firmly, 'I shall wait for you.' He saw mouths forming protests and raised a hand, 'I absolutely insist. I shall sit down again and await you. Please continue to look round and take no notice of me whatsoever.'

He sat and they continued their perambulations though the Apothecary could not help noticing that Mrs Anstey stayed well away from the high altar. Ten minutes later they were done and John led his troop out into the open countryside in which the church stood. They all paused for a moment drinking in the fresh Cornish air, looking about them to where sheep grazed in the fields, and the hills rose beyond. It was such a peaceful scene to encompass so much recent unpleasantness, yet in the Apothecary's experience this was often the way. His mind went back to the beauty of Gunnersbury House, standing in its own fine grounds, and he thought for a long moment about Emilia and how much he missed her. At that second he doubted he would ever marry again and he felt enormously saddened.

Realising that he was standing looking glum, John rallied. 'Ladies, are you ready to return?'

Mrs Anstey's voice drowned the replies of the others. 'I think, Sir, that we will call on the Colquites and the rest of our cousins. As you know, the brothers live locally. It is only a short step from here.'

For no reason that he could think of the Apothecary felt a thrill of unease. Yet there was nothing harmful about the men: the Colquites were a silly old couple, like a pair of spinsters. As for Sayce, he beamed joviality at all and sundry, while Reece was so neat, so tidy, so minute in fact, that he could pose a threat to nobody. Yet there was something about them collectively that John found disquieting. However, he thrust the notion away.

'Of course. I shall walk home alone. Good day to you.'

He bowed once more and parted company from them, proceeding back to The Angel solitary and deep in thought. On the way there he saw Tim Painter, striding up the street at a fair rate, going in the same direction as the three ladies. John wondered whether to hail him but thought better of it when he remembered their parting. He proceeded onward and was nearing The Angel when his attention was drawn by the arrival of a heavily built and somewhat old-fashioned coach. Importantly stepping from it was a mature man greeted with the utmost respect by the passing populace. Women bobbed and men doffed their hats, while a small child burst into tears at all the fuss. Drawing nearer, the Apothecary recognised him as the fellow who had been walking along the street the night before the Furry Dance. Turning to a passer-by, he said, 'Who is that man?'

'Baron Godolphin, Sir.'

'Hence all the bowing and scraping. I might have guessed.'

'He's the local peer of the realm. Baron Godolphin of Helstone.'

'Ah, that would explain it.'

Seized by the sudden idea that he could possibly be looking at Nicholas's actual father, who was definitely a local dignitary, John gave an elaborate bow and was rewarded by a cold glance from eyes hard as steel.

Just the type to have fathered a bastard child, thought John, and said 'Sarvant, Sah,' in an affected London accent.

'Do I know you?' asked the other nastily.

'No, Sir, you do not. I was merely passing the time of day.'

At this moment their conversation, if it could be described as such, was interrupted by the landlord appearing in the doorway, bowing and rubbing his hands.

'Good day, Lord Godolphin. A pleasure to see you again, Sir.'

'Good day,' his lordship replied briefly, and marched into the inn.

After a moment's hesitation, the Apothecary followed.

Lord Godolphin strode into the inner recesses but John, hearing a noise on the stairs, looked up just in time to see a shape covered by a cloth being carried down on a plank. Behind it came the Constable looking grim-faced. Catching sight of John, he called out, 'A word with you, Sir, if you please.'

'Certainly.'

He reached the bottom and the two men carrying the body came to a brief halt.

'To the mortuary, Will?'

'Aye.'

John asked, 'Have you informed the Coroner?'

'A message has been sent, yes.' William Trethowan hesitated. 'Do you think she did die naturally, Sir?'

'I'm not sure. There are no marks on her body as you probably noticed.'

For a large man, the Constable seemed to wither. 'I didn't look too closely.'

'Well I did and I can assure you that neither the doctor nor I could see any. But that doesn't rule out smothering.'

'But who could have done that?'

'I think,' John replied thoughtfully, 'that it could have been one of several people.'

That night, with Rose safely in bed and Jed keeping watch from the taproom, John and the Marchesa stepped out into the cool air.

'So what is your opinion?' she asked, as direct as ever.

'About Diana do you mean?'

'Her and the child.'

The Apothecary looked thoughtful. 'I'm not sure about either of them.'

'Is there a link, do you believe?'

'It's possible, though for the life of me I can't see what it could be.'

Elizabeth frowned. 'As they had apparently never met before they arrived it certainly presents a difficult problem.'

'But supposing there were some connection between them. That Mrs Pill knew Miss Warwick and they had come here by special arrangement. What then?'

The Marchesa shook her dark head. 'I don't think so somehow, though you might be right. Tell me all you have discovered about the woman.'

'As far as I can make out she was a poor prostitute from Truro, living as best she could. Then she was taken under the wing of Nicholas Kitto's mysterious father...'

'Who is he?' Elizabeth interrupted.

'That I am not sure of. You know I went to see young Kitto today...?'

She nodded.

'Well, he confessed to me that he was the bastard child of some local bigwig or other. He also told me that Diana was his father's mistress until Nick took her on.'

A lesser woman might have looked shocked but Elizabeth merely nodded. 'I see. A strange situation but not unheard of. Have you any idea who this mysterious parent is?'

'There's a local peer called Lord Godolphin. It could be him I suppose.'

'What makes you think so?'

'He's all ruffles and hard face. But you've seen him yourself. Do you remember the night before the Furry when Diana hastily crossed the road?'

'Yes, I do.'

'Do you recall a middle-aged man, probably about sixty, walking along on his own?'

'Yes.'

'That was him.'

Elizabeth looked extremely thoughtful. 'Quite a handsome fellow in his way. Perhaps Diana hurried away in order to avoid him. At the time it seemed an extraordinary thing for her to do.'

'It did indeed. But now it makes sense.'

'Yes, and it also provides a motive for murder.'

'You mean Lord Godolphin killed her for some reason or other?'

'Either him or Tim Painter.' The Apothecary braced his shoulders. 'I must have another look at the body. That is if I can get permission.'

'Do you know where she has been taken?'

'To the mortuary. I'll contact the Constable first thing in the morning.'

'A good idea.' The Marchesa smiled up at him. 'Now, we have spoken enough of death and murder. Let us talk of something else.'

'Our plans perhaps?' said John, turning his full gaze on her.

She shook her head and her dark hair was caught in the moonlight, giving it a silvery sheen.

'You'll be beautiful even when you're old,' he said.

She laughed. 'What are you talking about? I am old.'

'No you're not. You have the spirit of eternal youth.'

'I might have in your eyes but actually I am forty-seven in August.'

It was on the tip of John's tongue to tell her that next month he would be thirty-four but he held back. Instead he took her in his arms and kissed her. Then, laughing, they made their way downhill and made love quite naturally in the shadow of the trees that lay at the bottom, a rapturous experience to add their own sounds of pleasure to the noises of the night all about them. It was an unforgettable heightening of their relationship and afterwards, walking back slowly towards the inn, their arms round each other, John felt almost emboldened to ask her yet again if she would stay with him for ever. But once more he remained silent and as the evening came finally to an end, he could do nothing more than bid her goodnight and go quietly to his room.

Chapter Sixteen

John woke early, and putting his head round his daughter's door, saw that she was still asleep. But there was a stirring in the street below that was attracting his attention. Dressing quickly, he went out of The Angel's front entrance then stood, somewhat dismayed by what he was seeing. The blind fiddler and his band were leaving town, playing as they went. First came the Gaffer, his dark hair and his blackened spectacles gleaming in the early morning sunshine. A pace behind him, as usual, was Gideon – the monkey sitting on his shoulder and banging the tambourine. Behind him, in their turn, came the flautist and the kettle drums player, the mandora and fagotto players bringing up the rear.

The Apothecary's heart sank. The band's departure meant that there would be no further festivities, which, in turn, signalled the exit of most of the people who had come to Helstone to see the Furry. And, consequently, most of the people present when Isobel Pill had vanished and Diana Warwick killed. At any moment he was going to be left with both these mysteries to unravel and no witnesses to help him. In a sudden panic, John fell into step beside the fiddler.

'You're going from Helstone I take it.'

The head beneath its battered hat turned slightly and the darkened glasses flashed in the Apothecary's direction; for one incredible second John had the impression that he was being regarded.

'Mr Rawlings, isn't it?'

'Yes, how clever of you to know.'

'Ah, not just a pretty face, be I.'

The fiddler laughed and John saw a flash of white teeth, rather than the rotting brown stumps he had half-expected.

'May I ask why you are leaving?'

'Well, Sir, it be over. All dead and buried for another year. So what's the point in staying on?'

'Where will you go next?' John asked.

'Wherever there's a fair or festivity in Devon or Cornwall, that's where you'll find us.'

'Do you only travel in the West Country?'

'It's been known for us to go as far as Wiltshire, Sir, and to Dorset.'

Something about this remark struck the Apothecary as significant but for the life of him he couldn't place what it was. He dropped back a pace or two in order to speak to the others.

Gideon, of whom the monkey had obviously grown fond, had now retrieved his tambourine from Wilkes's leathery claws, and was banging and whirling it enthusiastically. The monkey, meanwhile, was chattering away, its face perpetually sad beneath its small tricorne hat. It bared its teeth as it saw the Apothecary but whether it was grinning or snarling he could not be certain.

John strove to remember the names of the rest. The little flautist was James and the craggy-faced kettledrum man with the wicked roving eye, was George. The aesthetic mandora player was called Zachariah, while his jolly fat friend, who puffed his cheeks out while he blew, was Giles. John turned his attention to the mandora man.

'Are you sorry to be leaving Helstone?' he asked brightly.

'No, Sir, I'm not. Seems like this Furry has been cursed what with the little maid vanishing and Miss Warwick dying so suddenly. A shocking affair.'

Giles, who had been blowing hard, stopped for breath. 'I reckon the Gaffer's right to move on. Mysterious though, ain't it. Do you know aught about it, Sir?'

'Not much more than you, I should imagine.'

The fat man looked slightly downcast. 'I thought you might, seeing as how you mixed with them.'

'I wasn't really that close,' John answered evasively.

A small crowd had started to cheer the musicians from the town and amongst them was Rose, still in her nightshift, but at least with a pair of shoes on. Unaware of her father's presence she ran straight up to Gideon.

'Oh dear, are you going?'

'Yes, we'm be off.'

'And you are taking Wilkes with you?'

'Of course we are. He's my little pet, ain't he.'

'Can I hold him once more?'

'Yes, you certainly can.' And Gideon handed the monkey to her.

It was almost as big as she was but for all that Rose cuddled the animal enthusiastically. John was vividly reminded of her mother who at one stage had wanted to adopt every stray creature they had come across. He rather feared that their daughter might well have inherited the same characteristic. He watched her as she fondled the monkey's ugly head and held one of its claw-like hands.

She looked up and saw him. 'Oh Papa. He's going away.'

'Yes, my dear. But he's happy with Gideon and the Gaffer. Now hand him back.'

She plonked a kiss on the grim little face, then did so. John looked at her and saw that a solitary tear was running down beside her nose.

'Don't be sad, darling. I am sure you will see him again one day.'

'I do hope so.' She brightened up. 'What shall we do today, Papa?'

'I have a commitment this morning. At least I hope I have,' he added in an undertone. 'But after that I will be free to do whatever you want.'

'Could we go to the sea again?'

'Provided Mrs Elizabeth wants to go, yes.'

'Is she going to become my mother?' Rose asked, her directness reminding John of the woman in question.

He looked at her, thinking she was young yet to know his true feelings on the matter, which were, to be honest, totally confused.

'Perhaps,' he said.

'I see,' Rose answered and flashed him a look which confirmed his belief that she was an old soul with ancient wisdom.

'The truth is that I don't believe Mrs Elizabeth wishes to marry again,' he found himself blurting out.

His daughter nodded, said, 'Poor Papa,' and taking him by the hand led him back towards the inn as if she were the adult and he the little child.

As soon as he had consumed a reasonable breakfast, John Rawlings went to see the Constable in his place of work. He came immediately to the point.

'I want to have another look at Miss Warwick's body, if that is agreeable to you.'

William straightened up and wiped the sweat from his brow. 'Why, Sir?'

'I need to see if there is any indication that she was smothered.'

'Have you informed the doctor of this?'

'I called at his house on the way here but he was out on his rounds. So I've come to you in the hope that you'll give permission.'

'I would rather Dr Penhale agreed.'

'That means a wait of several hours.'

The Constable hesitated, weighing up the pros and cons, then finally said with a sigh, 'Oh very well. But I insist on accompanying you.'

Glad that he had been given the opportunity of a second examination, John nodded with an enthusiasm he did not feel.

The mortuary was attached to the workhouse, situated in Meneage Street, a mere stone's throw from Trethowan's place of work. Walking side-by-side, John carrying a small medical bag with him, the two men made their way there, walking through the May sunshine in silence.

As always it was the overpowering smell of substances, used hopefully to counteract the stink of corrupting flesh, that the Apothecary disliked. Putting a handkerchief to his nose he walked amongst the slabs, each bearing a shrouded white figure, to the one that the mortuary keeper had indicated.

Turning back the cloth, Diana Warwick's face came into view.

She was still beautiful, even in death, though now – rigor mortis having been and gone – her cheeks had a fallen-in look and her features were drawing together round her mouth. John couldn't help but notice that the Constable turned away as the Apothecary leant over the body and peered into Diana's nostrils. If she had fought for breath as she died then surely some small particle of what had been pressed over her face would have been inhaled. And there it was, three tiny white feathers, indicating surely that a pillow had been held down. Giving a small cry of triumph John fished in his bag and produced a pair of tweezers. Inserting them gently, he pulled out the feathers and dropped them into a box. Then he turned to Trethowan.

'She was smothered all right.'

'How do you know, Sir?'

'Here's the evidence. See.' And he showed him the tell-tale feathers.

The Constable nodded his head slowly. 'This entirely alters the case. I will inform the Coroner immediately.'

'I think,' said John thoughtfully, 'that every man who saw her on the night she was killed should be interviewed.'

'But just who were they?'

'Tim Painter for one. And young Kitto, of course.'

'I'll see them directly.'

'And try Lord Godolphin,' the Apothecary added.

The Constable gave him an anguished glance. 'I wouldn't dare do that. Why, it could cost me my job.'

'Is the man so powerful?'

'He is in charge of a great deal of Helstone, that's for sure.'

'Would you like me to question him?'

'If you can get within a mile of him you're welcome to try.'

'Well, I can only do my best,' the Apothecary answered, none too confidently.

As it transpired he did not have far to look. John had crossed the road and was making his way back to Dr Penhale's house, hopefully to catch the man in, when a familiar carriage drew up in front of him. A servant leapt to the ground and pulled the steps down, and out got the familiar figure of his lordship, who proceeded, with a swagger, to make for the physician's front door. Seizing the opportunity John followed in his wake and arrived just a step behind him as the man rang the bell. He turned as he became aware of the Apothecary's proximity.

John bowed courteously. 'We meet again, Sir.'

The steely eyes regarded him. 'So it would seem.'

John, sizing the man up, decided he was arrogant and would probably respond to flattery. 'I hope your lordship is not in ill health,' he said.

'I am perfectly well, thank you.'

The Apothecary made a self-deprecating move. 'I thought as you were here...' His voice trailed away and he gestured to the doctor's name plate.

'I've come to see the quack for something for gout, if you must know.'

'May I suggest the juice of germander drunk over several weeks,' John replied smoothly. 'I have always found it extremely efficacious when prescribing to my patients.'

Lord Godolphin's eyebrows shot up but he was spared from making a reply by the door being answered by a woman servant. She curtseyed on seeing who stood there.

'Oh, my lord, the doctor is still out, I fear. I am expecting him soon, though. Would you care to come in and wait?'

'No, I would not.' Lord Godolphin turned away and was about to leave when he stopped abruptly and asked John a question. 'Are you a physician, Sir?'

'I am an apothecary, Sir, with a practice in London. I can certainly prepare you a concoction of germander to tide you over, should you so desire.'

His lordship hesitated, then said, 'Very well, I shall try some. I shall send a servant round this evening to collect it.'

'Not a bit of it, Sir. I insist on bringing it myself. Where do you live?'

'At Godolphin in Breage,' the other replied grandly.

'Very good, my lord. Shall we say six o'clock?'

'Yes. As good a time as any,' answered his lordship, and stepped into his carriage without further ado.

The servant, still standing in the doorway, stared at John questioningly.

'Could you tell your master that Mr Rawlings called with some information for him. I will return later,' he said, then turned on his heel and headed back purposefully for The Angel inn.

Elizabeth and Rose had gone for a drive to the sea which gave the Apothecary time to seek out some wild germander growing on an old ruined cottage. This he compounded using a small pestle and mortar which he had brought in his medical bag. Then he drained it as best he could and poured the juice into a clean empty bottle.

Having some time to kill, the Apothecary decided on a walk and found his feet leading him in the direction of the Loe Pool, that place of mystery and occasional tragedy, according to local legend. But he had only just got close to the bottom of the street when a familiar voice said, 'Buy my heather for luck, Sir.'

He turned and found himself looking into the clearwater eyes of Gypsy Orchard.

'How much?' he said, putting his hand into his pocket.

'As much as you care to give me,' she answered, and smiled at him.

There was something immensely attractive about the woman, John thought, and he wondered about her personal life; wondered whether she had a man or even children. He extended two shillings.

'Will that be enough?'

'More than plenty, Sir. I've charmed the heather for extra good fortune.'

'It will make me lucky, eh?'

'It helps to ward off evil spirits.'

'Surely there can't be any of those in Helstone,' he said, continuing to smile.

The look on her face removed his grin. 'I wouldn't be too sure of that, Sir.'

'What do you mean?'

'The Furry Dance attracts all sorts of people to see it.'

'Who exactly?'

'People who serve the Earth Goddess and also those who serve the Dark Master.'

'Do you mean witches?'

'I do, both white and black.'

John was silent, thinking about what she was saying, not consciously having realised before that there was a difference.

'Could you explain that?' he asked.

A cautious expression crossed Gypsy Orchard's face. 'No, it's not good to say too much, Sir. Remember, they hang witches still.'

And John did remember, and asked no further questions. Instead he said, 'Why should they be attracted to the Furry Dance, to Flora Day?'

'Because of its origins. It's pagan, don't forget. Some might think it is a form of devil worship.'

'What nonsense,' he exclaimed loudly. 'It is a tribute to the coming of spring, that is all.'

'And its roots are pre-Christian,' she answered with a secretive smile.

The Apothecary decided that further conversation on that particular subject was useless. He looked serious.

'Tell me again, do you truly believe that Isobel Pill drowned?'

Those amazing clear eyes gazed at him. 'I would stake my own life on it.'

'Then where is she?'

'That I cannot tell, Sir.'

He nodded. 'And now Miss Warwick is dead.' He decided to test her. 'Has she been murdered do you think?'

'I told her fortune the other night and all I could see was

darkness. I felt that all was not well but I denied it even to myself.'

'I see.'

'No, Sir, I don't think you do. Being a Charmer, having clear-sight, is not always easy. There are certain people who scoff...' She gave him a pointed glance. '...but fortunately not many round these parts. But the worst comes when you know that someone is going to die. Then you're hard put to it to know what to say.'

John's mind went back to the old crone who had foretold Emilia's death. She had had no trouble spilling out the dread words. At the time he had thought it was a friend playing a practical joke but now he could see that the gypsy woman had been absolutely right. Emilia had died as she had described and he had been left a widower. With a wrench he brought his mind back to the present.

'So you have nothing further to say on that matter?'

'Not at present. I shall consult my crystal and let you know what I see.'

John's curiosity overcame him. 'Tell me, Gypsy Orchard, where do you live?'

'In a little cottage not far from Loe Pool. Many think I dwell in the hedges but that life would be too unsettling for me. It's in that cottage that I keep my cats and my crystal and people know where to find me.'

'But your name suggests someone who spends a lot of time outdoors.'

'I do. But I was named after the place in which I was born. Does that answer your question?'

'Very adequately.'

'Then I'll be on my way, Sir. You know where to come looking should you need help.

And with that the gypsy picked up her basket, smiled, and was gone.

Chapter Seventeen

Godolphin was a truly magnificent house. John, having borrowed Elizabeth's coach together with Jed and his accompanying guard, could not help but feel impressed as they turned into the half-moon carriage sweep and a pillared white building, gracious and elegant of line, and bearing much in its architecture of the reign of William and Mary, stood before him.

The light in the sky was just beginning to fade and thus the beautiful place seemed to languish in its dark parkland like a lily that had been plucked and then discarded. The Apothecary, enraptured, called up to Jed, 'Stop a minute. I want to look.'

Candles had been lit and appeared to shine from every window so that the place had a fairy-like quality; a glittering breathless charm that left the Apothecary almost devoid of his senses. Indeed he felt quite weakened by the house's spell as the carriage moved forward again and deposited him at the front door. In response to the tolling of a bell a liveried footman appeared.

'Yes, Sir?'

'Lord Godolphin is expecting me. John Rawlings of Shug Lane, London.'

Much to his surprise the servant answered, 'Oh yes, Sir. If you would follow me.'

The Apothecary was led through an elegant and richly appointed hallway to where, in a library full of books, his lordship sat reading a newspaper, a pair of spectacles on his nose. He looked up and actually had the good manners to rise from his seat.

'Oh Rawlings, how nice of you to call. Do you have the physic with you?'

'I do indeed, Sir.' And John produced the bottle of juice from his coat pocket.

Godolphin held it up to the light. 'This will do me good, I

feel certain of it. Now, tell me, have you dined?'

'No, I was returning to the inn but…'

He hunched his shoulders and spread his hands.

'Then you can do so with me. Truth to tell I could do with a little company.'

John looked through the spectacles at the steely eyes behind. They were as hard as ever but a telltale flush had risen in the nobleman's cheeks.

'I should be delighted,' the Apothecary answered, glad that Elizabeth was a woman of resources who would not complain if he did not put in an appearance.

'Fact is,' Lord Godolphin continued, 'that her ladyship is away visiting relatives. Something she frequently does.'

John remained silent, unable to think of a fitting reply.

'I was hoping that you would tell me something of your life in London. I visit the capital from time to time but it is not the same as dwelling there in my opinion.'

'I would be delighted to do so, Sir. May I sit down?'

'By all means – how remiss of me. What can I get you to drink?'

'A sherry would be splendid, thank you.'

Lord Godolphin poured from a glittering decanter and passed John a glass, which he raised.

'Your health, Sir.'

'And yours. Now tell me of London.'

The Apothecary drew breath then started on a somewhat rosily painted version of the capital. He talked about the theatres, the pleasure gardens, the gaiety, the cutting fashions, but eventually he turned the subject to the whores of Covent Garden.

'Do you know the area, my lord?'

'Of course. Whenever I visit the capital I make my way there, simply to observe of course.'

With an effort John kept a straight face, thinking to himself that a splendid Madam at fifty guineas a night would probably be his lordship's meat. However, exercising a tight control of his features, he said, 'The woman are a sad selection of humanity, are they not?'

'Indeed they are.'

'Did you know one such was done to death in Helstone a few days ago?'

Lord Godolphin went the colour of stone and made much of sipping his sherry. 'Really?' he said eventually. 'And who might that have been?'

'She called herself Miss Warwick. Diana was her Christian name.'

Now it was his lordship's turn to keep a blank look. 'Not a local woman I take it?'

'No, not local,' John answered, giving him a straight glance.

'What was she doing in Helstone? Do you know?'

'Apparently she had arrived to see her young lover, an enamoured youth called Nicholas Kitto. The story goes that she was once the kept woman of his father – an anonymous character who sired him in bastardy it seems. Anyway at some point she transferred her affections from father to son and, it would seem, was murdered for her pains.'

All the while he had been saying this, his tone deliberately flippant, the Apothecary had been observing Lord Godolphin closely and had watched the range of expressions which had crossed the older man's features with interest. Now he added, 'Do you know young Kitto, Sir?'

His lordship's answer, when it came, was perfectly smooth. 'Yes, indeed. I know all the inhabitants of Helstone. It is my town after all.'

'And were you aware of the identity of his father?'

There was a long pause, then finally he said, 'Yes, I know him.'

'And?'

'And nothing. The matter remains a secret I have no intention of sharing with a stranger.'

John was at an impasse and knew it. Still he decided to ask one more question. 'You never met the lady, did you?'

'You mean Miss Warwick?' John nodded. 'I think I saw her in the street once. She was, as you say, radiantly beautiful.'

'A beauty that earned her her death,' said the Apothecary reflectively, and rose, following Lord Godolphin's lead, to go into dinner.

He arrived home at about nine o'clock to find Elizabeth sitting alone in the downstairs parlour, her amazing face alive with thoughts. Tonight, seen thus in repose, her scar stood out, highlighted from underneath by a candle which stood on a table beside her. A book lay open on her lap but she was not reading it, instead staring into the flames of the fire that had been lit in the grate. She looked up on hearing John's entry, then she smiled at him slowly and laid the book down. At that moment he felt her to be the most important person living and, crossing to her, gave her a kiss.

'Good evening, Marchesa.'

She looked at him intently. 'John, there is something you must hear?'

'What is it?'

'I have got into conversation with one of the maids. The maid who was on duty the night that Diana was murdered.'

All the Apothecary's inquisitive instincts rose. 'Tell me what she said.'

'No, I think you should speak to her yourself.'

'Very well. Where is she?'

'In her room. She snatches a few hours to herself before going on duty again.'

'She'll probably be fast asleep.'

'No, I gave her a guinea and told her to stay awake until she'd told you her story.'

So saying she took the Apothecary by the hand and led him up two flights of stairs to the rooms reserved for the servants who lived-in. They were small and mean as John discovered on entering the one at the end of the corridor. With no chair to sit on and no furniture other than for a single bed and a chest-of-drawers, he stood awkwardly in the entrance gazing at the girl within, wondering how much she was going to tell him.

She was little more than fourteen years-of-age and was not particularly appealing to look at. She was more than plump, indeed was extremely large for one of her tender years, while the fatness had spread to her face, giving her several wobbly chins. Despite being thrust into a cap, wisps of her dark hair hung down, and she was presently toying with one of these whilst rhythmically sucking her thumb. John thought it had been a while since he had seen such a messy creature, then took himself to task for being so stern a critic.

The girl looked up, removed the thumb, and said, 'Evening, Sir.'

'Good evening, may I come in?'

The Marchesa spoke from the doorway. 'This is the gentleman I told you about, Betty.'

The girl looked bewildered and rather frightened. 'As long as you're quick, Sir. I've got the passageway to scrub out in an hour when everyone's abed.'

She twiddled her hair and popped the thumb back in, staring at him wide-eyed over the comforting digit.

'We'll be rapid,' John answered, stepping into the space which was no larger than a big cupboard. Elizabeth, meanwhile, stayed by the door which she had somehow closed behind her.

'Now my girl,' said the Apothecary, deciding to try the masterful approach, 'tell me what you saw on the night that Miss Warwick died.'

The thumb came out, hovering moistly by the mouth in case it should be required. 'Well, Sir, I was coming down the stairs the first time and I saw Miss Warwick climbing up with that handsome gentleman with the lovely voice…'

'Mr Painter?'

'Yes. Well, I stands back in the shadows and I sees them go into her room, and they was kissing and cuddling and everything.'

'I can imagine,' John said, giving a lop-sided grin.

'When they'd gone in I continues on my way down and I could hear 'em inside.'

'What were they doing, do you imagine?'

'"It", Sir. You should have heard that bed creaking.'

'I see. Very interesting.'

The thumb went back in for a couple of rapid sucks, then was removed. 'But that's not all, Sir.'

'No?'

'No. I sees a couple of other men go in later.'

Now the Apothecary really was interested. He leaned forward. 'Go on.'

'Well, around midnight I was on my way up and you'll never guess who I sees.'

'Who?'

She lowered her voice conspiratorially. 'Lord Godolphin himself.'

John's mobile brows flew. 'Was he going in to Miss Warwick's room?'

'Yes, Sir. And she greeted him. I know 'cos I heard her.'

'What did she say?'

'Hello, my dear. I haven't seen you in an age.'

'Anything else?'

'I couldn't hear, Sir. I did try to make it out but their voices were too low.'

John smiled, he couldn't help himself, picturing the girl with her ear pressed to the door, sucking away in her excitement. But he returned to the matter in hand.

'You're positive it was Lord Godolphin?'

'I'm certain, Sir. I've known him all my life.'

John was still shaking his head over this latest revelation when the girl said, 'And that's not all.'

'It isn't?' he exclaimed, surprised.

'No, Sir. After seeing his lordship go in I went downstairs to scrub the floors. To be honest with 'ee, Sir, I fell asleep after I had finished. Anyway, when I wakes up it is about two o'clock in the morning. I make my way upstairs to go to bed and this time I saw another man coming out of Miss Warwick's room.'

'Good God. It sounds as if she was giving a ridotto. So who was this one?'

'It was the blind fiddler, Sir. I'd know him anywhere by his black spectacles. Though I must say that he went downstairs like he could see, which was strange.'

'What do you mean?'

'Just that he took the steps like a sighted man. But then they're very clever those blind folks.'

The thumb went in again and there were several minutes of silence while she sucked contentedly away, twiddling her hair the while. Then she spoke again.

'I hope you believe me, Sir.'

'I do,' said John, meaning it. 'Though what you have said perplexes me.'

'Why, Sir?'

'It's just that she had so many male visitors. And one of them killed her. But which?'

The girl took refuge in her thumb once more. Over it, she opened her eyes wide.

The Apothecary, realising that he would get nothing further out of her, reached in his pocket and drew out a guinea. 'This is for you. Thank you for telling me what you saw.'

Continuing to suck, the girl nodded. John turned to Elizabeth. 'Shall we go?'

'Indeed we shall.'

As they walked down two flights to the Marchesa's room he put his arm round her waist. 'She is probably the most important witness so far. It was clever of you to find her.'

Elizabeth said nothing, merely giving him her enigmatic smile.

Chapter Eighteen

John woke early, feeling utterly alert. He lay on the bed for a while, his brain turning over the information he had been given late last night. According to the maid Betty's story, the last time she had heard Miss Warwick speak had been to Lord Godolphin. Had he, then, snuffed out her life with a pillow? Or had it been the Gaffer? Or had, indeed, Tim Painter returned, unseen, and closed Diana's mouth for ever? Was it possible even that Nick Kitto's storms of tears had been fuelled by regret for something done in love play?

The Apothecary's attention turned to the missing child. Was she, too, dead and gone? And, if so, where was her body? Or had she been abducted by some corrupt being for a purpose he dared not even think about? And, above all, were the two occurrences linked in some extraordinary way? Sighing, John turned over and tried to sleep, but it was impossible. So, reluctantly, he got up and washed in cold water, ran a razor over his chin, combed his locks – which had grown beyond wearing a wig – and tied them back with a ribbon.

Going downstairs, having peeped in on Rose who was sleeping the profound and innocent slumber of childhood, he decided it was too early to break his fast and left the inn, turning left and surveying the scene. The town of Helstone lay before him, its cobbled streets and tightly packed houses presenting a charming vista in the early morning light. Yet somewhere, hidden, lay a murderer's cold heart. Unless, of course, the perpetrator of Diana's death was the blind fiddler, the Gaffer, who had left the place the day before. Yet what could his motive possibly be? Or had he known Diana from long ago? Was his connection to her stronger than it would appear? Weighed down with his thoughts the Apothecary marched on, not really seeing where he was going.

He became conscious of his surroundings as he approached the church where, despite the earliness of the hour, the Vicar was already up and walking round the surrounding grounds, gazing at a neighbouring sheep field and muttering to himself. John swept off his hat.

'Good morning, Sir.'

'Oh, good morning,' replied the reverend gentleman, somewhat flustered.

John regarded him closely, never having done so before, and found himself gazing at a good-looking man wearing a rather worn-out wig, beneath which was a fine pair of bright blue eyes fringed by a set of lashes of which a woman would have been proud.

The Apothecary bowed. 'Allow me to introduce myself. I am John Rawlings, an apothecary of Shug Lane, London.'

'Goodness gracious,' replied the other, 'you are a long way from home. I am William Robinson, vicar of Helstone.'

John bowed again, not too formally. 'We met recently when we were hunting for the little girl who ran away during the Furry Dance.'

'Yes, indeed. I hear the poor child has now vanished completely.'

'It's true enough. But no body has been found and I am beginning to wonder whether she has been abducted.'

The Vicar looked thoughtful. 'Of course we get people from all over the West Country coming to see the Furry. I'm afraid that what you suggest is not out of the question.'

'Remember that I have come from London. So any villains could be here.'

Realising what he had just said the Apothecary grinned broadly and after a moment or two Mr Robinson let out a circumspect giggle.

'Yes, how funny. But news of the child is indeed serious. Have you no idea of her whereabouts?'

'None at all. Her mother has gone to Wiltshire to get help.'

'That gentleman you were with the other night. Was he by any chance the little girl's father?'

'Not he. He is her mother's lover,' John answered

unthinkingly, then wondered if he had been too frank before a member of the church. But the Vicar looked unperturbed, merely placing the tips of his fingers together and saying, 'I see.'

The Apothecary asked another question. 'Have you lived in Helstone long, Sir?'

'All my life, man and boy, except when I went away to study theology. I was curate to the late vicar, Mr Halsall, and then took over his living when he passed away. I am very fond of the place, but I suppose that is obvious.'

'Indeed it is, Sir. Does Mrs Robinson care for Helstone as deeply as you do?'

'Alas, she too has been called to God.'

It was at that moment that John detected a movement in the distance and turning saw the door of Nicholas Kitto's house open and a woman come striding out, heading purposefully for the church.

Was this, the Apothecary wondered, Nick's formidable mother of whom he seemed more than a little frightened.

He watched her as she came resolutely up the path, then slowed her pace as she glimpsed the fact that the Vicar was not alone.

'Good morning, Madam,' he said, bowing handsomely and sweeping his hat to the ground. 'John Rawlings, at your service.'

She eyed him suspiciously and John found himself thinking that she was shaped exactly like an egg, going outwards both front and back from her head to her thighs. It was quite some while since he had seen such an unattractive contour and try as he might not to do so, he none the less stared.

Mrs Kitto, for that is whom he presumed her to be, said, 'Ah Reverend, good morning to you. May I have a word?'

'Certainly, Madam, if you can wait a moment or two. I am in the process of bidding farewell to Mr Rawlings here.'

The woman gave John a sickly smile. 'Good morning, Sir. I

am Harriet Ennis.' She curtseyed, very fully, and had some difficulty in rising.

The Apothecary bowed neatly. 'Forgive me, Madam. I thought you must be Mrs Kitto and Nicholas your...nephew.'

'That is partly correct,' she answered, just a shade too quickly as if what she was saying had been often repeated. 'Nicholas is indeed my nephew, he is my late sister's child. She was a Miss Ennis but married a Mr Kitto.'

John put on his best sorrowful face. 'And she has passed to her rest?'

'Yes, indeed. I attended her at the birth but, alas, it was too much for her.'

'And Mr Kitto senior?' asked the Apothecary in saddened tones.

The Vicar cleared his throat. 'He died before the child was born, Lord forgive us.'

'What a wretched tale,' said John, and gave Nick's female relation a beatific smile. He turned to Mr Robinson once more. 'Well, Sir, I must be off. It has been so nice conversing with you.'

'Likewise, my son. God bless you.'

'Thank you.'

Placing his hat onto his head with a flourish, John Rawlings started to walk away but not before he had taken a good look at the hair colouring of the ovate woman. It was, as he had known it would be, definitely red in shade.

So that was it. She matched the description Nick had given him exactly. She was more than likely the erring mother. It was rather difficult, the Apothecary concluded, to imagine her being sinful with anyone, let alone ending up saddled with a bastard. But then he knew from long experience that people changed with time and imagined that in her youth she must have been reasonably pretty. He tried to picture Lord Godolphin with her and somehow that particular pairing refused to come into his head. There was something too precise about the aristocrat to warrant such an action. The beautiful Diana Warwick he certainly could envisage, but not Mrs Humpty Dumpty.

As he neared Nick's house John looked at his watch and saw that it was now time for work to start. He was therefore not in the least surprised when the front door flew open and the young man uppermost in his thoughts appeared in the entrance. He was clad from head to toe in deepest black and his eyes were red and puffy with weeping. The Apothecary thought that if this was indeed a show, then it was one of the best he had ever seen.

He gave a short bow. 'Good morning, Nick. Off to work?'

'Yes,' came the abrupt answer.

'May I walk with you?'

'Of course you can. I'll be glad of the company.'

Now came the most difficult moment to contend with. He had not seen young Kitto since the discovery of the tell-tale feathers in Diana's nose, the feathers which revealed a pillow had been pressed down on her face and held there until she could no longer breathe.

John cleared his throat. 'Nick, there is something I have to tell you.'

A bleary eye regarded him. 'What?'

'It's rather bad news I'm afraid.'

Kitto slowed his pace and turned to stare at the Apothecary. 'It's about Diana, isn't it?'

'Yes.'

Nick stopped dead in his tracks. 'Oh God,' he said loudly. 'Oh my God.'

Surreptitiously the Apothecary felt for his salts and got his hand round them. 'I'm sorry to have to tell you…'

But he got no further. Nick let out a piercing scream and beat the air with his fists. 'She's been murdered,' he said, 'murdered. Oh woe is me!' he added theatrically.

Quick as a flash the salts came out of the pocket and were firmly implanted under Nick's nostrils.

'Breathe deeply,' the Apothecary ordered. 'Come along now.

Deep breaths.'

Willy nilly, the poor young man had no option but to inhale, a fact which made him cough appallingly.

'That's the spirit,' said John. 'There's nothing like a good lungful of brackish odour to clear the head.'

Nick produced a handkerchief and wiped at his streaming eyes and nose. 'That's enough, thank you,' he gasped.

The Apothecary withdrew the offending bottle, holding it at arm's length. 'How did you know?' he asked.

'What?' Nick asked, a touch belligerently.

'That she had been murdered.'

'I just guessed. As God is my judge, I just knew somehow.'

'How very perceptive of you.'

'What are you insinuating, Sir?'

'I'm insinuating nothing. I am merely pointing out that you are intuitive in your powers of instinct. Tell me, when you found Diana did you guess that someone else had played a part in her death?'

'No, you know damned well I didn't.'

John decided to change the subject. 'Look, Nick, are you fit to go to work? Or would you rather leave it for today?'

'No, I'd prefer to go,' said Kitto, blowing his nose loudly. 'It will be far better than my mother bellowing questions at me.'

'So I was right. I've just met her talking to the Vicar. You have her colour hair.'

'I hope the similarity ends there,' responded Nick ungraciously.

John did not answer, instead he said, 'If you are going to work you will have to hurry.' And young Kitto increased his pace.

They drew to a halt outside the offices of Penaluna Brothers and John held out his hand. 'If you feel in need of talking you know where I am staying. But in any event we must converse soon. I shall need to find out everything you saw that early morning.'

'Why?' said Kitto mutinously. 'And besides, why should I

talk to you? Surely it should be the Constable I converse with.'

It was a question that John had long been dreading and yet was at a loss to answer. In London he could claim quite legitimately that he was working with Sir John Fielding. But here, miles away in Cornwall's mysterious and cavernous depths, that reply would cut no ice at all. He cleared his throat.

'Let me just say that I have taken part in various investigations into unexplained deaths before.'

'Really,' Nick replied sarcastically.

'Yes, you have my word on it. I work for the Public Office in Bow Street, London.'

'Never heard of it.'

John ran out of patience, despite the man's obvious misery. 'Do you want to help me find who committed this crime or not?'

'Yes, obviously I do.'

'Then stop being so truculent and cooperate. When can we discuss what you saw?'

'Tonight. At eight o'clock, if that would be suitable?'

'Perfectly. I'll call at your house.'

'Say nothing about your true purpose until Mama has retired.'

'I shall remain silent as the grave,' said John, then regretted it when he saw the expression on Nicholas's face.

As the Apothecary turned into Coinage Hall Street he heard the rumble of carriage wheels and saw, coming at a remarkable pace, two coaches, one behind the other. Staring within he saw the pale profile of Mrs Pill together with several men, all bearing the same set expressions. So she had returned reinforced with her sibling and servants. The hunt for Isobel was about to recommence.

Arriving at the door of The Angel, John watched them dismount. Kathryn was helped down by a man so like her that he could only be her brother. John thought that in his case the plainness of feature didn't matter quite so much, cast as it was in a masculine setting. But poor Mrs Pill looked even worse than when he had last seen her; white as a daisy and her lips almost bloodless. She turned to the landlord, who was hovering.

'Have you seen Mr Painter about?'

'No, Mam. He's gone out I fear.'

'Well there was no way he could have known when I was arriving, I suppose.'

The brother looked grim. 'Don't make excuses for the bounder. He should have been waiting for you.'

John, not wishing to get embroiled in a family disagreement crept on down the road, heading for The Blue Anchor, but was unfortunately spotted.

'Oh Mr Rawlings,' Kathryn cried out, 'there you are. This is my brother Jasper Hughes.'

John bowed and said, 'How do you do, Sir.'

'May I present John Rawlings. He is an apothecary and has been most tremendously kind to me, as has been his travelling companion, the Marchesa di Lorenzi.'

'I am delighted to meet you, Sir,' said Jasper, bowing back.

Meanwhile an aged porter, assisted by the landlord and the bevy of servants accompanying Kathryn and her brother, were carrying in various bags and trunks. She turned to John.

'Tomorrow we start to search this town from top to bottom. Nowhere shall go unnoticed. I am determined to find Isobel.'

John looked sombre. 'Supposing she is in Loe Pool. Trapped beneath somewhere.'

Jasper spoke. 'From what you have told me I think she has been kidnapped.'

Yet again the picture of Gypsy Orchard's face came vividly into the Apothecary's mind. 'I don't believe that somehow,' was out of his mouth before he had time to think.

Mrs Pill looked sick. 'So you think my daughter is dead?'

The Apothecary shuffled his feet. 'Well…'

'It's not fair to quiz the chap so,' said Jasper. 'Now Kathryn, my dear, why don't you rest for a while. The journey has exhausted you. Meanwhile I'll locate Painter and tell him we are here.'

She turned to John. 'Yes, I'll go and lie down. But please inform the Marchesa of my arrival. She was so kind to me.'

The Apothecary bowed, 'Certainly Madam.' He said to Jasper, 'I think I know where he might be if you would care to accompany me.'

'I was going to suggest that you give me a tour of the town, Sir.'

'I will certainly do so later. But first I must speak to the Marchesa and also to my daughter. I was out before either of them were up.'

'But of course. I shall wash the stains of the journey from my person and meet you outside in thirty minutes if that is acceptable.'

'Perfectly.'

John walked into the entrance hall and was pleasantly surprised to see the Marchesa and Rose, dressed for the street and about to take the air. Elizabeth shot him one of her amused glances.

'Up early I see.'

'I've much to tell. But first a message. Mrs Pill is back with her brother and several male servants.'

'I shall seek her out later.'

Rose piped up. 'Have they come to look for Isobel?'

'Yes, sweetheart.'

'But she's drowned, isn't she?'

'I think so, yes.'

The Marchesa lowered her voice. 'Have you seen any of the men that Betty mentioned?'

'Only Nick.'

'And how is he?'

'Weeping and hollering fit to burst.'

'Is it to cover guilt?'

'I'll let you know later.'

He escorted the two females to the door and walked a little

way up the street with them. Then he turned and sauntered back to the inn where, after a few minutes, Jasper Hughes joined him and they made their way to The Blue Anchor. Very much as John had suspected and despite the earliness of the hour, Tim Painter was standing by the bar, holding forth to a group of cronies.

What happened next was so quick that nobody was prepared for it. On seeing him, Jasper entirely lost control and flew to where the man stood.

'You damnable bastard,' he shouted, and with that swung a fist into Painter's handsome face.

'Eh?' croaked Tim, and having said that plunged to the floor where he lay motionless.

'Good God!' exclaimed John, and fetching his salts from his pockets knelt down by Painter's prostrate form. Jasper, wiping his hands on his sides, calmly stepped over them.

'A jug of ale, if you please,' he said, and smiled benignly at the world.

Chapter Nineteen

It had all been so quick that for a moment no one in the room, with the exception of John Rawlings, said a word. Then a rumble of remonstrance came from the lips of Tim's cohorts.

'What 'oo done hit him for?'

'Aye. That's what I'd like to know.'

Jasper eyed them. 'I downed him because he is a trifler with women's affections. And the woman with whom he is currently involved happens to be my sister.' He looked down at where the Apothecary knelt at Tim's side. 'My dear chap, don't waste your valuable time. He'll come round soon enough.'

John shook his head. 'Whatever one may think of him he is temporarily my patient. And I am therefore obliged to do my duty.'

'Don't get into high stirrup over him. He's not worth the trouble.' Jasper drank his ale. 'Allow me to buy you a drink, old fellow.'

'Not just now. It's a bit early.'

'You're sounding a regular prat, Sir, and I'm sure you are not.'

John stood up. 'No, I don't think I am, though others may, of course. But forgive me if I attend to Painter. I agree with you he's a shiftless creature but for all that he's a human being.'

From the floor came sounds of groaning and John crouched down once more. With a flutter of eyelids Tim was regaining consciousness. His handsome gaze looked round, a glazed expression in its depths.

'What am I doing down here?' he said. Then memory returned and he fixed Jasper with a glare. 'You filthy bastard Hughes. I'll be revenged for this.'

'You already have, damn you.'

'What do you mean by that?'

'You did for little Isobel, didn't you? You've always hated the girl and made no secret of it. Now you've got rid of her, you devil.'

With some assistance from the Apothecary, Tim scrambled to his feet. 'How dare you make such accusations?'

'Because they're the truth. You've always considered the child in the way and now the way is clear.'

Somewhat shakily Tim rose to his full height, an impressive sight. 'Will you come outside, Sir?'

'What for?' said Hughes insolently, ordering another pint.

'Because I intend to give you the thrashing you richly deserve.'

'You? You wouldn't last five minutes.'

But Jasper got no further. A scream rang out from the doorway. Every head turned to see Kathryn, even paler, crying and wringing her hands.'

'Oh stop it for pity's sake. I have lost my child and now I am to lose the man I care for. Oh Jasper, don't step outside I beg you.'

Tim shot her a look of pure surprise. 'What makes you think that he'd best me? It's I who challenged him. I intend to beat him within a mile of an oak.'

She rushed up to him and quite literally threw herself into his arms. 'Oh darling, cease such talk. You two are all I have left in the world.'

John decided that the conversation was getting nowhere. 'Why don't the pair of you –' He indicated Mrs Pill and Tim Painter. '– step back to The Angel. I shall remain and take up Mr Hughes's kind offer of a drink.'

She and Painter looked at one another, she pleading, he uncertain, then Tim gave an elegant gesture. 'Very well. I withdraw my challenge.'

Jasper shrugged his shoulders. 'All the same to me whether you do or you don't. But out of respect for my sister I'll comply.' He turned to John. 'What would you like, my friend?'

'A glass of claret if you please.'

'Landlord, a glass of the best.'

A silence settled over the inn once the lovers, if one could indeed call them that, had departed. John leant forward.

'Do you really think Tim murdered Isobel?'

Jasper, onto his third pint of ale despite the early hour, said, 'I believe it is certainly possible.'

'But why? What motive could he have?'

'Money,' whispered Jasper sibilantly.

'What do you mean?'

'Simply this. As Kathryn's only heir Isobel stood to inherit a small fortune when her mother died. Tim Painter would have got less. But with the girl out of the way he is going to be very rich.'

'But suppose he dies before Mrs Pill?'

Jasper leant close to John's ear. 'I feel positive that it might have been arranged for my sister to go to an early grave.'

So they were back to the oldest motive in the world. John considered it, wondering whether Isobel had been disposed of by Tim Painter, thrown into Loe Pool tied down with a weight. Further he considered Diana and her strange death. But what motive could there have been for that? Unless she and Tim had known one another before. Yet one could say that of every man who visited her that night. Painter, Lord Godolphin, the Gaffer, they had all three paid her a call. As for Nick, had he perhaps caught her in the arms of another and decided then and there to do away with her, creeping in first thing in the morning and putting a pillow over her face while she slept?

Yet somehow what Nicholas said rang true. Knowing that he must keep an open-mind, John none the less felt that the answer lay somewhere with the other three. Desperately requiring the assistance of Sir John Fielding's acute brain, he determined to write and post a letter to him this very day.

He bowed to Jasper Hughes. 'Sir, will you forgive me if I leave you? I have to see my companion and my daughter as well as needing to write some letters.'

'Certainly, old man. Sure you can't manage another?'

'Thank you, but no. I'll say goodbye.'

But Jasper had already turned away and was ordering more ale. It seemed to John as he left the building that the man must have the constitution of a bull. Which was more than could be said of his sister, poor thing, particularly when it came to her choice of men.

No sooner was he outside than he spotted Elizabeth and Rose perambulating slowly down the other side of the street. He called and waved his hat and they heard him and stopped walking. Rushing across, John joined them.

The Marchesa looked at him in a rather odd manner, John thought. But she followed this with one of her spectacular smiles and he felt in harmony with her again. That is until she spoke.

'John, my dear, Rose and I have been talking.'

'Yes?' he said, instantly suspicious.

'And we have decided, if you are agreeable, to go back to Devon and leave you to your investigation.' The Marchesa lowered her voice. 'Truth to tell, the child is getting bored as there is precious little here for her to do. I think it would be better all round if we returned home. There she has her pony and other children I can call on, to say nothing of the delights of Exeter. So what do you think?'

John felt stunned and terribly hurt. Had he not after all done his best in every way to keep Elizabeth happy? But no, that was clearly not good enough. Then he felt saddened by the thought of Rose growing bored and depressed. He bent down to her.

'Are you tired of this place, Rose?'

'I am a little.'

'But you loved it when we first came here.'

'Then there was the Furry Dance to look forward to. And besides there was Wilkes.'

'Wilkes?' repeated her father, thinking of the politician.

'Yes, the monkey. He had such a thoughtful face.'

Despite what he was feeling, the Apothecary could not help

but laugh. He straightened up.

'It seems that whatever I say the decision has been made,' he said.

Elizabeth looked a little annoyed. 'I was thinking of your daughter's wellbeing, Sir.'

'And only that?' asked John childishly.

'Certainly. What other reason could there be?'

'Perhaps that you too are feeling constrained by Helstone.'

'Yes, as a matter of fact I am. But I would have stayed on were it not for Rose.'

'I see.' He bent down to his child once more. 'Would you be happier in Mrs Elizabeth's house, sweetheart? Tell me truly.'

'Yes, Papa, I would. There's so much more to do there.'

'Then of course you must go.' He looked up at Elizabeth, presenting a cold face. 'When will you be leaving?'

'First thing tomorrow morning if that is agreeable.'

He shrugged. 'Do as you wish.' Standing straight he said, 'And now if you will excuse me I have some urgent letters to write. Good day.' And he stalked away feeling more displeased than he had in an age.

Crossing the road he went into The Angel and was just making for the guests' parlour when he was waylaid by Tim Painter.

'Thanks for coming to my rescue, old chap.'

'Think nothing of it. I only did my duty. Where's Mrs Pill by the way?'

'Lying down. This would be a great opportunity to have a drink. Will you join me?'

The Apothecary, who had had no breakfast, thought that if people continued to ply him with alcohol he would probably end up drunk or dead, or both. Yet, on the other hand it was an excellent chance to speak to Tim on his own.

'Very well. I have a half hour or so.'

He followed Painter into the tap room which fortunately was deserted other than for a couple of workingmen, clearly not working. Leading the way to a quiet corner, John sat down.

'Have you heard of Sir John Fielding?' he said abruptly.

'The Blind Beak? Yes, I've been up before him,' Tim replied nonchalantly.

The Apothecary was so surprised that he practically dropped his glass.

'You've what?'

'I said I was up at Bow Street.'

'What for?'

'Some damnable Duchess – old as the hills but still rampant for a man – accused me of stealing her diamonds, would you believe.'

'And had you?'

'Of course not. I'd my eye on greater things than a few paltry stones.'

'What?'

'Her fortune, you foolish fellow. The old Duke had died and left her every penny he had. I was introduced to her at a ball and the rest you can guess. But some footman or other told her I was a thief and she lodged a charge at me at Bow Street.'

John swigged his drink. 'What happened?'

'I came up before the Beak – looked on by every member of the *beau monde* it seemed to me, for they were packing the public galleries – and he said there was insufficient evidence to condemn me. So I sallied forth from the dock and shortly after that I met Kathryn.'

He smiled, displaying a set of perfect white teeth.

John said, 'I, too, know Sir John but in rather a different context.'

'Oh? What is that?'

'I occasionally work for him, solving murder cases. Years ago I was a suspect in a murder which I eventually helped him to unravel. Since then he has called on me for help from time to time.'

'How interesting,' said Tim unenthusiastically.

'And now I feel obliged to solve this one. So tell me, Sir, how was Diana Warwick when you finally left her?'

An unhealthy flush crept over the handsome face and Painter took a good draft of ale before he muttered, 'What do you mean?'

'I mean that night you dined with her alone, then went to her bedchamber. The night she was done to death.'

Tim looked up sharply. 'I thought her death was accidental.'

'Then you thought wrong, my friend. I have found incontrovertible evidence that she was killed.'

Tim suddenly flared up. 'Well, don't put the blame on me. Alright, I did go to bed with her, and enjoyed it too. I am a man, after all. But I left her alive and that's the truth.'

'What time would that have been?'

'About twelve or so. Why?'

'Because Miss Warwick had several callers that night.'

Tim looked decidedly relieved. 'Really? Who?'

'I don't believe I should tell you that.'

'You must do as you think best. But I'll warrant one of them was the blind fiddler.'

It was John's turn to be surprised. 'What makes you say that?'

Tim leant forward confidentially. 'He's not all he appears to be, you know.'

'What do you mean?'

Painter looked vague. 'I'm not sure. But I'm certain I've met him before somewhere. And doing something entirely different too. Anyway, Diana Warwick knew him. I caught them when I was wandering around town, talking in a most conspiratorial manner.'

'Did you now! Did you manage to hear what their conversation was about?'

'No. They stopped as soon as they saw me – or should I say as soon as she saw me.'

John sat silently, then said, 'It's a pity he's left Helstone.'

'He's not gone far though,' said Tim helpfully.

Once again the Apothecary was amazed and his svelte brows rose high. 'You know where the Gaffer is?'

'Yes, he's in Redruth, playing at some gypsy gathering.'

'So that's where I can find him,' answered John slowly.

An hour later, still having eaten no breakfast or midday repast, John rolled upstairs and fell on his bed and to sleep. But much had been achieved in that hour. Trusting his gut that Tim Painter, for all his bad behaviour and naughty ways, was not capable of murder, he had arranged to travel to Redruth in his company the next morning in order to question the Gaffer. They had decided to ride there, hiring horses from the Helstone Livery Stable. In fact just before he dozed off John felt a definite kick of excitement in the pit of his stomach. He was going adventuring and needn't bother with pleasing any women, or rather one woman in particular.

Two hours later he woke with a start. That particular woman and he were presently on bad terms and he was not going to make it up to her by being late for dinner. Hurriedly John pulled on a pair of fitted silk stockings, then dressed in a rich emerald green suit trimmed with delicate embroidery of pink and silver flowers. He completed the ensemble by putting on a pair of soft leather shoes with flat heels, rounded tongues and silver buckles. Then he examined himself in a long mirror.

The new fashion for fitted breeches and short waistcoats left little to the imagination, but for all that suited the Apothecary superbly. His one fault was his hair which had grown so long that no wig would sit on it. He determined to go to the barber as soon as possible. Despite this he felt pleased with his appearance and set off confidently down the stairs.

But as he entered the dining parlour and saw Elizabeth, gleaming in crimson, her low square neckline giving a tantalising glimpse of breasts, her skirt decorated with black ruched and pleated silk, his heart gave a lurch.

Surely she had dressed to please him as much as he had dressed for her. Their eyes met and she gave him that slow tantalising smile that he loved so well. John bowed, then smiled crookedly. He approached her table.

'May I join you?'

'Is your humour restored?'

'Somewhat.'

'Why were you so angry earlier?'

He sat down, and leaning across the table covered her hands with one of his. 'Because you were leaving me.'

'But my darling I thought I explained. Your daughter was becoming bored and restless. I couldn't bear to see it.'

John looked serious. 'Tell me, do you resent having to spend so much time with the child?'

'Not at the moment, no. But as for the future I couldn't say. I have always been free and unfettered. A longing for that time might return.'

'But what about when your son was small? Surely you were tied down then?'

'That was different. I loved him with all my heart. Besides he was all I had left after my husband was killed.'

'Would you not consider having a husband again?'

Again came that stupendous smile as Elizabeth answered, 'No, never again. I have reached a stage in my life when I want my independence. I wish to be unattached to live and love as I please.'

'I shall do my best to persuade you otherwise.'

'That,' answered the Marchesa, 'I look forward to enormously.'

It was so exhilarating to feel horseflesh beneath him and to be cantering, wild and free, towards Redruth. Early that morning John had seen Elizabeth and Rose off in their coach, well protected by Jed and Rufus, then he had posted his letter to Sir John Fielding, written late at night. After that he had gone immediately to the livery stables where Tim Painter, looking stunning in riding gear, had been awaiting him, as arranged on the previous morning when the two men had decided to go in search of the Gaffer.

'Have you been excused from the search for Isobel?' the Apothecary had asked.

'Jasper wouldn't let me within a mile of it. He is so convinced I murdered the brat that he thinks I would deliberately lead them in the wrong direction. So I told Kathryn I was taking off for a few days.'

'Does she know where and for what purpose?'

As he mounted Tim raised an elegant shoulder. 'No, there was no need to tell her.'

'She must trust you a great deal,' John answered, as he wrestled to mount a large grey mare with an unfriendly eye, considering that he was never really lucky when it came to hiring horses.

'She is far too preoccupied with the search for her child to give me much attention,' had been Tim's casual reply as he had clattered out of the stable yard, with John, presenting a somewhat awkward figure in comparison, following him towards the open countryside.

But the small Cornish town was now no bigger than a thumb on the horizon and they were there, on the moor land, making for Redruth and feeling the morning air, sharp and somehow sweet, surround them. John felt glad to be out of Helstone's confines, glad to be doing something positive even if the trail were to go cold and he found that the blind fiddler had moved on somewhere else.

Everywhere he looked he could see sweeping green hills, with the occasional cluster of cottages, accompanied by fields of sheep contentedly grazing. To him this typified his beloved West Country and a part of him yearned to stay for ever more. Yet another side, the practical side which had made him sit for lonely hours silently studying herbs and books, told him that as soon as this case was solved he must head back for London and his shop in Shug Lane. But would this case be solved? The murderer of Diana Warwick he felt positive he could track down. Yet what of the death of Isobel Pill? And was she indeed dead?

Tim was shouting something over his shoulder and John hastened to catch him up.

'What did you say?' he asked, drawing alongside.

'I said who's that.' And he pointed.

John looked along the line of his finger and saw a very distant but somehow familiar figure plodding along the narrow path that led from hamlet to hamlet.

'I can't say for certain but it appears to be Gypsy Orchard.'

'By Jove I think you're right.'

And so saying Tim Painter wheeled his horse and covered the distance at a gallop. John, doing his best to keep up, watched the man dismount and make a low bow before the Romany woman. Then he saw her nod her head and the next minute she was up in the saddle, basket and all, while Tim climbed up in front of her. John panted up to where they stood.

'Look who I've found,' said Painter, epitomising charm.

Surely, thought John, this clear-eyed intelligent woman is not going to be taken in by such an obvious performance. But to his disappointment the gypsy smiled and said, 'It was most kind of 'ee, Sir.'

And then momentarily she caught John's eye and he knew that she was fooling, that she knew perfectly well what Tim Painter was and that he hadn't deceived her for a moment. Unreasonably glad of that, John gave her the merest hint of a wink before he turned his horse's head in the direction of Redruth.

Two hours later they entered the ancient town and made for a tavern, the gypsy entering the place quite unselfconsciously with her basket of wares on her hip, regardless of the stares of the other occupants, all of which needless to say were men.

Tim hovered over her. 'What can I get you to drink, my dear?'

'A draught of cider, Sir.' As soon as he was gone she leant forward to John. 'So you're here to search for the blind fiddler?'

'Yes.'

'May I ask why?'

'I want to question him about something, that is all.'

'I see.' And John had the extraordinary feeling that she actually did, that she knew precisely why he was here and the reason for his wanting to see the man.

'What do you know of him?' he asked.

'The Gaffer? Oh he appeared at the Furry one year and has been coming regular ever since.'

'How long ago was this?'

She smiled slowly, shaking her thick plait of dark hair. 'It would be about ten years or so.'

'And where was he before that? Do you know?'

'No, Sir, I don't. Some people said he come from London but nobody was quite certain.'

'London,' repeated John, and became thoughtful.

Tim Painter rejoined them with three foaming glasses. He raised his to Gypsy Orchard.

'To the most charming gypsy it has been my good fortune to meet,' he said, his handsome eyes all over her.

'Well met indeed, Sir. I was on my way to join the others but you saved me hours of walking.'

'You were going on foot to Redruth?'

'Yes, Sir. How else would I get there?'

She said it so simply that John laughed but Tim creased his brow in a frown. 'But you must walk miles.'

'Oh I do, Sir,' she answered earnestly, though something told John that she was actually mocking.

'How many miles a year?' Tim persisted, genuinely interested.

'Hundreds, Sir,' replied Gypsy Orchard, and sighed.

John was dying to laugh, enjoying the company of this intelligent woman and admiring her for the way in which she conducted herself. Tim, however, was determined to make himself memorable.

'One day, when I have money, I shall buy you a small cart and horse.'

'That will be nice, Sir. But surely you have money now.'

'Er…yes. But not quite enough.'

At this John did laugh, in fact was in the middle of letting out a great guffaw when he saw something that wiped the smile off his face. Into the tavern had come the brothers Colquite, of all people. Today they were dressed very similarly, in matching coats of a neutral shade of dun.

'Good heavens,' he whispered, and indicated to the other two exactly what was happening.

'What are that couple of old buggers doing here?' said Tim, clearly astonished.

'For what purpose are they come?' Gypsy Orchard muttered, almost to herself.

John looked at her, observing that she had lost colour while her hand had flown to her neck and was grasping something on a chain that hung round it. Obviously uneasy, she gazed with her great clear eyes to the place where the brothers had found seats.

'I'm going to speak to them,' said Tim, showing off. And getting up he smoothed out his riding breeches, which fitted tight as skin, and sauntered over to where they sat.

'How do, gentlemen? What brings you so far from home?' he asked jovially.

They jumped guiltily. Then one of them smiled and said, 'We've come to visit an ancient aunt.'

'Ancient aunt,' echoed the other.

'And have you brought the rest of your party?' Tim enquired blandly.

'Mr Sayce and Mr Reece are with us. The ladies are at leisure.'

Tim bowed. 'Well, I'll bid you good day, gentlemen.'

'One moment, Sir. May we ask the reason for your visit?'

Painter gave a broad grin. 'Just surveying the scene,' he said, and bowed once more. John looked at him as he returned. 'You treated that with great elan, Sir.'

Tim, appearing mighty pleased with himself, whispered, 'They say that they are here to visit an elderly relative.'

'Is there any reason to disbelieve them?'

Gypsy Orchard spoke. 'They are not to be trusted.'

John and Tim stared at her. 'What do you mean?'

'What I say. There is something odd about them.'

'In what way?' asked Tim.

While John added, 'Surely they are just a couple of harmless old eccentrics.'

She uttered one word, but it was a word that made the Apothecary's hair rise on his scalp. 'Wicca,' she said.

There was total silence, then Tim asked, 'What exactly does that mean?'

But Gypsy Orchard wasn't going to answer. Instead she rose to her feet, tucked her basket on her hip and said, 'Thank you for giving me a ride into town. Good day, gentlemen,' and left the ale house with her usual swinging gait.

Painter watched her go. 'A damn fine looking woman that. I wouldn't mind taking a stroke with her.'

John rolled his eyes. 'As long as it's female it will do.'

Tim appeared slightly annoyed. 'That's not true. I like my women good looking.'

It was on the tip of John's tongue to ask what he was doing with Mrs Pill in that case, but he simply hadn't the unkindness. Instead he said, 'Yes, of course. And do you want to know what Wicca means?'

'Yes.'

'It means witchcraft,' answered John, and had the satisfaction of seeing Tim look more than a little startled.

They booked themselves into a coaching inn, The Lion. Tim, who had risen early and drunk a good deal, went to bed, presumably to sleep, leaving John free to roam. Knowing that there was to be a gathering of gypsies he went through the town looking for anyone with brown skin and dark hair. But though he saw several there was no sign of the Gaffer, his actual quarry. In fact he was getting a little desperate when very faintly, borne on the summer breeze, there came a distant but distinctly recognisable air. Following it, the Apothecary found himself in an open courtyard beyond which lay an important-looking house, built fairly recently judging by the architecture. Here were not gathered the gypsies but rather the gentry, sitting on chairs and listening to the music of the blind fiddler and his troop.

They were all there: Gideon, James, George, Zachariah, Giles and, of course, the Gaffer. Today the blind fiddler was giving his all, indeed he seemed to have subtly altered his repertoire to suit the different type of audience. Holding the violin in his small and beautiful hands he coaxed out of the instrument a strange sobbing melody that held the listeners transfixed. Even John, with dark thoughts on his mind, felt himself uplifted by the wild song, and applauded heartily with the rest of the audience when eventually it came to an end. Next the band played a jig and Wilkes came out with the hat and danced a few sad steps, allowing several of the ladies present to embrace him. In this manner the monkey raised a large collection and scampered back to his associates with the hat bulging. John followed him at a more leisurely pace.

The first to see him was Gideon, who shook his tambourine in greeting and said, 'Greetings, Mr Rawlings. What are you doing in this neck of the woods?'

'I followed your music, of course.'

'Now that, Sir, I don't believe. Not all the way to Redruth.'

'No, you're right. But I heard that you were playing here and I came along on the off chance. And now I've found you.'

Zachariah came up. 'Well, Sir, this is a surprise.'

'Indeed. But for all that I am delighted to see you all.'

The mandora player let his hand wander over the strings, producing a delightfully quaint little melody. 'And there we all were thinking how sad it was to leave our friends behind us in Helstone. And lo and behold, most of you are here.'

John looked casual. 'I have already seen the brothers Colquite. Who else has arrived?'

'Their three ladies are in town.'

'Are they,' said the Apothecary, surprised.

Zachariah changed the tune to something sentimental. 'One of them was asking about you.'

'Oh, and who might that be?'

'Anne Anstey, of course. I think perhaps she has a swingeing passion for you.'

'Oh God forbid.'

'She says you saved her life one night at dinner.'

'She was choking; I assisted her. That is all. Anyway, it was Sayce who saved the day. But I must have a word with the Gaffer, if you'll forgive me.'

'Naturally, Sir.'

Zachariah bowed and retreated but John could feel his eyes boring into his back as he crossed to where the blind fiddler stood alone, turning his head to where the crowd was slowly starting to leave, chatting to one another on the way.

'Good evening, Gaffer,' he said quietly.

The man jumped and wheeled round. 'Do I know you, Sir?'

'Aye, you do. My name is Rawlings.'

The fiddler chuckled quietly, a sinister sound. 'Ah yes, from Helstone. How kind of you to follow me, Sir.'

'How do you know that I did?'

'I just had a feeling that I hadn't heard the last of you when we said our farewells.'

'I've come to talk to you about Diana Warwick,' said the Apothecary quietly.

'Well bless you now, Sir. I rather thought you might.'

The shadows were creeping over the great, somewhat mysterious, courtyard as John Rawlings turned to the blind fiddler and said, 'How well did you know her? Was she a friend of yours from the past? Is it true you met in London?'

The musician didn't answer, instead saying, 'Would it be all the same to you, Sir, if I sat down?'

Feeling discourteous and suddenly disadvantaged, the Apothecary answered, 'Yes, of course. How remiss of me. Here, let me.'

And he led the blind man to a nearby seat and took one himself.

There was silence and then the fiddler said eventually, 'Aye, I've know Diana a long time. From London, and also from Truro.'

Memories of Nick Kitto saying that she had been a poor young girl from that very town until his father had rescued her, came back.

'Were you one of her clients?' John asked boldly, deciding it was better to state the facts rather than mince words.

The darkened spectacles turned in his direction and stared silently. 'Now what would she be wanting with me?' And the Gaffer chuckled quietly.

John peered at him, seeing the jungle of dark hair and darkened skin. Beneath all that, however, he could see a strong face. A face dominated by the glasses which the fiddler wore. The Apothecary suddenly longed to see the man without the concealing spectacles. For a wild moment he thought of snatching them off, but restrained himself.

'I think you are probably fairly handsome beneath all that grime,' he said, somewhat thoughtlessly.

The Gaffer laughed aloud. 'Am I mucky then, Sir? I do apologise to 'ee for that. It's not that I mean to be but my fellow musicians don't really bother about dressing me.'

'But somebody shaves you,' John pointed out.

'Once a week I'm done by young Gideon. And that's the extent of my beautifying.'

All this was said with much good humour but there was something about the recital that didn't quite ring true. The Apothecary realised with a start that he had been entirely led away from his original question.

'I'm sorry if I am being indelicate but I have a witness who tells me that you visited Diana Warwick in her room on the night she was murdered. Or rather I should say in the early hours of the next day.'

The Gaffer nodded slowly, then said, 'It's true enough. I did go in to see her. But she was already dead.'

John sat silently for a moment or two. 'How did you know?' he asked eventually.

'I knew by her stillness, Sir.'

'I see. Can you describe to me exactly what you found.'

The Cornish fiddler sighed. 'I went into the room – the door was not locked – and I called her name, but she did not answer me. I crossed over to the bed and shook her gently by the shoulders, but she made no response at all. Eventually I found her wrist and took her pulse but there was nothing. So I concluded, Sir, rightly or wrongly, that the poor girl had been done to death.'

'But why presume that? Why did you not think she had died naturally?'

'Because women of forty, in good health, rarely do so.'

The Apothecary was silent, thinking of the exceptional gifts of those who are blind. 'How did you know Diana?' he asked eventually.

'She and I were old friends,' the Gaffer replied firmly.

'Then you had been her client,' the Apothecary said.

The black spectacles shifted once more, turning in John's direction and fixing him with a sightless gaze. 'I was once – long ago. Before my…accident.'

'So you weren't born blind,' John exclaimed, interested because of Sir John Fielding's catastrophe when he had been aged eighteen.

The Cornish fiddler shook his head. 'No, I was in my late twenties when it happened. Oh, that was a grievous day I can tell you. Anyway, I put on my black spectacles and walked away from the whole thing. I took to the road, playing my violin, and have been living by my wits ever since.'

'What happened exactly?'

'That I'd rather not say, Sir. It is a subject too painful to discuss before a comparative stranger.'

'Of course. I quite understand.'

'Do you, Sir? Well, that's very good of you I must say.'

John looked up sharply, certain that he had heard a certain mocking tone underlying the Gaffer's speech. But the expression on the face of the man was utterly bland, almost emotionless. Inwardly he sighed. He felt as if the blind fiddler had given him a certain amount of information and no more. He also felt that it was impossible for him to ask any further questions. That, for want of a better phrase, he had been out-manoeuvred.

The Apothecary got to his feet. 'Thank you so much for telling me what you have. I am extremely grateful to you.'

The fiddler also stood up. 'Most kind of you to say so, Sir. Now, would you give me your arm to the nearest ale house. I can hear by the silence that my fellow musicians have gone on ahead.'

John took the fellow's hand and tucked it through his arm, then proceeded slowly out of the courtyard, looking around him as he went.

'A fine place, this,' he said. 'Who owns it?'

'It used to belong to the Marquis of Dorchester but it changed hands after a game of cards.'

'Really?' said John, intrigued.

'Yes, it is owned these days by Lord Lyle. A dull fellow but an excellent gambler.'

'What happened to the Marquis?'

'He vanished, Sir. Out he went into the night and nobody ever heard of him again.'

'God's wounds. And the title?'

'Inherited by his cousin, another dull fellow.'

'Was the Marquis then presumed dead?'

'Oh yes, Sir. This all happened fifteen years ago at least. Mind you –' The Cornish fiddler laughed once more. '– the cousin didn't get much other than the name. It had all been gambled away.'

'He sounds a bad lad, this Marquis.'

'Oh he was that all right, Sir. A very naughty chap.'

They turned into the street and John spotted an alehouse. 'I think I can see what you're seeking.'

And sure enough there was little fat Giles coming out and staring about him.

'Here,' called John, and the jolly man saw them and waved.

Handing the blind fiddler into his care, John made his way back to The Lion to find out what, if anything, Tim Painter had been up to.

As he might have suspected there was a woman involved. John made his way into the inn only to stop short. There ahead of him were Muriel Legassick and Tabitha Bligh. Seeing him as soon as he appeared, the women came up, all giggles and grins. 'Why, Mr Rawlings, this is a regular reunion. We came here to visit some elderly relatives only to discover that Mr Painter and your own dear self had booked in. What a splendid thing.'

It was Mrs Legassick, eyes enormous behind her glasses, who spoke. Tabitha Bligh had her say.

'It's so nice to see you again, Sir. I was wondering what we would do for some gay company.'

They nodded and smiled at him but it was to Anne Anstey that John's eyes were drawn. She and Tim were sitting side-by-side, rapt in deep conversation, staring at one another intently. She glanced up as the Apothecary entered and gave him a look which proclaimed her triumph in securing a man. In fact she positively sneered at John that he had missed his chance, a fact which infuriated him as he had never even liked the wretched woman.

She moved largely and made a fanning motion with her hand. 'Well, Sir, we meet again. How nice to see you.'

John gave a curt bow. 'Madam.'

'I was just saying to Mr Painter here that Helstone had grown very dull and we were hard put to it to raise a smile. We therefore decided that Redruth would suit us better. But where, may I ask, are the Marchesa and your daughter?'

'They have returned home, Madam. They left early this morning.'

'And you allowed them to go unescorted. My!'

'Jed was driving the coach and Rufus carried shotgun. I think they are reasonably well protected.'

'My late husband would never allow me to travel alone. He insisted on accompanying me wherever I went.'

'How awkward for you,' John said tartly.

She shot him a look from her great slumberous eyes which for some reason made him feel uncomfortable, then she turned away.

Tim Painter, meanwhile, was inviting her to dine with him.

'I couldn't possibly, Sir. I have my friends to consider.'

'Oh Rawlings can look after them, can't you old chap?'

Horrified, the Apothecary gave a hasty bow. 'Alas I have a previous engagement. I'm afraid I cannot oblige. Forgive me.' And turning on his heel he marched out of The Lion leaving Tim Painter to sort out the problem.

Despite the horrid thought of spending the evening in the company of Mrs Legassick and Mrs Bligh, he felt guilty and a little ashamed of himself. After all they had done nothing to him. It was just that he found them utterly boring. He was on the point of turning back and making an excuse about his engagement having been cancelled and facing the evening like a man, when a rotund figure, in company with another, rolled out of an alehouse just ahead of him. John was just about to call out when something furtive in their manner reduced him to silence. Instead, the Apothecary found himself slinking into a doorway until they were several yards ahead of him. Then, walking quietly and not drawing attention to himself, John started to follow Messrs Sayce and Reece as they made their way through the back streets of Redruth.

Ahead of him the couple walked quite straightly, as if they had purpose and also as if they knew precisely where they were going. It seemed to the Apothecary, straining his ears, that they proceeded in silence, almost grimly in fact. Wondering where on earth they were bound, John walked along behind them, keeping his distance. And then to his amazement they turned into the courtyard where he had been earlier and made their way up to the front door of the big house. They pulled the bell and after a short interval were admitted, leaving the Apothecary quite literally standing. Wondering what to do next, he made his way into the nearby alehouse and ordered himself a large glass of Gascon wine.

The Cornish fiddler and his gang had all left and the place was practically deserted. John decided to converse with a serving wench who was wandering about idly.

'Good afternoon, my dear.'

She gave him a suspicious glance. 'Afternoon,' she said in a broad Cornish accent.

'Not many people about.'

'No. They'm been gone for their dinner.'

This reminded the Apothecary that he hadn't eaten and at that moment as if to endorse the fact, his stomach rumbled loudly. He patted it.

'Excuse me.'

The girl smiled and looked a bit more friendly. 'Hungry, are you?'

'Ravenous.'

'I got a bit of rabbit pie.'

John gave her a grin which twisted up on one side. 'I'd like that very much, please.'

'Then you shall have it, young Sir.'

She disappeared into the back and John was left alone with his thoughts. The blind fiddler had told him that the house was owned by Lord Lyle. So, though he wouldn't have put them down as the people who might be on calling terms with the nobility, it was possible that Sayce and Reece knew the man. It was even possible – just – that the aged aunt might be a resident at Lord Lyle's house.

The Apothecary, while he was waiting, ran through a list of excuses as to why he should visit Lord Lyle, but none of the reasons seemed legitimate. In the end all he could do was wolf down his belated dinner and sink a pint of ale, still in a quandary as to what action to take. Eventually he decided to watch the house against the moment when Sayce and Reece should reappear.

Standing outside, discreetly hidden from prying eyes, John waited until dusk fell but there was still no sign of the two visitors. Eventually deciding that they must have come out while he was in the alehouse, he turned disconsolately in the direction of The Lion. And then, behind him, he heard the front door open quietly. Wheeling round and at the same time hiding in some sheltering darkness, he looked rapidly across. A hooded figure had come out. A figure that sent a shiver down John's back from the silent way it stood framed in the doorway before it made its way through the gardens and out of his line of sight.

Back in The Lion he found the two ladies looking round madly for someone with whom to play cards. Greeted like a long-lost brother, John felt that he had no option but to agree and sat down reluctantly at the table. Being a poor player and not really enjoying himself, he decided to make the best of it by asking one or two questions.

'Where is Mrs Anstey?' he began.

A look shot between the duo together with an audible giggle.

'She has retired,' said Mrs Bligh, barely suppressing a laugh. 'She had a megrim.'

'Dear me. And what of Mr Painter? Did he have a megrim too?'

Now they laughed aloud. 'Oh, Mr Rawlings, you are so droll,' said Mrs Legassick, wiping her eyes. 'What will you think of next?'

'Who knows, Madam,' John replied, laying a card. 'Whatever fancy catches me, I daresay.' He changed the subject. 'By the way, do either of you ladies know the name of a great house belonging to Lord Lyle? It stands just outside the town.'

Was it his imagination or did a frisson run between the two of them? After a few seconds silence Mrs Legassick spoke. 'I know the place of which you speak but I do not recall its name.'

'It's called Tryon House I believe,' said Tabitha Bligh.

He looked at her and decided to change the subject.

'And how are you enjoying your stay in Redruth?' he asked.

'Very well, thank you Sir. It is a most pleasant town.'

'Which reminds me,' said John, laying another card but at the same time watching their expressions. 'I saw two of your many cousins, namely Herbert Reece and Eustace Sayce, tonight.'

'Oh really?' said Mrs Bligh. 'And where were they then?'

'Strangely enough they were going into Tryon Place,' John answered, and was rewarded by the look of frozen horror that appeared on both their faces.

Chapter Twenty-Two

That night John slept particularly heavily and woke late. Putting a hand out to seize and look blearily at his travelling clock he saw that it was after ten and that he had missed his favourite meal of the day. Even getting out of bed was an effort, in fact every muscle in his body ached, as if he had been given a severe kicking. Yet he had done nothing more strenuous than play cards with the ladies and drink a little wine. Feeling ghastly, John washed and dressed and went downstairs. There was nobody about and his need to take some fresh air was critical. Hoping he did not look as bad as he felt, the Apothecary made his way into the street.

The town was particularly deserted and he walked along aimlessly, then found that his steps were leading him towards Tryon House, almost of their own accord. Suddenly he decided on the reckless venture of taking a closer look at the place. Of making an attempt to get into the grounds to see where it was that the hooded figure had been heading. As so often happened with the Apothecary, action followed immediately on the thought and he quickened his pace, walking with more determination.

As he made his way he thought of the word uttered by Gypsy Orchard. She had said Wicca and had appeared quite nervous at the sight of the Colquite Brothers. Could they really, thought John, be involved in magic? Apparently such a pair of harmless old duffers, they seemed stupid more than anything else. But was this an act? he wondered. Did their bland silly old-man act mask something far more sinister?

At last he was heading out of town and Tryon House appeared in the distance. Once again, the Apothecary gazed on its pillared entrance and the large courtyard that stood before it. Yesterday it had been packed with people while the Cornish fiddler played, but today it stood empty other than for a stable boy listlessly sweeping away the signs of recent habitation. Boldly, John approached.

'Good morning, my man. Is Lord Lyle within?'

'No, Sir. He'm be gone for his morning ride.'

'Oh really. Whereabouts did he head?'

'Out to the countryside beyond. Shall I say you called, Sir?'

'Yes,' John called over his departing shoulder. 'Tell him John Rawlings wants to see him.'

But the Apothecary was running, seized by an idea and determined to put it into action. He sped back to The Lion and round to the stables, where an hostler was idling round in the yard, sucking a straw and whistling.

'Quick,' called John. 'Saddle up my horse, would you?'

Looking slightly astonished, the man complied and fifteen minutes later the Apothecary was mounted and making his way out of town. How he would know Lord Lyle when he saw him, he had no idea. But he was determined to find the fellow and somehow or other get into conversation with him.

Countryside lay all round Redruth, it being a small town, though considerably bigger than Helstone. Further, there were several horsemen out and about and the Apothecary was beginning to think he had taken on a hopeless task when he spotted two riders in the distance. Somehow he knew that one was Lord Lyle, the lucky man who had won Tryon House gaming at cards. Indeed, he recognised the fellow from the crowd of people listening to the music on the previous evening. So certain was he that he had found his quarry that he urged his horse into a canter. However, he had not taken into consideration the temperament of the beast. Liking to go at its own pace, the grey horse with the uncertain eye sped off into a gallop leaving the Apothecary to be tossed about like a ship in a gale. Clinging on for all he was worth he shot past the two men, giving them a frantic look as he did so. They laughed, he heard them do it, but for all that they set off in pursuit, presumably to try and slow the horse up. And then the creature stopped short and John went sailing over its head, landing in the grass below with a thud.

'Are you all right?' called a voice, and John, looking up, saw that a tall man with a young but worldly face was dismounting and coming to his side.

'I think so,' he answered, heaving himself into a sitting position and feeling his arms and legs.

'You took a nasty tumble, Sir,' said the other, also getting off his mount.

'I'm afraid I'm not a very good rider.'

'Not local then?'

'No, I come from London.'

'Well, let's get you on your feet and see what damage has been done.'

They put a hand under each arm and hauled the Apothecary upwards.

'Can you stand?' asked the worldly man.

'Just about.'

'Nothing broken then.'

'No, I don't think so.'

And then came the stroke of good fortune that John had been hoping for. The second man turned to the tall one and said, 'Should we take him back to the house, my Lord?'

'Why not? I could do with a bit of company. Here, you get on my horse. I'll ride that grey beast.'

And the next thing John knew was that his foot was in the stirrup and he had been half-lifted by the second man, presumably a servant, into his lordship's saddle. With the effortless ease of someone who had been riding almost as soon as he could walk, Lord Lyle swung himself into the saddle, pulled the reins tightly, and said, 'Don't you play tricks on me, you brute,' before setting off at a trot towards civilisation.

Half an hour later they were back, seated in the drawing room, while several male servants fussed round the Apothecary looking for injuries. Meanwhile milord, draped languidly in a great chair, observed the process and sipped a morning glass of sherry.

'You've had a lucky escape, my friend.'

John, thinking to himself that his lordship would never know how lucky, said, 'I must thank you, Sir, for your gallant rescue. It was immeasurably kind of you. Allow me to present myself. My name is John Rawlings, Apothecary of Shug Lane, Piccadilly.'

'Antony Lyle,' answered the other carelessly. 'Would you like a glass of sherry?'

'Very much. Thank you.'

Lord Lyle waved a lazy arm. 'Pour one, Simmons. And you can refill my glass at the same time.' He turned to John and laughed. 'An apothecary, eh? Well, have you broken anything?'

John felt his arms and legs once more. 'No, I can honestly say that I'm in one piece, though I'll be many shades of purple tomorrow.'

'A fine sight indeed. Good thing that I happened to be around. Where are you staying?'

'At The Lion.'

His lordship raised his brows and nodded, making no comment. 'And what is your purpose in visiting Redruth?' Before waiting for a reply, he went on, 'I come here for a month or two now and then. But our family seat is in Worcester and naturally I have a town house.'

John decided to be daring. 'Is it true that you won this place gambling?'

Lyle let out a short laugh. 'Perfectly. I was eighteen at the time and had staked all I had on the turn of a card. Fortunately it worked my way and I won everything, leaving the Marquis of Dorchester minus the place.'

'But surely he had other homes to go to?'

An extremely sly grin crossed Lord Lyle's face. 'He not only wagered this house.'

'Poor devil. You mean you took everything?'

'Everything. People said I had the luck of Satan himself that night.'

He laughed robustly and John, looking at him, thought the man a typical example of his class, a younger member of the aristocracy who would gamble his life away to relieve his perpetual boredom.

'You certainly seem to have done. Was Lady Lyle pleased with your new homes, Sir?'

Milord shrugged. 'She moves from one to the other as she wishes, usually choosing a house where I am not resident.'

The Apothecary felt faintly amused that anyone could live such a shallow life. 'You do not get on?' he asked boldly.

His lordship let out a snort. 'Get on! We detest one another. She is thin and simple and was foisted on me by my father. I can't stand the sight of her.'

'I take it there are no children?'

'There's one sickly boy who follows his mother around as if he were tied to her. And that is that. I have provided the heir and done my duty.'

He held out his sherry glass which was duly refilled, crossed his ankles and grinned at the Apothecary. John, peering at him over the rim of his glass, wondered just how much emotion he actually felt about his current situation.

Lord Lyle seemed to come to a sudden decision. 'I like you,' he said. 'Come and look over my estate.'

Knowing that all of this had once belonged to the Marquis of Dorchester, John stepped out of a huge pair of French doors and into a vast garden. It was laid out in terraces full of yew hedges, rose borders brimming with buds, while over the balustrades climbed clematis, much of it in full bloom. A pillared folly, in which stood iron garden furniture, lay before them. This, in turn, led onto an alley whose lush green grass was bordered by Irish yews. Lord Lyle, glancing at his companion's awe-struck face, led the way down to an ornamental lake on the banks of which was moored a little rowing boat.

On the far bank were some ruins, standing dark and strangely mysterious, contrasting with the beauty of the rest of the surroundings.

'What are they?' asked John, pointing.

'All that's left of Roskilly Abbey. Do you want to have a closer look?'

'Yes. I'd like to see.'

'We'll go by boat then. It will be quicker than walking.'

They climbed into the small vessel and John, almost automatically and despite the aching in his limbs, picked up the oars. Meanwhile milord dipped his fingers idly in the water and hummed to himself as they skimmed the surface. Coming to the other bank John saw a mooring post and a jetty, and somehow or other managed to scramble out and secure the craft. Lord Lyle, taking his time and clearly conserving his energy, followed at his own pace.

The Abbey had obviously been big and important in its day but the death blow delivered by Henry VIII meant that now only a skeleton of its former glory stood to tell the tale of a once proud history. John, looking up at what had been the chapter house, walked along decayed and deserted cloisters, staring at the remains of the great church. And then he had an optical illusion. He could have sworn that a hooded figure dressed in a monk's habit had passed quickly round the corner of the church and vanished from his sight. He stared, then looked round for his lordship, who had sat down in the sunshine, taking his ease, his back turned. John stood uncertainly for a moment then made his way to where he had seen the apparition.

There was nothing and nobody there. The ruins of the church were deserted and empty. All that John could sense was a faint smell, like incense, permeating the brickwork. Yet there was nothing surprising about that, he thought. After all, this had been the place where the monks had prayed. Yet the ghost – if indeed it had been such – had made him uneasy. Involuntarily, there in the bright sunshine, something walked over John's grave.

He made his way back to where Lord Lyle, apparently asleep, sat leaning against the stonework, eyes closed. He opened one as the Apothecary approached.

'Like it?' he asked.

'Yes, it's a very fine ruin. Tell me, is it haunted?'

'Zounds, yes. The locals won't come near the place. There's talk of ghostly processions of monks, chanting and carrying lanthorns. It has a terrible reputation. Why?'

'I thought I saw something.'

'Did you, by Jove. Well, you aren't the first and you certainly won't be the last. What was it?'

'A hooded figure wearing a habit.'

Lord Lyle looked wise. 'That would be Brother Mark. They say he was killed when Henry VIII ordered the Abbey to close. He died fighting before the altar, so legend has it.'

'Oh, I see.'

But the Apothecary was not happy. The story of Brother Mark gallantly losing life in the most holy place in the Abbey somehow did not match what he had seen. For there had been something furtive and almost sinister about the apparition. A something that made him shiver again despite the unexpected warmth of the morning.

'Seen enough?' asked his lordship.

'Not quite. Can you spare another ten minutes?'

'Certainly. I shall doze. Wake me when you are ready to go.'

As Lord Lyle once more closed his eyes John hurried back to the place where he had seen the supposed ghost. There was nothing there, of course, but despite that the Apothecary started to search the building thoroughly. Then he dropped to his knees and hunted along the ground, running his fingers over the soil as he did so. It was painstaking and hard but eventually he was rewarded. His hand closed over a tiny stump of candle. Swiftly he picked it up and slipped it into a pocket.

It proved nothing of course as it could have been dropped by an earlier visitor to the Abbey. But nevertheless it was some indication that the ghost may well have been mortal. Slowly John made his way back to where Lord Lyle sat, eyes closed in the sunshine and loud snores emanating from the noble nostrils. But he woke at once and clambered into the boat, taking his turn to row back cheerfully enough. John sat facing him, watching the Abbey grow more distant, thinking about what he had seen and determining to go back to the place after dark to find out more about the creatures of the night.

Having been warned by Lord Lyle's hostler that the grey horse with the unfriendly eye had an erratic temperament, John walked back, leading the creature by the reins. Having thankfully handed her into the care of The Lion's stables, he made his way within. As usual, Tim Painter was recounting some yarn or other in the taproom. He turned as John entered and gave the Apothecary a meaningful wink.

'My dear chap, where have you been? I was about to organise a search party.'

John looked at him in amusement. 'Last I saw of you was deep in the clutches of Anne Anstey. How did it go?'

Tim waved a hand in front of his face. 'I cannot discuss it. Let me merely say that I feel utterly exhausted.'

John grinned. The fellow was such a reprobate and was clearly going to get worse over the years.

'I've spoken to the blind fiddler,' he said.

'Have you, by God. Then our work here is done?'

'Not quite.'

And drawing Tim into a private corner, John told him his adventures since he had got up that morning. To give the man his due he listened intelligently and in silence, nodding occasionally. Finally he said, 'So you think there's something strange going on in the Abbey ruins?'

'It's just an instinct I have. It's not based on much but I feel compelled to go back at night.'

Tim scratched his chin. 'Do you think Lord Lyle is involved?'

'I would imagine he is. Remember I saw a robed and hooded figure leave his house. He's rich and idle and incredibly bored. In my view he's either part of what goes on or is turning a blind eye.'

'Then let's to it.' And Tim Painter rubbed his hands together.

'Tonight?'

'Why not. Anne Anstey is playing cards with friends so I shan't be seeing her. I am at your disposal, Sir.'

'We'll have to gain access to his grounds.'

'An easy task.' Tim was silent, then said, 'Pity we haven't got habits and hoods ourselves.'

John nodded. 'I don't see us finding any at this late stage. We'll just have to wear black.' And suddenly he laughed, feeling incredibly young and reckless. 'Tally ho,' he said.

Tim raised his glass. 'To the chase.'

'Indeed,' answered John, and clinked his in response.

Chapter Twenty-Three

The night had grown unseasonably cold and rowing across the lake in the little boat proved a thoroughly chilling experience. Entry into the huge parkland owned by Lord Lyle had been as easy as Tim Painter had predicted. They had simply chosen a place where the wall was in need of repair and climbed over it. John had stood for a minute, disorientated, then a glimmer of water in the moonlight had been enough to set him on track and the two men, keeping within the shadow of the trees, had made their way towards the lake.

Once on it, the Apothecary realised, they would be clearly visible. Not from the house, which lay back amongst the huge and sheltering gardens, but from any other pairs of eyes that might also be watching that night. Never the less to walk round the stretch of water would take rather a long time and might also place them in danger. After a whispered discussion, the two men decided to row across and take their chance.

Night on the lake was very different from its daytime aspect. Banks of reed, habitat of ducks and waterfowl, became inky black pools; while the water itself, by daylight quite blue and sparkling, turned into something dark and unfriendly. The small boat became wet round their feet and Tim was forced to bail while John rowed, the sound of his oars loud and clear in the silence of the night. Meanwhile the shape of the derelict Abbey reared tall and terribly menacing as they approached the jetty.

'What are you hoping to find?' whispered Tim.

John shrugged his shoulders and put his finger to his lips as the boat slid into the mooring spot and he leapt ashore. Tim, no doubt to prove his athleticism, followed suit but slipped on the dampness making an unmistakeable crash. Furiously, John glared at him and plucked him into the shadows of the chapter house wall where they crouched, side by side, waiting for something to react to the noise. But only silence echoed back at them and after a few minutes they both relaxed.

'Nobody here,' Tim muttered.

'Not yet,' John answered meaningfully.

'What do you mean by that?'

'I'm not sure.'

'How long do you think we should wait?'

'At least an hour.'

'Thank God I brought a hip flask,' Tim answered, and took a swig.

They changed to a sitting position and stayed like that for a while, then Painter stood up. 'I think I'll go for a look round.'

'Why?'

'Because you've got some idea of the size of this place while I have none.'

'Then I'll come with you. But for heaven's sake be quiet.'

'Don't be silly, man. There's no one about.'

John replied, 'I'm not so certain.'

Together they crept out of their place of concealment and began a moonlit tour of the Abbey, which was even larger than John had at first realised. Many of the buildings were minus a roof but still had four walls standing; others were crumbling into total decay.

'It must have been a powerful order in its day,' Tim commented, gazing up to where beautiful windows – now totally without glass – had dominated the rooms beneath.

But John did not answer, instead straining his ears to catch a faint sound.

'Listen. Can you hear anything?'

Tim relapsed into silence. 'No, I don't think so.'

'There. There it is again. You must be able to hear it.'

Painter turned a panic-stricken face towards him. 'It's chanting – and it's getting nearer.'

'Quick,' said John, and seizing his companion by the elbow, hurried him into the great and gloomy ruined church.

'Is it ghosts?'

The Apothecary made a sound of disgust. 'They're as human as you and me.' And so saying he dragged Tim Painter into the dark recesses of a side chapel and crouched behind a tomb. Tim ducked down beside him.

'Who is it?' he whispered.

John shrugged once more and motioned him to be quiet, all his attention focussed on the church's arched and doorless entrance.

Scarcely breathing, he and Tim watched fascinated as two figures dressed as monks, one of them bearing a lanthorn, came in. The other carried a censer swinging on a chain, which he shook as he proceeded along. Behind them came a procession of people all dressed similarly. But it was their chanting that sent a shiver through the Apothecary; low and deep, it was a chilling sound that seemed to penetrate through to his very soul. Stealing a glance at Tim he saw that the man was pale as a shadow.

Behind this initial procession, which numbered about two dozen, came people in ordinary clothes, their faces disguised by masks. For those who had none, the device of pulling hats well down had to suffice. John, watching them, was seized by an idea and as the last drew level and passed where he was hidden he, too, joined them at the back of the line, bending his face so that it was hidden by shadow. Tim Painter, clearly losing courage, remained where he was.

The leaders halted before the altar and threw back their hoods, revealing none other than Lord Lyle and a dark stranger, who produced a crucifix from within his robe and deliberately and slowly turned it upside down. John's blood ran cold. He was about to witness the Black Mass.

He could not look. He was not a religious man but something in him rebelled against anything so profane taking part in a place that had once been used by deeply religious men to celebrate the love of God. Yet his eyes could not help but be drawn as a figure stepped out of the line and threw back its cassock, to reveal Anne Anstey, naked, her flesh overflowing. Without pausing she threw herself backwards on the altar and parted her legs, writhing about as if Satan himself were pleasuring her. From the chapel to his left John could hear Tim Painter gasping.

The smell of incense filled the air and the sound of chanting grew louder as the witches formed a circle. He heard words that he did not understand, saw the crucifix passed round so that the celebrants might spit on it, heard Christ denounced and the congregation swear fealty to Satan. Then one of the males did in fact copulate with Anne Anstey in full view of the rest of the coven. As he jerked on top of her his hood fell back to reveal Geoffrey Colquite. Sickened beyond words, the Apothecary attempted to move away but was forced to remain where he was because the man in front of him turned at the sound of John's feet.

Eventually, though, all was done and pulling up their hoods, the coven processed out of the church and away, leaving Mrs Anstey, who appeared to be in some form of cataleptic trance, still lying naked on the altar.

John, who had loitered behind, hurried to Tim Painter's side to find him sitting on the floor with an expression of horror on his face.

'By God's life, I've never seen the like of it.'

'That was the Black Mass.'

'And *her*.' He pointed to the inert body. 'Zounds, we've all been naughty in our time but that was utterly flagrant.'

'I think she was having some kind of seizure.'

Tim giggled loudly. 'She had a seizure all right.'

It was a blessed relief to laugh and John did, enjoying the normality of it. 'What shall we do with her?' he asked.

'Leave her, of course. Presumably one of her friends will return for her. I can't see you and I lugging that mass of flesh back in such a little boat.'

The mental picture was so vivid that John had to suppress another fit of laughing.

'Come on. Let's go while the coast is clear.'

Tim struggled to his feet, glancing as he did so in the direction of the altar. From it came the noise of low moaning.

'Oh rot the old bitch,' he said with contempt.

But John was already making for the arched entrance, moving quietly but with determination. Painter followed and they reached the landing stage without meeting anyone. But there a shock awaited them. Two cowled figures stood in readiness, guarding the boat, waiting for whoever it was who had rowed across in the moonlight.

'I'll take the one on the right,' John whispered, and without further ado leapt on the man and wrestled him to the ground. Meanwhile Tim swung a mighty blow to the other man's chin, rendering the fellow insensible, then he turned to assist his companion, jumping on his assailant's back and pummelling him with his fists. In the end they overpowered him, though he was built like an ox and was equally as strong. Gasping, John Rawlings tied the man's hands behind him with his monk's girdle, then mopped his bloody mouth.

'I was utterly wrecked by falling from my horse – and now this.'

'A gallant endeavour, my friend,' Tim answered as they got into the boat and pushed off. He took the oars. 'What do you think about what we have just witnessed?'

'Well, Lord Lyle is deeply involved, as are Anne Anstey and the brothers Colquite.'

'But what about the rest of that cosy nest of cousins?'

'All of them I should imagine,' John answered gloomily.

A thought occurred which he did not speak aloud. Could Isobel's disappearance be linked to the fact that a coven of witches had been in Helstone to see the Furry Dance? Surely they had not been into human sacrifice? But remembering the final scenes of the Black Mass he had just witnessed, when Anne Anstey and Geoffrey Colquite had lain shrieking on the altar, almost anything was possible.

As if he had read the Apothecary's thoughts, Tim said, 'You don't think they captured Isobel do you?'

John looked at him out of an eye that was swelling up rapidly. 'I believe it's possible.'

'Then she's dead,' Tim answered flatly.

'I'm afraid she is,' came the bleak reply.

They reached The Lion safely and despite their truly dishevelled appearance made at once for the tap room where they restored themselves with cognac, a particularly good French one John noticed, wondering how far the smuggling trade extended.

'That,' said Tim, after his third, 'is something I never want to witness again.'

'Nor I. But they knew we were there, you know.'

'But not till afterwards surely.'

The Apothecary made a face. 'I'm not certain about that. But the presence of the boat was all they needed. Then they were positive.'

'We've been seen, of course.'

John nodded. 'I know. That's why I think it wise if we get out of town early tomorrow morning.'

'My thoughts entirely.'

'Then I suggest we get some sleep,' the Apothecary answered.

But even though he was utterly exhausted he could not lose consciousness, his mind full of the events of the evening, his brain so powerfully charged that it worked on regardless of the fact that he was longing for rest. Thus he was awake when he heard the sound of the lightest of footfalls in the passageway outside his bedroom. In an instant John was out of bed and reaching for his pistol when the door, which he had omitted to lock, was flung open and two men appeared in the entrance.

'Don't move,' said a gruff voice. 'And put your arms high.'

John instantly complied, thinking it far better to obey at this stage of the proceedings.

'What's all this about?' he asked with as much dignity as he could muster.

'Lord Lyle wants to see you. Now,' came the reply.

And without further ado they had seized him by either shoulder and hustled him downstairs, still only wearing his nightshirt. A coach was waiting outside and before John could as much as protest he found himself bundled in, one guard mounting the box, the other sitting opposite him with a loaded pistol pointing at his ribs.

The Apothecary thought frantically. Nobody who knew him, even by sight, had witnessed him being present at this evening's terrible ceremony. It must be description alone, probably from the men guarding the boat, that his lordship was acting on. His best way was to bluff it out and hope that he sounded convincing.

At Tryon House he received the same treatment, being roughly handled into a drawing room, where he was pushed into a chair and told to keep quiet.

'I wouldn't dream of speaking to you,' he stated. 'I shall deal with Antony Lyle and nobody else.'

The guards exchanged a look but said nothing, and a voice behind him responded icily, 'Well, what do you have to say for yourself, Mr Rawlings?' and Lord Lyle strolled into view.

He was dissolute, that much was certain, and tonight his lordship was pale. Yet he had covered this paleness – or rather accentuated it – by a smearing of face paint, complete with carmined lips and pencilled eyes. In short he looked frightful, a travesty of the man who had rescued John from his plunge off the horse.

The Apothecary went straight in on the attack. 'May I ask the meaning of this, Sir?'

Milord looked at him languidly. 'I think you know.' He gestured with his hand and the two guards withdrew immediately. 'I think you were present this evening.'

John assumed a haughty expression. 'Would you be kind enough to explain that remark.'

'There's no need for all that bravado. You were there all right.'

'Where?' John demanded, determined to pin the man down.

'You know damned well,' came the snarled reply.

'If I knew what you were talking about I might be able to respond. But if you want the facts, I spent the entire evening in company with my friend Mr Painter. We dined together, we played chess and then we retired. So what is the meaning of this outrage?'

For the first time a look of uncertainty crossed Lord Lyle's face. 'Are you telling me that you did not go to the Abbey?'

John's expression of righteous indignation was masterly. 'The Abbey? Why should I want to return there? I've seen the place.'

His lordship poured himself a drink and the Apothecary saw that his hand was shaking. 'Then who was it?' John heard him mutter.

He stood up. 'I've a mind, Sir, were it not for the fact that you rescued me when my horse had thrown me, to lay a charge against you.'

Lord Lyle made one last attempt to win the day. 'I'd like to see you try.'

'Don't tempt me,' John answered, and thrust his face close to that of his captor.

His lordship backed away. 'Is it possible that I owe you an apology?' he said, his voice full of disbelief.

'Sir, you do. I have been seized from my bed by two blackguards and brought before you to answer some ridiculous accusation of visiting that God-forsaken Abbey. Merciful heavens, Sir, can you not see that I am in my night attire?'

Lord Lyle downed his drink in a single swallow. 'Mr Rawlings, what can I say? You have been mistaken for some trespasser upon my property. Please accept my sincerest regrets. I would not have had you treated so.'

Be magnanimous in victory, John thought. Aloud he said, 'If I may have a drink before I return to bed. Mr Painter and I are off early in the morning.'

'Oh really? And where are you heading to?' asked Lord Lyle as he poured a goodly measure into a glass.

'We are returning to Helstone,' said John.

'Ah,' said his lordship, his face quite ghastly in the candlelight, 'I have a little property there. I visit it from time to time. In fact you have decided me. I shall follow you some time tomorrow.'

'Really,' said John, sipping his drink. 'And may I ask where your house is situated?'

'Of course,' answered Lord Lyle. 'It overlooks Loe Pool.'

Chapter Twenty-Four

To say that Mrs Pill looked drained of vitality would have been to half-state the case. Indeed she seemed to have lost the will to live. Tim, who had slipped once more into the role of feckless lover, stood about looking helpless while John returned to the room he had ordered be kept for him to fetch his medical bag. Administering salts, he said, 'I presume that your search was in vain?'

'She has vanished off the face of the earth,' came the heartbroken reply.

And John, remembering Lord Lyle's face as he had described his house overlooking the Pool, thought perhaps he ought to tell her what he suspected. But somehow, probably the piteous sight that the poor woman represented, stopped himself. Instead he asked the whereabouts of her brother.

'He is around somewhere, I believe with the servants. He wants us to depart tomorrow but I can't bear to go.' Her voice broke in a sob.

'Madam,' John said quietly, 'I think perhaps you should.'

'But it would mean leaving…'

Tim Painter spoke up. 'Kathryn, it's time you faced reality. You're not going to find Isobel.'

'Do you mean that she is dead?'

'Yes,' her lover answered bluntly.

He could have spared her the pain somehow, though how John could not at that moment guess. In response to his words Mrs Pill crumpled up, her face contorted into an almost simian cast of features.

'Oh God,' she cried.

John put his arms round the wretched woman, holding her tightly against him. 'Come now,' he said soothingly.

It was utterly inane but he could think of nothing else to say, certain as he was that Tim was right.

At that moment Jasper joined them, casting a look of immense dislike in Painter's direction. 'I thought something smelt bad,' he said.

Tim lost his temper quite suddenly. 'Take that back or I'll floor you,' he shouted.

'Why, you rotten little upstart...'

It was enough. With a flying leap Tim crossed the distance between them and grappled with Kathryn's brother. At this she let out a dismal wail, beating her fists on John's chest.

'Oh no, oh no,' she howled. 'This on top of everything else I have to bear. Jasper for the love of heaven stop fighting.'

But it was no use. They were whacking one another like a couple of schoolboys. Extricating himself gently, the Apothecary attempted to part them, feeling far from up to doing so. As well as the bruises he had obtained from falling from his horse, he had been involved in a fight the night before which had damaged both his eye and his lip. In fact he looked a sorry spectacle as he strained to part the warring couple, not very successfully. Indeed it was the landlord of The Angel who, just stepping out into the street as he was, finally parted them. John, defeated, turned his attention back to Mrs Pill.

'Why don't you go tomorrow, my dear?'

'And with whom should I travel? You've seen those two for yourself.'

'Travel with Tim and let Jasper go with the servants.'

Kathryn's miserable little face came close to John's own. 'I don't know that I want him any more. I think he is a liability rather than an asset.'

Seeing sense at last, thought the Apothecary.

'But then,' she added brokenly, 'where else would I find such a man to be with? I am no beauty when all's said and done, and Tim is handsome, is he not?'

'Very,' John answered dryly.

'Then there we are. You have hit on my dilemma.'

I have said nothing, John thought. Aloud he remarked, 'You must weigh the situation carefully, Mrs Pill. After all the whole of the rest of your life depends on it.'

At this point Tim came over, his beautiful face somewhat

beaten round the edges. 'Your brother has extremely hard fists, Kathryn. As far as I am concerned I never want to see the oaf again.'

'Why make my life even more difficult?' she asked, rounding on him.

'I? I have made it difficult? I think you exaggerate, Madam. Surely it is your brother who is the founder of your problems.'

Mrs Pill's trembling chin stuck out. 'Jasper is merely trying to protect me.'

'Then let him,' said Tim suddenly. 'I've had enough of this conversation. I'm off to The Blue Anchor. Coming, Rawlings?'

'I'll follow you,' John answered. He turned back to Kathryn. 'What are you going to do?'

'I don't know,' came the miserable reply. 'I'll have to think about it. I shall come to my decision in the morning.'

Yet something in her tone of voice told the Apothecary all he needed to know. Mrs Pill would rather suffer all kinds of indignities than be without a man, particularly one so very good looking as Tim Painter. Come what may she was going to remain with him.

The journey back to Helstone had been uneventful. Tim had ridden the grey horse while John had travelled on his mount, a more successful arrangement. Also they had taken their time about getting back and had stopped at a wayside inn for refreshment.

Thus, though very different people, they had shared a great deal and John could honestly say that he liked the fellow, for all he was shiftless and idle and no doubt represented a nightmare to any woman.

'You know I spent the night with Mrs Anstey,' Tim had said after his fourth jug of ale.

'So I gathered.'

'And to think the next night she was thrashing about on the altar with horrible old Colquite. It's enough to make me ashamed.' He had grinned. 'Almost.'

Now, a day later, in the confines of the Blue Anchor, he said,

'Helstone is very quiet without that witchy bunch of people. Shall we move on?'

John shook his head. 'You may do as you please, Tim, but I have still to see Lord Godolphin and have another chat with Nicholas Kitto.'

Tim had given him a dark look. 'You don't think that I killed Diana Warwick, do you?'

'Not really. According to the witness she was alive when his lordship visited her.'

'What time was that?'

'About midnight. But he was gone by two in the morning when the blind fiddler went in and, if we are to believe him, found her dead.'

'She must have been a great slut,' said Tim, and chuckled, long and deep.

'What time did you leave her?'

'At about half past eleven. Funnily enough she seemed very insistent that I went.'

'Hardly surprising if she had another admirer coming at midnight.'

'No, but it was more than that. It was as if she were nervous.'

'Do you think she was frightened of Lord Godolphin?'

'She could have been.' Tim struggled with a memory. 'No, I think it was from the time she heard a noise.'

'What sort of noise?' asked John, suddenly intensely interested.

'I don't know for sure. I'll spare you the details but my attentions were otherwise engaged. But she heard something and – yes, I remember now – she looked towards the door.'

'Was it locked?'

'No, I don't think it was. I think we went in in rather a hurry and we forgot.'

'What happened then?'

'I asked her what had disturbed her but she said I was imagining it. So I just got on with things.' Tim grinned, unabashed.

'But looking back you think that the door opened and somebody stood there?'

'I'm not certain. As I said, I saw nothing.'

'Um.' The Apothecary was deeply thoughtful. 'If that happened – and I repeat if – then that person might well have been her murderer.'

For the first time Tim looked serious. 'Zounds, you may well be right. What a ghastly notion.'

'Not very pleasant I admit.'

'Poor Diana,' said Tim, and fell to musing over his ale.

John was silent, thinking hard. If the door had opened while Tim and Diana had been *in flagrente delicto* and a jealous man had stood there, then look no further for the murderer. But who, that was the question? What pair of eyes had observed them and decided to act later that night?

Full of uncertainty, the Apothecary decided that he must see the two remaining witnesses, namely Lord Godolphin and Nicholas Kitto – probably father and son in his opinion – as soon as possible.

Nick was obviously going to be the easier subject to find so, without ado, John Rawlings set out from The Blue Anchor and made his way up Coinage Hall Street, past the building that had given the place its name, then along Church Street until he came to the house at the top. Here he rang the bell which was answered by the usual servant.

'Is Mr Kitto in?' the Apothecary asked, adding crisply, 'I do not have an appointment.'

'I will see if he is at home, Sir.'

And the maid, who was elderly, disappeared into the depths of the house. A few minutes later Nick himself, looking older and dressed entirely in black, came to the front door.

'Oh it's you, Rawlings. Come in, come in.'

He led the way into the drawing room and said without preamble, 'It's Diana's funeral tomorrow. The Coroner has agreed on it. The delay has been caused by an abortive attempt to find her relatives. But none have come forward and no further waiting can be brooked.'

'Indeed not,' said John, thinking of the state of the body.

'Will you be attending?' Nicholas continued.

'Yes, of course. Do you know who else is going?'

'I have no idea. A mere handful I expect.'

'And where is it to be held?'

Nicholas looked surprised. 'Here, in the local churchyard. The ceremony will be conducted by the Vicar. It is at half past ten in the morning.'

'I shall make a point of being there.' John cleared his throat. 'Tell me, my friend, are you coming to terms with her death?'

'I have accepted the fact that I shall not see her any more but it has not made life any easier to bear. To tell you the truth I am missing her terribly.'

'I'm sure,' the Apothecary answered soothingly. 'Now tell me again, you went to her room at about six o'clock in the morning, is that correct?'

'I've already told you, yes.'

'And you saw no one about as you ascended the stairs?'

'I passed some little maid with her thumb in her mouth. That was all.'

'And you found Diana dead?'

'Yes. Why do you want me to repeat everything?'

'What would you say if I told you that someone else had discovered the body some four hours earlier?'

Nicholas looked utterly astonished. 'Who for God's sake?'

'The blind fiddler,' John answered slowly.

Kitto's face was a picture of disbelief. 'The blind fiddler?' he repeated. 'Why him of all people? What was he doing there?'

'Much the same as you I imagine.'

'What are you inferring?' snarled Nick Kitto, his face suddenly white and savage.

'I am saying that you were not Diana's only visitor that night.'

The attack was as unexpected as it was swift. The Apothecary, covered with bruises and with a cut lip and black eye to boot, was suddenly knocked to the floor by a hammer blow to his jaw.

'Oh God help us,' he bellowed, holding his face.

But Nick was on top of him and pounding his head on the wood repeatedly. Every tooth the Apothecary had shook violently and his senses had started to swim when there was a sudden shout from the doorway.

'Nicholas! Whatever are you doing? Stop it at once, do you hear me?'

It was Mrs Ennis, looking formidable in a purple gown with which her hair clashed violently. Her son, however, continued to crash away regardless. John felt himself to be on the point of losing consciousness when the rough treatment suddenly came to an end and he was vaguely aware that Nick had been hauled to his feet and sent to stand a good few feet away. The Apothecary had never been so glad to see anyone as his extremely unlikely rescuer. He looked at Nick's mother, glassy-eyed.

'Thanks,' he managed from a mouth totally swollen.

'My dear young man, whatever happened? Why was Nicholas attacking you?'

Nicholas rolled his eyes at John, a pleading in their depths.

'A slight argument over a game of chance,' the Apothecary muttered inaudibly.

This reply was treated with contempt as there were no cards or dice visible. 'How about the truth,' said Mrs Ennis fiercely.

Nicholas growled from the corner in which he had been sent to stand, 'It was my fault. I attacked him.'

'Why for heaven's sake?'

'He was maligning a friend of mine.'

'I was telling the simple truth,' answered John from the floor.

Mrs Ennis swelled up, resembling an egg more closely than ever. 'Now what is this all about? Mr Rawlings, please explain.'

She helped him to stand and he collapsed into a nearby chair, very much the worse for wear. Shooting a look at

Nicholas he saw that the young man was standing in the corner like a truculent little boy, sticking out his lower lip and generally pulling a sour face. No wonder he hadn't been man enough for Diana, John thought cruelly.

Mrs Ennis turned to her son. 'Well, Sir, as your friend will not speak, what do you have to say?'

'Nothing.'

'A fine how-do-you-do indeed. Both remain silent when it comes to the cause of the quarrel. Well you can leave my house, the pair of you. Go and fight in the street for all I care.'

'What about the neighbours?' muttered Nick.

'Oh they must take their chance,' Mrs Ennis snapped in reply.

Weakly, John got to his feet and staggered towards the front door. Holding his somewhat crumpled hat in his hand he made his way out, then turned towards the church, desperately needing somewhere quiet to sit for half an hour. But he had got no further than a few yards when a voice said, 'Oh my dear Sir. You seem fit to drop.'

He looked up and into the clear eyes of Gypsy Orchard.

'I don't feel too good,' he replied weakly, before everything went black and he lost consciousness, seeing nothing but the stars whirling round his head. He came round lying comfortably on a chaise, a cooling bandage on his forehead, some soothing ointment applied to both his eye and his lip. Watching him anxiously were the Vicar and the gypsy, a rather odd combination thought the Apothecary wryly.

'Ah, my dear Sir,' said Mr Robinson, 'you are back with us.'

Struggling, John sat up. 'Yes, I apologise. I've had rather a harsh time of it in the last few days. It all started when I fell off my horse and everything has grown progressively worse since then.'

Gypsy Orchard smiled. 'Ah, the things you men get up to. Anyway, Sir, I'll give you a little pot of my special ointment for your eye and your mouth. Apply morning and night and you'll soon be feeling better. Now I'll leave you in the capable hands of Mr Robinson. I must be on my way.'

'Where are you going?' John asked, genuinely wanting her to stay.

She shrugged. 'Wherever the fancy takes me. Goodbye,' and she turned and left the room.

John propped himself upright. 'How did I get here, Sir?'

'The gypsy rang the doorbell and told me there was a sick man in the street. I carried you in with the aid of a servant.'

'Thank you very much, Sir. Mr Robinson...' John hesitated, not quite sure whether he should tell him.

'Yes, my son?'

'Sir, I have reason to believe there is a witch's coven based in a house near Loe Pool.'

The Vicar sighed wearily. 'So I understand. The trouble is, catching them at it.'

'There,' said John, 'I might be able to help you.'

'Really? Good heavens! What do you know of them?'

The Apothecary pointed to his swollen eye and lip. 'One of their number gave me these. I attended a ceremony of theirs in the ruins of Roskilly Abbey. Only as a hidden observer,' he added hastily as he saw a look of panic rise in Mr Robinson's eye.

'Really? How did you get there?'

'It's a long story,' said John. And suddenly he felt a great deal better to be discussing the matter with a clerk in holy orders.

'First I shall get us a glass of cordial each and then you can tell me everything,' Mr Robinson answered.

He rang a bell and an ancient servant answered and took the order.

'Now,' said the Vicar, seating himself opposite John, 'tell me all you know.'

'Gladly, Sir.'

And John launched into his tale, leaving out nothing, despite the fact that Mr Robinson lost colour at some of his more lurid descriptions and once went so far as to put his hands over his ears, his expression one of total disgust.

Chapter Twenty-Five

The story was told and John, seeing the look of both horror and fear on Mr Robinson's face, regretted telling it.

'I'm sorry, Sir,' he said. 'It is rather a ghastly tale.'

The Vicar made an effort to pull himself together. 'Well, I'm glad you related it for all that. Now, I don't usually imbibe at this time of day but I feel on this occasion a small sherry might not come amiss.'

'I think that sounds like a very good idea,' said the Apothecary, reviving somewhat.

Despite Mr Robinson's words two large helpings were poured from a decanter standing on a side table. Handing John a glass, the Vicar took a seat opposite his.

'The point is, my friend, short of doing what you did in Redruth, how do I catch them at it?'

'I think you should involve the Constable, Sir. After all those who practice witchcraft are breaking the law of the land.'

'And of God.'

'Indeed,' John replied solemnly. He drank his sherry and began to feel a great deal better. 'Forgive me, but you have lived in Helstone all your life, have you not?'

'Yes indeed. As I have already told you I was curate here until the Reverend Halsall passed to his rest when I secured this place for my living.'

The Apothecary looked round him. 'You have a fine house here.'

'Yes, but it is not the vicarage house which I considered unsuitable.'

'Oh,' said John, longing to ask why but not daring.

As if in answer to his unspoken thoughts the Vicar said, 'Mrs Robinson did not care for the other place. But she liked this house very much.'

'Oh I see. How long has she been dead, Sir?'

'Twelve years at least,' the Vicar replied gloomily.

'And you have no children?'

It was a natural enough question but Mr Robinson looked slightly irritated and replied, 'No, none,' rather shortly.

John, observing him, wondered why.

'Have some more sherry,' said the Vicar, refilling the Apothecary's glass without waiting for a reply.

'Thank you, Sir. I'll have this then I really must be getting along.'

'My dear chap, do you feel up to walking back?'

'I'm sure I'll be fine. As long as I can get past the house of my assailant without being attacked.'

'You didn't tell me who it was.'

'Nicholas Kitto.'

A very odd expression came over the Vicar's face. 'That young scoundrel,' he said. 'I don't know why he behaves so badly. I truly cannot think.'

'Don't be too hard on him, Sir. I was telling him an unpleasant truth about the love of his life.'

'The woman I am to bury tomorrow?'

'The very same.'

Mr Robinson was silent for quite a while, then said, 'I knew her, you know.'

'Did you?' asked John, intensely interested.

'Yes. I found her wandering the streets of Truro and brought her back to Helstone to give her a decent Christian education. But alas she caught the eye of a certain noble gentleman, though what the arrangement between them was I was never quite certain. For Diana, set up by him no doubt, spent some of her time in London, going to theatres and so on. But she always came back here and when Nicholas was about seventeen he met her and fell in love with her.'

Even while the Vicar was saying the words they were striking the Apothecary as odd. For surely Nick had told him that his father, Lord Godolphin, had rescued Diana from Truro. So somebody wasn't telling the truth and it could not possibly be the reverend gentleman. Or could it? John listened avidly.

'What did the noble gentleman do in that situation?' he asked.

Mr Robinson shrugged, quite elegantly for a man of the cloth. 'I have no idea. Perhaps she saw them both, perhaps she dropped the older man for the younger. Who knows?'

And John, his head in a whirl, thoroughly agreed with the last statement. For why should Nick tell him a tissue of lies unless it was to protect someone. But it was no use bombarding the Vicar with questions. The Apothecary decided to change the subject.

'Are you expecting a large number at the funeral, Sir?' he asked.

'A mere handful if we're lucky,' came the rather sad reply.

'Well I shall be there,' said John, rising somewhat shakily to his feet.

'My dear boy, allow me to walk with you.' And Mr Robinson stood up too.

True to his word the Vicar escorted John up the street, then on to The Angel. There was no sign of Nick Kitto anywhere and the Apothecary rather imagined that his mother must be holding him under lock and key. If it hadn't been for the aching in his head he almost could feel sorry for the wretched young man.

'Well, good afternoon, my friend. I shall see you tomorrow.'

'You will indeed,' answered the Apothecary, as he and Mr Robinson bowed to each other and parted company.

A far bigger crowd turned up than John or the Vicar had anticipated. Mrs Pill, accompanied by her brother and the entire retinue of servants, came. There was Lord Godolphin and Nicholas Kitto, of course. Tim Painter arrived, a few minutes after Kathryn, sitting in a different pew and smiling amiably at the world. These people together with the landlord of The Angel and several of the regulars made quite a goodly collection, John thought, as he made his way to his customary place at the back of the church, where he could observe everyone but not be seen himself.

Mr Robinson, rather pale, his blue eyes like glinting sapphires in his face, began the customary funeral oration. Today his voice seemed weak and he cleared his throat several times until he finally got a grip on himself and began to speak in normal tones. John thought over the story he had heard of the Vicar saving Diana from begging on the streets of Truro. Then the other tale of Nicholas Kitto's father doing exactly the selfsame thing.

Lord Godolphin was sitting almost directly in front of him, dressed to the inch, his face emotionless. In fact it looked almost deliberately blank, as if the man were trying to disguise what he was feeling. Across the way from him was Tim Painter, no longer grinning but managing for once to appear quite serious. John stole a look at Mrs Pill who seemed bowed with grief, her head in her hands as people rose to sing a hymn. All in all the Apothecary supposed they were pretty typical of a bunch of people attending a funeral. And yet there was something wrong, as if everyone were playing a part, trying to appear something that they were not.

The service came to an end and it was time for the committal to earth. Six burly village lads carried the coffin in the absence of male relatives while the Vicar led the way to the graveside, walking slowly and sorrowfully. John followed the rest of the doleful procession trailing along behind. Mrs Pill was leaning heavily on Jasper's arm, weeping copiously and staggering slightly as she threw in the obligatory handful of earth. Lord Godolphin cast a large portion but Nick Kitto, by now in floods of tears, threw in a red rose and glared defiantly out of moist eyes at the rest of the company. Tim Painter, looking quite shaken, emptied some earth from stiff fingers, while John Rawlings passed by, never sympathising with the ceremony and not feeling moved to do so on this occasion.

The dismal walk from the graveyard to the church began. The Apothecary, proceeding alone, felt a tug at his elbow and saw that a shame-faced Nick Kitto had joined him.

'I'm sorry I attacked you, Sir, and I hope I did no damage.'

The Apothecary smiled as best his damaged lip allowed. 'Other than for giving me a thundering headache, no harm done.'

'I wanted to ask you...' Nick started, but there his voice was drowned by a much louder sound. From beyond the church came the noise of a band playing a funeral march at full volume, above the rest of the cacophony rising the sweet, sad voice of a violin. He knew even without seeing who had gathered there, that the blind fiddler had heard of Diana's funeral and had come to pay his respects.

He turned to Nicholas. 'The Gaffer is here with his band. Now I beg you to restrain yourself. Ask him questions by all means but pray do so in a civilised manner.'

But young Kitto had already broken into a run and was heading along the path that went round to the front of the church. John, following at a slightly more leisurely pace, concluded that the young man had quite literally gone mad with love. But when he got round the corner he saw that even wild Nick had been halted by the sheer sobbing beauty of the fiddler's music. The rest of the band were playing softly beneath the soaring notes of the violin, which seemed to be offering a prayer direct to God, far more effectively than those just said in the church, the Apothecary thought. The rest of the funeral party, coming up from the graveside, were also stopped by the sight of the blind fiddler, in fact everyone stood in silence until the air was concluded, when one or two people burst into spontaneous applause.

The Gaffer lowered his bow and turned his head. 'I hear we have company lads.'

'Yes, Sir,' said Gideon. 'It's the funeral party.'

The blind man took a step towards them. 'How de doo, ladies and gentlemen. I've come to pay my respects to Diana Warwick.'

At that Nicholas broke ranks. 'What did you mean by going into her bedroom in the small hours? It was me who found her dead, not you.'

There was a stunned silence, broken by the fiddler saying, 'I knew Miss Warwick when you were still a twinkle in your father's eye, young man. And I felt free enough with her to visit her in her room at any time I pleased.'

Nicholas literally ran towards him, fists raised. 'I'll have you for that.'

'No you won't,' the Gaffer responded and sidestepped so adroitly that Nick fell flat on his face in the churchyard.

The Apothecary could not resist it. He chuckled under his breath. The fiddler looked over in the direction of the sound. 'Mr Rawlings, is it?'

John stepped up to him. 'Yes, it's me.'

'I thought I recognised that laugh.'

'So you've concluded your business in Redruth?'

'Aye, 'tis all done. Is yours?'

'Yes,' John answered briefly, his attention drawn by the fact that Lord Godolphin had gone to assist Nicholas Kitto and was helping him to stand upright.

The Gaffer put a hand on John's arm. 'There's dark doings there, my friend.'

John could only whisper, 'I know,' before the figure of Nick charged up once more.

'You dirty blackguard,' he said.

The blind fiddler turned on him. 'No, Sir, that I am not. In fact I've probably done more honourable things in my life than you can conceive of. Now you listen to me, young sir. The woman whom you have just seen buried was a great friend of mine. She was also a whore. If you can't accept that, if you want to put her on a pedestal, then that is entirely your choice. But one day reality will creep in and you must accept her for what she was. Until that happens, I bid you good afternoon and I take my leave of you. Goodbye, Mr Kitto.'

The unexpected happened then. Nick collapsed into a sobbing heap on the breast of the blind fiddler who held him as tenderly and tightly as if he had been a wayward son coming home to learn a lesson at the hands of his father. John stared amazed.

'You're very patient,' he said, somewhat daunted, to the Gaffer.

'Aye, Sir. I've learnt how to be.'

And with that the fiddler passed the boy gently to the Vicar, who had approached meanwhile, and putting his bow to the strings started to play a wonderful and soul-stirring lament.

There was no wake, as such, though several of them – including the Gaffer and his band – got together in the parlour of The Angel. The Vicar, who had joined them, particularly, or so it seemed, to keep an eye on Nick, took a little sherry. But the fiddler's men drank ale by the pint, then burst into spontaneous playing, so much so that other people wandered in to listen. Lord Godolphin, who surprisingly had graciously attended for a half hour, took his leave at that point, bidding his fellow mourners farewell.

John, observing him closely, found himself puzzling more and more as to whether he was the natural father of Nicholas or not. Because, ever since that extraordinary embrace in the churchyard, he was wondering if the blind fiddler could possibly be the man. Yet a conversation with his lordship regarding Mrs Warwick was essential. As Lord Godolphin left the room, John slipped out also.

He caught up with him in the street, waiting for his carriage to come round.

'Excuse me, my Lord,' he said politely, 'would it be possible to have a word with you?'

'By all means. When did you have in mind?'

'Now, if that would be convenient.'

'My carriage is about to take me home.'

'May I ride with you? I can find my own way back.'

'Yes. It will help pass the journey if nothing else.'

Wondering exactly how he was going to handle this somewhat supercilious being, John clambered aboard, taking a seat opposite that of his lordship.

He decided to pander to the man's vanity. 'It was very kind of you to see me at such short notice, my Lord.'

Lord Godolphin waved a deprecating hand. 'Think nothing of it. Now, what was it you wanted to talk to me about?'

'The woman whose funeral we have just attended.'

'Miss Warwick? What about her?'

'How well did you know her, Sir?'

Milord's face became a study in careless insouciance. 'I remember now that I knew her, something I did not recall when last we spoke of her. She came here when she was a young girl. I believe she was rescued by the present Vicar before he was promoted to the post.'

'Rescued from what?' John asked innocently.

'Oh God knows. One of those things that men of the church are concerned about. She lived in Helstone for a while.' Lord Godolphin's voice became suddenly warm. 'She was such a beautiful creature, you know.'

'I suppose a great many people were in love with her,' John said quietly.

'The future Vicar, certainly. And one or two others beside.'

'The Vicar!' the Apothecary repeated in astonishment.

'Oh yes, it was perfectly obvious. His wife was alive then; a sickly creature. Robinson worshipped the ground the girl walked on.'

'And you?' The words were out before John Rawlings had time to control them, and he instantly regretted what he had just said.

Lord Godolphin gave him a steely glance and looked out of the window. When he turned back John saw that he was smiling.

'I was young and foolish and I adored beautiful things. Yes, I admit it. I fell in love with her as well.'

The Apothecary knew the rest of the story and felt no need to pursue the matter. But there was one thing he desperately needed to find out. He leant forward, his expression earnest.

'Sir, you can throw me out of the coach on the instant but there is one further question I have to ask.'

'Yes?'

'Did you visit Miss Warwick on the night she was murdered and was she alive when you did so?'

His lordship looked down the length of his aristocratic nose. 'What right have you to ask those questions of me?'

'None at all, Sir.'

'You're an impudent rogue, Sir.'

'Indeed I am, my Lord. But the question is burning at my soul.'

'I suppose you have a witness who saw me.' John nodded mutely. 'Well the answer, my friend, is yes to both. Diana was alive when I went to see her. Are you satisfied?'

John nodded. 'I certainly am. Thank you, my Lord.'

'And now you can get out of the coach. The walk back should put some colour in your cheeks. You're looking terrible by the way. Have you been in some sort of accident?'

The Apothecary grinned painfully as Lord Godolphin banged on the ceiling with his stick and shouted instructions to the coachman.

'It would be fair to say that I have, Sir. Good day to you.'

When John returned to Helstone after walking briskly for an hour he found that at last the post boy had delivered the long awaited letter from Sir John Fielding. It read as follows:

> *My dear friend Mr Rawlings,*
> *What you say to me gives me Cause for Concern. I had Imagined you taking your Ease in Devon but I read that Instead you are Involved in a Series of Strange Events. Take my Advice and Do Not Confuse one with the Other. For it seems to Me that two Separate Hands are at Work. I Would send You the assistance of two Brave Fellows but Alas all are Out About their Business. I Fear for the Child but Fear More the Murderer of the Woman. At this Distance I can offer no Further Advice but I do Caution You to be careful.*
> > *Your very respectful Servant,*
> > *J Fielding.*

It was rather disappointing, John thought, giving no real advice but offering instead a warning. He had rather hoped that in consulting Sir John he might be given some assistance but even this was to be denied him. He must hunt for the murderer of Diana alone. And then, as he sat deep in thought, an idea occurred to him that began to take root in his mind and refused to go away. So he missed the hour to dine and continued to brood over his latest notion until the shadows began to lengthen.

He awoke next morning feeling refreshed and went down to breakfast ravenously hungry. There was no one about and John was able to catch up with a local newspaper. Having read it through, however, he put it down and gazed into space, deciding on his plan of action.

If the idea which had seized him so strongly on the previous evening was correct he needed to act fairly swiftly. The question was how exactly? In order to clear his mind the

Apothecary decided to go for a ride. Walking round to the livery stable he hired the most docile creature they had available – a patient-looking roan that plodded towards him when fetched from its loose box – and proceeded out of Helstone, away from the sea and up the hill.

Panting and gasping, his horse, which had the whimsical name of Rajah, gained the top and refused to move another step. Feeling sorry for it, John dismounted and led it into the shade where it started to chew grass in a ruminative fashion. Sitting on a fallen tree trunk, John stared about him at the rolling and challenging landscape. He could see for miles, having a bird's-eye view. From this point the town of Helstone looked small and unimportant. Yet contained within its heart was at least one murderer, and probably more if his theories about Isobel were correct.

The Apothecary's attention was suddenly drawn to a small coach coming in on the road from Redruth. He stared at it fixedly, wishing he had brought his telescope. Sure that he recognised it he remounted the now refreshed Rajah and proceeded downhill in the general direction of the road. As he drew nearer he was convinced he was right and called out, 'Jed. Stop. It's me. John Rawlings.'

He saw the coachman look round and then pull the horses to a halt. Rather as he thought would happen, Elizabeth's head, gorgeously hatted, was thrust out of the window. She was just about to ask what was happening when she saw him.

'John!'

He swept the covering from his head and bowed from the saddle. 'Madam Marchesa.'

'I didn't expect to see you. Not yet, at least.'

'Nor I you, Madam. What brings about your early return?'

In her usual frank manner she answered, 'Your child is not happy without you, it seems. She is a dear soul but she craves your company.'

He was half pleased and half saddened. He longed for Rose to be independent but on the other hand fully appreciated the fact that the poor child had been left motherless and probably clung to him more than was customary. At that moment the little imp, grinning and hatless, thrust her head out above Elizabeth's.

'I'm sorry, Papa.'

'Don't be. I'm delighted to see you.'

'And I you, Sir,' she responded bravely, and his heart went out to her.

He rode behind the coach which rattled over the cobbled streets of Helstone till they came to the main thoroughfare and finally pulled to a stop in front of The Angel. Elizabeth dismounted, leaving the child to the mercies of Rufus, riding shotgun once more. She turned to the Apothecary with a smile.

'My dear, I am going to disappoint you. I am leaving you as soon as I have refreshed myself.'

He could only stare, certain that she, too, had been coming back to join him.

'I have much to do at home,' Elizabeth continued, smiling even more delightfully. 'And I really need time to concentrate on it on my own.'

John immediately felt guilty. 'Rose? Was she too much for you?'

'Not at all. She is a joy to have around the place and is most popular with the staff I can assure you. But it is just that I need time to myself. Do you understand?'

'Of course,' he answered. But inside he felt disappointed; disappointed that the Marchesa was returning his daughter to him and had found it impossible to be a mother to her. Disappointed, too, that his love for her was, now, clearly doomed to fade away. However, he hoped that he was showing none of this, continuing to smile as she went on speaking.

'I knew you would. So, my dear, let us have some coffee together before I depart.'

'Of course. I'll order some immediately.'

He took Rose's hand, looking down at her with much

affection. 'So you missed me, did you?'

She stared back up at him and for a minute, despite her red colouring and general aspect, Emilia peeped out. Seeing that, John felt suddenly totally depressed with everything but particularly with the development of this enquiry. He was swimming through molasses and every stroke he took was making things worse. He made an instant decision to reveal none of this to Elizabeth however hard she pressed him.

No sooner were they seated at a table, Rose happily sitting beside her father, than the Marchesa turned to him.

'Tell me, my dear. How is everything going?'

'Extremely well,' John answered over-confidentially.

'Have Mrs Pill's party found Isobel?'

'No, and I don't think they ever will. I reckon she is a victim of Loe Pool.'

'And what about the murderer of Diana Warwick? Are you any further forward?'

'As a matter of fact I am,' said John, and meant it.

'I see. What do you intend to do about it?'

'I shall go to the Constable, of course.'

Elizabeth shot him a look full of unexpressed thoughts. 'You enjoy all this,' she said eventually.

'You know I do,' he answered shortly, then deliberately changed the subject. 'May I call on you before I return to London?'

'But of course, I would be deeply wounded if you did not do so.'

But I am the one who is wounded, he thought. Your whole attitude to me and my daughter has hurt me immeasurably. Yet deep down he knew that it was his pride that was damaged rather than anything else.

'Then I shall,' he said, and stood up. 'If you will forgive me, Madam. Rose and I must visit the Constable and make a report.'

She looked frankly surprised, much to John's delight. 'Well, I suppose this is goodbye.'

'For the present,' he replied stiffly, and kissed her hand.

Rose rather spoiled things by flinging her arms round the Marchesa's neck and embracing her warmly on the cheek.

'Thank you for looking after me, Mrs Elizabeth.'

'It's been a pleasure, sweetheart. Come and see me soon.'

'I shall come with Papa,' the child answered, and put her hand into John's.

It hadn't been a very dignified exit, John thought, as he walked to William Trethowan's place of employment. He had left the Marchesa sitting alone, staring at him with a somewhat bemused expression on her face, as he and his daughter had set off purposefully.

'And that's the way I'll treat her in future,' John muttered angrily.

'What did you say, Father?' Rose piped up.

'Nothing, sweetheart. Tell me, was Mrs Elizabeth kind to you when you stayed with her?'

'Very. She is really nice. Are you going to marry her?'

'Most certainly not,' he replied forcefully, and strode forward.

He discovered the Constable at work and found himself considering that there must be little crime in Helstone, otherwise the man would be far busier about his duties. Trethowan put down his hammer and wiped his brow.

'Good afternoon, Mr Rawlings. What can I do for 'ee?'

'Quite a good deal.' John turned to Rose. 'Look, darling, at the old cat over there. She's had a litter of kittens. Go and have a closer inspection.'

With his daughter out of earshot, the Apothecary rapidly described all that had taken place in Redruth, watching the Constable's face as he did so. The man's expression became more and more horror-struck as he listened. Eventually he spoke.

'I know Lord Lyle's place up by Loe Pool. I shall make it my business to call there.'

'Don't go alone, I warn you.'

'I wondered if you might come with me, Sir.'

'Provided we take some more men, the answer is yes. But I've got something else to tell you about the death of Miss Warwick.'

And John put forward the theory he had been considering the night before. William's face fell as he listened.

'It's a good conjecture all right. But how to prove it, that's the question. I can't very well go and accuse the person concerned.'

'But there are ways of eliciting the information.'

'You would be better at those than I would, Sir.'

John gave a resigned sigh. 'You want me to find out for you?'

'If you would, Mr Rawlings I would deem it a personal favour.'

Rose was heading towards them holding a kitten. Once again John was vividly reminded of Emilia who had had a weakness for all animals.

'Oh, Papa, isn't it sweet.'

'It would not be possible for us to adopt it, Rose,' John said firmly, cutting to the heart of the matter.

She pulled an adorable face, quite deliberately. 'But…'

'No buts. The answer is no.'

'Oh, Papa.'

William Trethowan bent down. 'Don't worry, little maid. The mother cat lives in the yard. The little 'uns can stay with her till they'um be bigger.'

'Can I come and visit every day?'

'That depends on your Papa.'

John gave a crooked grin. 'We'll come as often as we can, Rose. Will that do?'

'Oh, very well,' she answered, and kicked a stone, though only slightly.

Somewhat amused by this tiny show of temperament, the Apothecary took his daughter firmly by the hand and led her away.

Having called at The Angel to check that Elizabeth had

departed – which he was somewhat glad to see she had – John returned to the livery stables and rehired the aged horse, together with a small, resolute pony for Rose. Then he rode with her at a circumspect pace, heading down Coinage Hall Street to the open countryside surrounding Loe Pool. There, saying nothing to his daughter, he ambled round the waterway's circumference looking at the various dwellings built overlooking it. He spotted Lord Lyle's house almost straight away. Set up high and surrounded by trees, it looked a grand residence even in the distance.

'Why are you looking at that house?' Rose asked.

'I know the man who owns it.'

'Is he nice?'

'No, not at all,' John answered, remembering their last meeting and how he had finally managed to bluff his way out.

'Oh dear,' she said, but got no further, for from behind them John could hear the pounding of hooves. Instinctively, he put out his hand and took the pony's rein and led Rose into the shelter of the trees. Peering through the leaves, he sat silently, motioning his daughter to do likewise.

A man was coming hell for leather along the track, clearly an excellent rider. John had a moment of envy before he recognised the fellow as Lord Lyle. It was surprising to see him alone but his destination was obvious. Where the lane divided he took the left hand fork uphill and started the climb to the house that John had been watching. So his lordship had returned to his home in Helstone.

The Apothecary thought rapidly. He had managed to talk his way out of trouble when he had last seen the man. But what of the seven – the three women and four men involved in witchcraft. He had played cards with the satanic ladies and they had known perfectly well that he was in Redruth. But none of them had seen him at the ruined abbey. Could he continue the pretence of merely being an innocent visitor? It was worth trying, he decided.

'Was that the wicked man?' asked Rose.

'Yes, sweetheart. That was him.'

'Can we come out of hiding now?'

'He's gone, so yes we can.'

As they trotted into the late May sunshine, John's daughter said, 'I enjoyed that.'

'What?'

'Hiding. It was exciting.'

The Apothecary looked at her in amazement. Most children would have been afraid of suddenly being told to take cover in the trees, might even have burst into tears. But not Rose. She was truly his daughter, a daughter to be proud of. With the thought of having many years to watch her grow and develop, John Rawlings burst into song as he continued his ride round Loe Pool.

With Elizabeth gone he was naturally going to find the evenings more difficult to organise. Having given the thumb-sucking little maid a handsome tip to check on Rose every half-hour once the child had retired for the night, John made his way to the taproom. There, sitting looking somewhat doleful, was his erstwhile travelling companion, Tim Painter.

'Ah, my dear friend, how goes it?' the Apothecary enquired cheerfully.

'We're leaving tomorrow,' Tim responded gloomily.

'Are you now,' John answered. He had been half-expecting the reply yet still it came as something of a shock. 'How have you persuaded Mrs Pill to go?' he added.

'She has finally given up hope.'

'She has accepted the fact that Isobel is dead?'

Tim nodded silently.

'I'd like to see her before she leaves,' John said.

'She's dining late with her beastly brother.'

'How are you going to live like that in future? The man clearly detests you.'

Tim turned his handsome eyes in the Apothecary's

direction. 'Not as much as I detest him. But to answer your question, who knows what lies ahead?'

John looked at him with shrewd amusement. 'What are you saying to me?'

'Just that. Kathryn and I are together for the moment.'

John could not help but laugh. 'Are you saying that if something better were to present itself then you would be off? Have you no shame, Sir?'

'None at all, I'm delighted to say.'

'But surely the poor woman has done a great deal for you.'

'And so have I for her,' Tim protested. 'After all she was pretty short of suitors after the death of old man Pill. Then I came along.'

'Oh happy chance,' said the Apothecary, and raised a dark eyebrow.

Still the thought of their imminent departure left him with a great deal to do. Plunging his face into his wine glass, John thought rapidly.

The blind fiddler was still in town, as was Lord Godolphin. Nick Kitto was sulking miserably in his home but was easily reachable. Tim Painter was currently sitting beside him. John thought frantically of some excuse to get them all together but came up with nothing. Then Tim said nonchalantly, 'Fancy a game of cards?'

'Why not?' John answered, then he said, 'Shall I go and find some more who'd like to play?'

Tim looked surprised. 'Yes, if you can raise anyone. It would be amusing to gamble the night away.'

'I'll see who I can discover. Listen, I shall have to leave for a short while. Can you listen out for my daughter? She's fast asleep but it is possible she could wake up.'

A foxy grin crossed Tim's face. 'Not so easy without your light-o-love, is it?'

'No,' John answered with feeling. 'It's not so easy.'

Chapter Twenty-Seven

Walking purposefully, the Apothecary went up the road then down Church Street, all the time turning over in his mind the names of the men who had visited Diana Warwick on the night she had been killed. Indeed he was just conjecturing what excuse he could possibly use to lure Lord Godolphin to play cards with a handful of ordinary citizens when, as good fortune would have it, he saw the man leaving the doctor's house. Sprinting to catch up before his lordship got into his coach, John arrived panting and gasping just as Lord Godolphin put his foot on the step. Turning, he saw the Apothecary.

'Oh, it's you,' he said.

'Yes, Sir. How are you?' John answered, not being able to think of anything else to say.

'My damnable gout is playing up again. Not that it's any business of yours, mark you.'

Putting on his honest citizen face, the Apothecary gave him a sincere look. 'Oh but it is my business, Sir. I prescribed a remedy for you. I hope it worked.'

'It worked well enough, thank you. But as you will be leaving us soon I have returned to my doctor.'

'I have enjoyed meeting you, Sir. In fact it has been one of the highlights of my trip.' John was getting desperate and thought that the only thing he could do was to act like a sycophant, much as it went against the grain.

'I'm delighted to hear it. Now if you'll excuse me.'

'I will excuse you, Sir. But first I must ask you a favour…an enormous favour. Would you allow me to buy you a drink in The Angel?'

His lordship heaved himself up into his coach, leaving John in the undignified position of leaning in through the conveyance's door.

'Just a little drink,' continued the Apothecary sweetly, thinking he was about to be sick, the words were sticking in his mouth so badly.

'Oh very well. I shall see you there in a quarter of an hour. I have another call to make first.'

'I am your servant, My Lord.' And John bowed low. The minute the coach had drawn away however, he straightened up and removed the sickly grin from his face. Adopting a much more determined expression, he headed straight for the home of Nicholas Kitto. An ancient retainer answered the door this time and was still asking John who he wanted to see when Nick himself came into the hall.

'Oh it's you,' he said, using identical words to Lord Godolphin.

'Yes, as you see,' John answered. He held out his hand. 'Nicholas, let our quarrel be at an end for pity's sake – and for mine. I've come to invite you to have a drink with me and maybe play cards. It will do you good to get out.'

Nick turned a morose face in his direction. 'I feel at the moment that I wouldn't care if I never ventured forth again.'

'Well I'd be obliged if you could make an effort tonight. I shall be off in the next few days and would like to think that we parted on good terms.'

Nick shuffled from foot to foot, then looked up. John knew at once that the fellow was desperate to leave the house and was longing for an excuse.

'I'll have to think about it,' he said slowly.

The Apothecary put on his no-nonsense face. 'I'm afraid that won't do, my friend. You'll oblige me and say yes immediately. I'm determined to have a little gathering before my departure. Lord Godolphin will be there,' he added.

'Oh very well then,' said Nicholas, quite promptly.

'Good. Then I'll meet you at The Angel in quarter of an hour. There's just one other person I want to invite to my party. I'll bid you farewell.'

And with that he had turned on his heel and hurried back up the street before Nick could change his mind.

He found the band in The Blue Anchor, playing, as was their wont, to please the other customers and at the same time make a few pennies to pay for drinks. The sound was a great deal noisier and more cheerful than the one they had made at the funeral. Without hesitation John went straight up to the Gaffer as soon as they had finished the rendition of their jolly air.

'My dear Sir,' he said, 'we meet again.'

'Mr Rawlings, isn't it?' asked the Cornish fiddler with that strange perception that blind people seem to have.

'The very same.'

John bowed and the Gaffer did likewise. 'What can I do for 'ee, Sir?'

'You can come and play at a little gathering I am organising at The Angel.'

'When, Sir.'

'In ten minutes or so.'

'That's very short notice, Sir. Now, will you be wanting all of us or is it just me?'

'I thought just you.' John leant closer and whispered in his ear, surrounded as it was by black locks and swarthy beard.

'Oh I see,' said the Gaffer, when the Apothecary was done. 'It's a sprat to catch a mackerel, is it?'

'I hope so. But then, who can tell? Nothing may come out at all.'

The blind fiddler turned towards John just as if he could see. 'You're a wise young man, Mr Rawlings. Has anyone ever told you that?'

'There have been one or two in the past, yes.'

'So there should have been.' The Gaffer turned to his band. 'Listen lads, I'll be leaving you for a while. I'm going to play at a little gathering of gentlemen up at The Angel. You stay here and entertain the folk. Right?'

'Are you getting paid, Gaffer?'

'I am getting well rewarded, never fear.'

And the Cornish fiddler winked an unseen eye at the Apothecary.

Lord Godolphin was alighting from his coach as John and the Gaffer made their way, arm in arm, up to the hostelry door. His lordship raised his quizzing glass.

'Oh it's you, my good man. I wondered who could be perambulating up the street in that odd manner.'

'Yes it's me, Sir,' John answered. 'The fiddler is coming to play for us while we drink and play cards.'

'Cards, is it? You didn't tell me that.'

'Would you be so kind as to make up the fourth, my Lord?'

'I don't see why not,' Lord Godolphin answered jovially, and John suspected that the man might have a weakness for gambling.

Hurrying into the taproom where Nick had now joined Tim Painter, John ushered the men into one of the snugs and took over the one and only table. Seeing a card party setting up, the other occupants left the room, thus giving them the privacy they needed. Standing a little apart the blind fiddler started to play very softly.

John handed the cards to Lord Godolphin and asked him to deal.

'Shall we play whist, gentlemen?'

'Certainly,' replied Nick, and there were noises of assent from the others.

Wondering how he was going to broach the subject of Diana Warwick and the night on which she died, John – a bad card player at the best of times – could scarcely concentrate on his hand. It was clear from the outset that Tim and his lordship were both exceptionally good players, however, and soon the Apothecary and young Kitto found themselves hopelessly outclassed. Tim executed a Bath coup which Lord Godolphin countered, thus winning the rubber. There was a general exclamation and they paused to recharge their glasses.

'Gentlemen,' John began, 'I had a motive in inviting you all here tonight. It was…'

But he got no further. There was the sound of pounding feet coming along the corridor, then the door burst open. Framed in the entrance was the figure of William Trethowan, the constable.

'Mr Rawlings,' he panted, out of breath. 'Can you come at once. There's a ritual going on close by Loe Pool.'

John leapt to his feet while the others turned startled faces in the direction of the speaker.

'It's a witches coven,' the Apothecary said by way of explanation. 'I came across them in Redruth and now they have obviously made their way here.'

'I'll come to Loe Pool with you,' Tim stated without hesitation.

'Me too,' said Nick Kitto, rising.

'I may as well join you all,' Lord Godolphin remarked majestically.

'There's no time to waste.' This from Trethowan. 'We must catch them in the act and then I can charge and arrest them.'

'I'll call for my coach,' said his lordship.

But the others had already left, running behind the Constable down Coinage Hall Street to the countryside beyond.

'I'm glad there's a few of you, Sir,' William remarked, as he sped down the road beside the Apothecary.

'Are there a lot of them then?'

'About twenty I think. I didn't have time to count exactly.'

'You're going to need all the help you can get in that case.'

'I've a few men hidden up there but not nearly enough.'

They had left the little town behind them and were making their way through the open land towards the Pool, following the course of the River Cober. Faintly, borne on the breeze, could be detected the sound of chanting.

Beside him John felt Nick stiffen. 'Can you hear that?'

'It's them all right,' Tim answered him meaningfully.

Avoiding the marshland and bearing to the left they could see the glint of water through the trees. And there, up on the hill, shaded from Penrose House by parkland but standing almost immediately opposite it, was the dwelling belonging to Lord Lyle.

'The ritual is taking place in the woods,' whispered the Constable, pointing.

'Did you see it?' asked John.

'I climbed up a little way. There're some old ruins in the grounds. It's being held inside them.'

'Like Redruth,' the Apothecary answered grimly.

They had reached the fork in the road and began the ascent to the house. Wondering where Lord Godolphin had got to, John climbed upward. The sound of the chanting was growing louder, blotting out the distant voice of the sea, and he was filled with a sense of unreasonable terror. Glad to have stout companions, he continued the march uphill. And then panic broke out. There was a scream from one of the Constable's assistants who began to run downwards as fast as the others were coming up.

Breaking through their ranks, he bellowed, 'He's after me. Oh God help me. He's after me.'

Chaos broke out. The four men ascending, namely the Constable, John, Tim Painter and Nick, stood their ground but the other fellows, ordinary men of Helstone who had been dragooned into helping Trethowan, broke ranks and started to scurry downwards.

'Stop!' bellowed the Constable, but to no avail. The volunteers, thoroughly frightened, were heading off as fast as they could go in the direction of town.

John turned to Trethowan. 'What shall we do?'

'There are just the four of us, Sir. We won't have a hope against that lot.'

'You're right,' said Tim Painter promptly. 'Let's return and have some claret.'

'And make a plan,' said Nick.

'Yes,' answered John, relieved in a way. 'I think it would be best if we got out of here.'

It appeared that Lord Godolphin had started off in pursuit of his card-playing friends and had then lost a coach wheel at the bottom of Coinage Hall Street. Indeed it was being repaired as the quartet made their way back to The Angel. It was clear that his lordship had given up the chase early in the day and had made his way back to the snug where he had sunk a bottle of wine without any difficulty whatsoever. He looked up as the others came in.

'Tally ho, gentlemen. Did you track down the wrongdoers?'

'No, Sir,' answered Trethowan, suddenly very formal. 'There was a commotion at the other end and my assistants ran away. We had no option but to follow.'

'A commotion, eh? What was all that about?'

'I questioned one of them on the way back and he said he saw the ghost of Parson Jago mounted on horseback.'

'Parson Jago?' interrupted John, for the clerk of Bow Street court was also called Jago, an old friend of the Apothecary's.

'We've had several parsons of that name hereabouts. And there's a legend that one of them could exorcise ghosts and to this day can still be seen mounted on his mare,' answered his lordship.

'What a strange coincidence.' And John related the story of his acquaintanceship with the clerk.

'Jago is a Cornish name,' said Nick Kitto. 'It means James.'

'Well, well. I never knew that.'

'You must ask him whether he comes from these parts.'

'I will indeed.'

'I thought we were going to make a plan, gentlemen,' said the Constable plaintively.

'I'll give you a plan,' said Lord Godolphin, thumping the table with his fist. 'I'll call on Lyle tomorrow and ask what the devil he's playing at.'

'Forgive me, Sir, but I think that would be dangerous,' said Trethowan seriously.

'Damn foolhardy,' put in Tim, who had taken a seat and been pouring himself glasses of claret with great enthusiasm.

'Then what shall we do?'

'I think we should raid the house in force and look for evidence.'

'You won't find any,' John replied. 'They're too clever for that.'

'Then, Sir, what do you suggest?'

'We've got to catch them at it. In fact we missed a great opportunity tonight. I wonder what it was your man saw, by the way.'

'Perhaps he truly saw Parson Jago. Perhaps the ritual conjured him up.'

'You can't believe such superstitious nonsense.'

Lord Godolphin spoke. 'Cornwall is alive with legends and ghost stories. They are as old as time. You would do well to mark them, Rawlings.'

The laugh that John had been about to give froze on his lips when he saw the serious expressions of both his lordship and William Trethowan, and he thought again of Gypsy Orchard.

'I'll try my hardest, Sir,' he answered contritely.

'Well, I'd best be getting back. I'll consult with you in the morning, gentlemen.'

'Excellent plan,' said Tim, pouring himself another glass. 'If I say I am on special duties I might be able to delay my departure.'

'I leave that to you, Sir. Good night.'

And Trethowan made to go out but was interrupted by the thumb-sucking maid. 'Oh, Sir,' she said to John, 'your little girl is awake – and she's frightened.'

The Apothecary cursed himself. In the excitement of the dash to the Loe he had forgotten entirely that Rose had returned and was lying asleep upstairs. Before anyone could question him he had left the room and gone up the flight two at a time. He could hear her crying quietly before he even opened the door.

'Oh Papa,' she said as soon as she saw him, and she jumped out of bed and hurled herself into his arms.

'There, there, sweetheart. There's no need to be afraid. I'm here.'

'But it was so horrid, Father.'

'What was, darling?'

'My door opened and a woman stood there. And... Oh, Papa.' Rose wept again.

'What, dearest? What did she do?'

'She beckoned for me to go with her but I was too afraid and I told her to go away.'

'What happened then?'

'She just laughed and said that she would be back. And…'

'Yes?'

'That she would take me to join Isobel.'

Chapter Twenty-Eight

That night the Apothecary slept badly, dreaming vivid dreams of Emilia in which she begged him to take care of her child. Waking up in a sweat, seeing from his travelling carriage clock that it was two in the morning, he gazed to where Rose slept peacefully. He had moved himself into her room after she had told him the story of the old woman who had beckoned her, certain – though he had said nothing to the child herself – that the female had been a member of that ghastly coven of witches. Then, during the night, a terrible thought had occurred to him. If one supposed that they were into human sacrifice, could that have been the fate of Isobel Pill? Had she, after all, met her end on some unconsecrated altar and her defenceless body been disposed of afterwards? It was a hideous idea and yet the more John considered it the more sense it made.

He sat bolt upright in his makeshift bed, perspiration starting out all over his body, his hand reaching for a glass of water. A shaft of moonlight was shining in through the curtains, which had not been properly drawn, and getting out of bed the Apothecary silently crossed to the window and looked out. Helstone slept, apparently at rest, yet John was more than aware that beneath its blameless facade there currently dwelt a band of people with evil in their hearts. Looking back over his shoulder he saw that his child still slumbered, and at that moment determined that he would never leave her alone again until he had departed from that Cornish town for ever.

Which shouldn't be long, he thought to himself. In fact he had only one task remaining before he and Rose could return to Devon. And this idea set him thinking about Elizabeth and the hopelessness of his situation with her. What had started out as a powerful attraction was clearly doomed to end in disaster. In fact at that moment of bleakness the Apothecary could imagine no future with her at all. He sighed quietly and turned to go back to bed. But just as he did so something moved in the street below and, turning back to the window, he gave it his full attention.

It was a strange figure dressed in a long concealing garment which hid the fact whether it be male or female. Yet, despite this, John had the distinct impression that he was regarding a woman. She stood motionless, gazing at The Angel, not moving at all as she stared. Seized with the idea that it was she who had earlier beckoned to Rose, the Apothecary threw a cloak over his nightshirt and sped downstairs. Grappling with the heavy bolts on the front door took him some time but eventually he got it open and gazed out on Coinage Hall Street. She or he had gone, and though he stepped outside and looked round the place there was no sign of the stranger. Shivering, despite the warmth of the night, John Rawlings returned to bed.

True to his word he stayed by Rose's side next day except when she went to the water closet. But even then he remained outside the door until he heard the crank of the plunger, when he pushed the partition open and his child was restored to him. Privately he thought it quite marvellous that a remote inn like The Angel should have had such a thing installed, it not being his experience in other places in which he had stayed.

Having finished an early breakfast John decided to take his daughter for a walk before the one item of business left to him. In the street, she turned to look at him as they left The Angel and headed up the town.

'Papa, have you much left to do here?'

'Only one thing,' he answered, taking her hand and holding it fast.

'Will it take long?'

'No, I shall do it this morning and then we will leave tomorrow.'

'Shall we catch the stagecoach?'

'Yes, my darling. We will cram in with the rest of the passengers.'

'I look forward to that.'

'We can catch it to Truro and from there make our way to Devon.'

'We are going to say goodbye to Mrs Elizabeth, aren't we?'

'Of course we are, sweetheart. But after that we must return to London and resume our old life.'

'I want to see Grandpapa again.'

'Do you love him?'

'Very much indeed,' and Rose tightened her grip on the Apothecary's hand and gave him a look of such sincerity that he felt the tears sting his eyes.

They walked in silence for a while and then John's daughter said, 'Oh look, Papa. Here come Mr Sayce and Mrs Anstey.'

And there to the Apothecary's utter amazement came two members of the coven, strolling along as if they hadn't a care in the world. But then, he realised, nobody was aware of their secret other life, nobody except Tim Painter and himself. He decided to behave as if he knew nothing.

'Mrs Anstey, Mr Sayce,' he said, and swept off his hat. Beside him he felt Rose give a small curtsey as she had been taught.

Today the older man looked decidedly deflated, John thought, though the woman stared at the Apothecary as lecherously as ever.

'Mr Rawlings, we were just talking about you.' And Anne ran her oddly small tongue over her lips in a manner that John could only think of as obscene.

'Really? What were you saying?'

'That we hadn't seen you since that night in Redruth when we played cards.'

'I have been quite busy,' he answered, dropping his eyes.

He found it hard to return Anne Anstey's gaze which, though strangely cold, had still an unpleasant fire in its depth. He recalled her lying stark naked on the altar, coupling with a Colquite and had to control himself not to shudder visibly. But despite his efforts he must have made some movement because he felt Rose glance up at him questioningly.

'Hello, my dear. How pretty you look today.' Mrs Anstey was speaking to his daughter.

'Thank you.' And the child curtseyed again.

It was at that moment that the Apothecary caught Sayce's eye and, briefly, the expression within. To say that the man looked strained would have been an understatement. There was genuine fear in his glance. John could not help but notice that the older man's lips were forming soundless words.

Anne bent down and picked up one of Rose's rich red curls. 'Beautiful,' she crooned. 'You have such beautiful hair, sweetheart.'

The child pulled back against John's legs. 'Thank you,' she whispered again, but the Apothecary could tell that she was genuinely frightened.

He bowed abruptly. 'I'm sorry. I have an urgent appointment. Come Rose.' And replacing his hat, he hurried up the road.

'I didn't like it when the woman touched my hair,' the child said quietly.

'It wasn't she who came to your room, was it?'

'No, Papa, it was somebody much thinner and older.'

'I wonder,' he said to himself, as into his brain came a picture of the unappealing features of Mrs Legassick.

Returning to The Angel, he discovered the coaches in which Mrs Pill had arrived drawn up outside. Now he knew that he had little time. His problem was going to be what to do with Rose, for what he had to say was not suitable for her ears. Eventually he found the thumb-sucking fat maid and asked her if Rose could stay with her for half an hour. On the production of a coin the girl rapidly agreed.

'You are not to leave her alone, you understand?'

'Oh, I won't, Sir. I promise.'

'Not even for a second.'

'No, Sir.'

He went downstairs and eventually found Tim Painter taking his ease in the parlour.

'Aren't you leaving?' John asked in some surprise.

'No,' Tim answered lazily. 'Thought I'd stay and give what assistance I could to hunting down these wretched witchcraft people. I mean to say, one can't have this sort of thing going on in decent society.'

If he had not been about such serious business, John would have laughed uproariously. How a reprobate such as Tim could have the bare-faced gall to sit and pontificate about moral standards was almost beyond him. As it was he grinned broadly.

'Glad you'll be with us,' he said.

'Think nothing of it, dear boy.' And Tim flapped a languid hand.

'Have you told Mrs Pill?' asked John.

'Yes. I said I would follow on later.'

'And how did she take that?'

'Not well, not well. However the wretched Jasper came to the rescue and said it would be a much easier journey without me. For once I was totally in agreement with him.'

The Apothecary shook his head. 'Why do you really want to stay?'

Tim shifted in his seat. 'I don't know exactly. I think it was the thought that I might, at last, be of some help. Which reminds me, why did you really call us all together last night?'

John's face remained impassive. 'Because I would have present the four men who visited Diana Warwick on that fatal night. I wanted to run through the sequences of events with you all for the last time. But it's too late for that now.'

'What do you mean?'

'I'll explain later.' The Apothecary stood up. 'Do you know where I will find Mrs Pill and Jasper?'

'They're in the hall somewhere, I think. But you'd better hurry. They'll be leaving shortly.'

'Thank you.'

They were indeed getting ready for departure, though Mrs Pill, looking terribly white and thin, had taken a seat in a snug, leaving Jasper to organise the servants getting the trunks onto the two carriages. Catching her alone, John sat down beside her.

'So you're departing from us, Madam.'

'Yes,' she said, and her voice sounded broken and fragile. 'I realise there is no hope for my poor Isobel. So I am taking my leave of this accursed place.'

John nodded. 'I quite understand how you feel. Helstone can hold nothing but unhappy memories for you.'

She lowered her head, staring into her lap. 'I shall think of it as the town in which my heart was broken.'

'And not just because of Isobel,' he said quietly.

She looked up and just for a second he peered into those small, sad eyes, today partly hidden by a pair of spectacles. 'What do you mean?' she asked.

'I think perhaps you know.'

'I don't understand what you are talking about.'

'I speak of the death of Diana Warwick,' he said, still in that calm, quiet voice.

'What about it?'

Leaning over, John took one of her thin-fingered hands in his. 'Why don't you tell me what happened? It would be much easier if you did.'

She stared at him and he saw her try to control herself, and fail.

'You know, don't you,' she said at last. 'How long have you known?'

'Not long,' he answered truthfully. 'It only came to me recently in fact.'

She started to tremble, resembling nothing so much as some poor small creature out in the cold. John started to pat her hand.

'I think I had the first intimation when Tim Painter said that Diana suddenly looked at the door then afterwards hurried him away as soon as possible. Yet I knew she was alive when Lord Godolphin called on her, but was dead by the time the Gaffer went to visit. That suggested to me that somebody opened the door while she was *in flagrente* with Tim and she saw that person look into the room with an expression of pure horror. Horror, perhaps, mixed with something else.'

'Oh yes, I looked on her with hatred,' Kathryn said quietly. 'After all, Tim was the only man I have ever really loved.'

'And she was taking him away from you.'

'How could she have been so cruel? Yet her beauty was such that men followed her wherever she went. But when all was said and done she was just a common whore.'

'So you went in later – after his lordship had left – and put a pillow over her face.'

'Yes.' The shrivelled, white visage turned to the Apothecary and he saw for the first time that she was slightly unbalanced. 'And shall I tell you something, Mr Rawlings? I enjoyed smothering the life out of her. Enjoyed seeing the end of her dangerous, fatal beauty.' Slowly she got to her feet, removed her hand from his grasp and held it out to him. 'Goodbye to you, Sir, it has been most pleasant knowing you. Perhaps we will meet again somewhere.' Then she walked past him and made her way out of the front door.

Just for a moment John sat motionless, then he sprang to his feet and ran after her. But he was too late. Mrs Pill had taken possession of the front carriage waiting outside the inn. Climbing up onto the vacant coachman's box she had whipped up the horses and gone clattering down the street towards the open countryside at the bottom. John stood staring after her, in company with Jasper, her brother. The bird had clearly flown.

Chapter Twenty-Nine

For a second John and Jasper stood staring as the coach disappeared down Coinage Hall Street. Then together, just as if they had rehearsed the move, they leapt into the second conveyance, shouting to the driver, who was already in place, to pursue at all speed. He shot forward so quickly that the pair was obliged to cling onto the upholstery in order not to end up on the floor. Ahead of them they saw Kathryn's coach career wildly into the fields that lay beyond the town, heading in the direction of Loe Pool. Even as he saw it, the Apothecary had a terrible premonition of the thought that might be in her mind.

They followed into the meadowlands which grew progressively more boggy as the coach moved forward. Eventually the wheels ground to a halt, arrested in the marshy terrain. Ahead of them, a much lighter weight than that of the two men, Mrs Pill's conveyance lurched its dangerous path onward. John, descending as best he could, started to run behind it but realised the futility. Despite the fact that it was of necessity travelling slowly, he still found it hard to keep up. Behind him he heard Jasper clambering down.

'What shall we do, Rawlings?'

'We must go in pursuit. She won't be able to drive much further.'

'Come on then.'

They hurried forward but their way and also their line of sight was barred by trees. Occasionally, though, the woodland cleared and they could see Mrs Pill's abandoned coach standing somewhat forlornly on the edge of the lake.

Jasper turned to John. 'Oh my God! You don't think she…'

But the Apothecary didn't answer, resolutely pushing his way forwards. He came out of the trees and rushed to the lakeside. And there, floating on the surface, was a sad dark shape. Without hesitation John kicked off his shoes, tore off his jacket and dived in, to be followed a minute later by Jasper, who reached Kathryn first and hauled her to the shore.

Dripping wet, John did everything in his power to restore life; turning her on her face and pumping her back, waiting for her to cough up water. But it was to no avail.

Looking down into her plain, pale face, the Apothecary thought that she had endured a wasted life culminating in two terrible acts of violence, one brought about by a kind of desperate jealousy, the other to end the suffering which she must have been subjected to since losing both Isobel and Tim Painter. For surely that is how she must have seen his betrayal of her in the bedroom that night, as a total loss of loyalty. Yet surely, John considered, still gazing at her, she must have known what she was taking on in Tim. That was most certainly not the first time he had been unfaithful to her but – and this idea struck him with some force – it was destined to be the last. Then he remembered Anne Anstey in Redruth and he stopped his mind going down that path of deceit and concentrated on the present.

Jasper had lifted the inert body up in his arms and was openly weeping.

'Why did she do it, Rawlings? She was my sister. We spent all our time together until she married Hubert Pill. Oh God, my poor little Kathryn.'

'She did it because she had lost Isobel, Jasper. The child meant everything to her,' John lied.

'I know that. But I thought she was starting to recover. Felt sure that with time and patience I could coax her back into a normal life.'

John looked at him, thought of all that had happened and knew that he was utterly right to remain silent about the actual reason for Kathryn's death. To Jasper he said, 'Come on, my friend. We must carry her body back to Helstone. I'll drive her coach. The coachman can bring back the other.'

So they set off in dismal procession, manoeuvring the coaches with care through the unfriendly undergrowth until at last, and after a great deal of effort, they found their way to

Coinage Hall Street. Here they parted company; John to find Tim Painter, Jasper to go to the undertakers to arrange for Kathryn's body to be coffined up before he took it home to Wiltshire.

It was in a very sombre mood that the Apothecary, having drawn a blank in the taproom of The Angel, made his way to The Blue Anchor, feeling certain that he would find the extraordinary character that made up Painter in the hostelry chattering to his crowd of cohorts. As he walked down the street he had been mulling over whether to tell Tim all the facts and was still not certain as he went through the front door and saw him, seated at a table, regaling some gullible individual with how he had been promoted to Constable's assistant. John sighed heavily and took a seat beside him.

'How do, John my friend? How goes it with you since this morning?'

'Not well, I'm afraid.'

'Really? What's up?'

'I would rather discuss that in private.'

'Oh. Oh, I see.' Tim leant across the table to his crony. 'Would you mind, old boy? Got some confidential business to talk about.'

The cohort, having given John rather a dark look, shambled off to a corner where he disconsolately supped his ale.

'I suppose you want to discuss the witches,' said Tim in a loud whisper.

'No, it's something else I'm afraid. Tim, you must prepare yourself for a shock. I am sorry to have to tell you that Kathryn is dead.'

To say that the ne'er-do-well gaped at him would have been a gross understatement. His jaw quite literally dropped and for once in his life he looked utterly devastated.

'Dead? But that's not possible. I only saw her an hour ago. She was perfectly well then.'

'Yes, I saw her too remember. But after our conversation she went to Loe Pool and threw herself in.'

Tim let out a terrible cry, then turned his head away and John could see that he was weeping. He leant forward. 'I'm sorry, believe me. It must be a terrible blow.'

'It is. Poor Kathryn. What had she done to merit such an end?'

She met you, thought John, but would rather have died than say it aloud. Instead he said, 'I think it was principally the death of Isobel that unhinged her.'

'Yes.' Tim dried his eyes. 'You're right. But where did the child go? That is something we have never discovered.'

John shook his head slowly. 'I believe she drowned in Loe Pool.'

'And her mother followed her,' Tim said quietly. He sat up straight. 'Let us have another drink and toast her memory.'

'Yes,' answered John, but inside his head he was thinking how extraordinary Tim Painter was. But then, he considered, the entire nation, indeed the world, was made up of such individual people that one should never be surprised by the behaviour of anyone.

They raised their glasses. 'To Kathryn,' said Tim, 'may God rest her soul.'

'Amen to that,' answered John. He drained his glass and stood up. 'Now, are you going to be alright?'

'Yes. I intend to drown my sorrows. You won't join me?'

'No, I must get back to my daughter. We plan to leave –' John pulled his watch out and looked at it '– this afternoon. Now I see it will have to be tomorrow. I'll bid you farewell in case our paths do not cross again.'

Unbelievably Tim's eyes filled with tears once more. 'Oh no, we cannot part like that. I shall come and wave farewell to the stagecoach. After all, I consider you a close friend.'

He suddenly seemed unbelievably sad and lonely, and John thought that he probably had few male friends having spent most of his adult life concentrating on women.

'That will be most kind of you. Thank you.'

'It will be my pleasure. We must meet when I am next in town.'

John bowed, Tim made to stand up but couldn't quite achieve it. None the less he gave a small salute before he addressed himself once more to his wine, another bottle of which had been ordered on the Apothecary's arrival.

Back in the street, John ran the short distance to The Angel, suddenly full of fear for his child. But she was playing happily enough with the landlord's wife, a dark comely creature of some forty years. They both looked up as he approached.

'Oh, there you are, Sir. I was feeling somewhat worried.'

'Is Rose all right?'

'She's perfectly well, Sir. I had to remove her from the custody of the girl because she had so much to do the poor thing was at her wit's end. So I took Rose from her. I hope you don't mind, Sir.'

'Mind? I am more than grateful to you, Madam.' He produced a guinea from his pocket. 'I wonder if I could ask you a favour. Would it be possible for you to care for Rose tonight? I have to go out later and I am very nervous of leaving her on her own. If you could, perhaps, sleep in her room.'

The landlord's wife looked askance. 'Why, Sir? Surely you're not afraid once the child has bedded down.'

'But that's when I do worry. Suppose some stranger were to come in off the streets.'

'Bless you, Sir. They're all locals.'

John thought wildly and came up with the answer. 'It's ever since the disappearance of Isobel Pill. She vanished as you know. I couldn't bear it if anything like that were to happen to Rose.'

The woman looked thoughtful. 'Aye, Sir, 'ee do have a point. I'll sleep with the child tonight.'

'Just this once. We're leaving tomorrow. Can you tell me at what time the stagecoach departs?'

'Are you going to Truro or Falmouth, Sir?'

'Truro.'

'Then your luck holds, Sir. The Truro stage leaves in the morning at nine o'clock.'

'And we'll be on it,' said John, and felt a sudden uplifting of his heart.

He never afterwards could tell what drew him back to Loe Pool. But immediately after dining with his daughter and handing her into the care of Mrs King, who fussed over the child, presumably thinking that another guinea might be on the way, he set off on foot to see that stretch of mysterious water for the last time. The sun was just going down and the lights were transforming the Loe into a glittering mirror. All around him the trees were etched darkly against the fading light, sinister sentinels of the night that was to come. From where he stood John could glimpse Penrose House and immediately opposite it, almost hidden by the undergrowth, the home of Lord Lyle himself. Penrose was lit by a shaft of dying light but the other house lay in gloom. Suddenly, for no reason, John needed to go there to see the owner and tell him that the game was up. That he should get out before the wrath of the law descended on him. Almost without knowing it, his feet started to walk to where the steep path ascended upwards.

It was almost dark by the time he reached it and in the undergrowth on either side of the track he could hear the little rustlings of wild creatures. For no reason the sounds made him nervous and he would have turned back had he not been over half way up. As he drew nearer the Apothecary could see that the place was in total blackness, not a candle lit anywhere. This made him even more frightened and he stood still for a second. Then he pulled himself together, thinking he had come this far and really must continue on his way. Gritting his teeth, John proceeded towards the house.

As he drew nearer he realised that the place was deserted. No light shone from the windows, which gazed out onto the night, shutters open. Drawing closer, John peered in through one of them, seeing dim reflections of the room beyond. He was staring into a library for the walls were lined with books, a high stool drawn up before one wall. There were two chairs standing on either side of the fireplace, which had been cleaned out and laid but remained unlit. John leant closer, his face pressed against the glass, peering into the room. As his eyes adjusted to the light he found that he could see the interior more and more clearly, and he allowed his gaze to wander, picking out individual items of furnishing. Then suddenly he started forward, staring with total concentration. For in front of the chair with its back to the window he could see a pair of buckled shoes – shoes with stockinged legs inside them.

John pulled back into the shadows, his heart pounding. So the house was not empty after all. Whoever it was in there obviously preferred sitting in the dark, his only light coming from the unshuttered windows. He waited silently, listening for the noise of the occupant stirring. There was none and after a few minutes he ventured another cautious glance inside. The legs and feet were in exactly the same position as they had been when he had last seen them. It occurred to him then that the legs' owner was asleep and so he had nothing to fear. None the less John's hand went into his pocket checking that he had brought his pistol. He allowed himself another quick peer and saw that, yet again, they were just as they had been when last he looked.

Now he began to feel slightly worried. Supposing, just supposing, that the man sitting in the room had had a seizure and was incapable of movement. Or, even worse, that he had died in the chair and would slowly be starting to stiffen. It was too much for someone trained as the Apothecary had been. Cautiously, for he was very far from certain that the man *was* ill, John made his way round to the front door.

It was open, just a crack, but open for all that. Moving cautiously John pushed it and the door swung back with a loud creak. He stood motionless, half expecting the man from the library to stagger to his feet and come into the reception hall to see who had arrived. Nothing moved.

'Lord Lyle,' called John quietly.

There was no reply and walking softly over the wooden

floor the Apothecary, losing his sense of direction, began to open doors and peer into the rooms thus revealed. Eventually he came to the library which he recognised from the close covering of books on the walls.

'Lord Lyle,' he said again.

Nobody stirred. Moving with extreme caution, John went into the room.

Lord Lyle was asleep in the chair wearing that same cruel make-up with which he had been adorned on the last occasion they had met. An enamel white macquillage, carmined lips and looping black brows completely blotted out his natural colour, while a white wig atop only added to the general ghastly effect. Creeping forward, calling his name softly, John wondered at the deepness of his sleep.

And then he drew level with him and saw that the head had fallen to one side at a most unnatural angle, and that round his lordship's throat was a black scarf pulled tightly. As if released from a catalepsy, the Apothecary rushed to Lord Lyle's assistance. Snatching off the scarf, he felt for the pulse but, much as he had expected, there was none. Someone had done for his lordship, someone who had come, perhaps, as the shadows began to fall, and then, deed finished, had hastened away into the roseate evening.

John stood up. There was nothing further he could do. His mission now must be to get back to Helstone in the darkness and raise the alarm. For a moment he felt desperately sorry for William Trethowan, whose troubled plate was already overflowing with disaster. But then he thought it was the man's turn to do the job of Constable and there was nothing for him but to get on with it. However, this matter put a slightly different complexion on his leaving town tomorrow. Suddenly overcome with worry about Rose, about the situation in general, John left the house, closing the front door behind him.

The night had become treacherous – or at least he imagined it had. Trees and bushes scratched his face and hands and he seemed to lose his path several times. But at long last he found himself in open fields and the lights shining from the houses of Helstone seemed as bright as if they had lit every candle in Christendom. Hurrying up Coinage Hall Street, John made his way into The Blue Anchor. There was no one there he knew, Tim Painter and the man he most wanted to see – William Trethowan – being all too clearly absent. Turning round abruptly John ran towards The Angel.

It was strangely quiet within, indeed there was hardly anyone around. With a feeling of growing panic John went into the taproom. A few huddled locals sat about but they too seemed oddly restrained. Deciding he would have to go to Trethowan's home – a small dwelling in Meneage Street – the Apothecary was aware that he must first check on his daughter. Going upstairs, he went to his room to change his coat and breeches which had become somewhat soiled by his encounter with various pieces of undergrowth.

The place was in darkness but striking a tinder, he lit the several candles that were dotted round the room. And then he saw that a letter had been pushed under his door. With a sudden rush of fear, the Apothecary picked it up and broke the clumsily applied seal.

'Sir, take care of your child, I beg you. She is in mortal danger,' he read.

There was no signature, no address, no date, nothing. But the very sight of it had John running, half-dressed, to the room next door to his. He flung open the door without ceremony, gazing at the white bed where Rose's small figure should have lain. It was entirely empty. His daughter had vanished.

Chapter Thirty

A cry of sheer despair broke from the Apothecary's lips, then turning abruptly he left the room and hurried down the stairs, the sheet of paper still clutched in his hand.

'Mrs King,' he called. 'Mrs King, where are you?'

There was no answer and he started to run through the inn, shouting the landlady's name, his panic rising with every passing second. She appeared from the kitchen, wiping her hands on a cloth.

'Mr Rawlings, whatever is it? What's the matter?' He saw her expression change. 'It's not Rose surely? I only left her for a minute. There was a crisis I had to attend to.'

'Rose has gone,' he said, and sat down suddenly in a chair, his face drained entirely of colour.

'Oh no!'

'And this letter was pushed under my door.'

He handed it to her and watched her expression as she read. Then she looked up at him, her eyes wide and frantic.

'Oh my God. I feel so guilty. What shall we do?'

'We must rouse everyone we can and search for her. I will go to the Constable straight away.'

He stood up, realising that he felt utterly weak, his limbs heavy and useless. But despite this the Apothecary knew that to act quickly was essential and that he must overcome this feeling. Hurrying back upstairs he put on his jacket and went out into the night.

From the moment he left The Angel John started calling his daughter's name. Yet he was racked with indecision, longing to start searching for her but knowing that he must get William Trethowan's assistance, and get it promptly. With this thought in mind he ran as fast as he could to the Constable's cottage and arrived there sweating profusely and gasping for breath.

He had just put his hand to the knocker when he heard a strange rustling sound down by his feet and looked at the cobbles to see what was causing it. There, of all things, was the blind fiddler's monkey picking round for food. For some reason John drew back into the shadows of the cottage wall and watched.

A few seconds later the blind man came down the street calling, 'Wilkes, Wilkes. Where are you, you little wretch? Come here.'

Once again, John stood quietly, not knowing why he did so. In total silence he watched the fiddler draw near. The monkey meanwhile had ceased its scrabbling and now sat up, its head on one side, watching as the Gaffer approached.

The fiddler looked up and down the street rapidly, then he bent and picked the monkey up. 'You're a naughty boy, running away like that.'

In that one movement, done without witnesses except for himself, John knew that the blindness was assumed, that the Gaffer could see as well as he could. Yet now he had more pressing things on his mind. Waiting till the fiddler was out of earshot, he banged the knocker and called out, 'Mr Trethowan, please come to the door. It's John Rawlings. My little girl has disappeared.'

Surprisingly it was thrown open almost straight away to reveal the Constable, still fully dressed and smoking a long clay pipe.

'What's happened, Sir?' he asked.

'It's Rose. She's been taken from her room. And this was put under my door.' And he thrust the letter into the Constable's hand.

Moving back into the light of the hall, Trethown scanned its contents. Then he said, 'Have you any idea where she might be?'

'None. None at all. All I know is that she has been taken and I must find her quickly. I am certain her life is in danger.'

'I'd agree with you there, Sir,' William answered, struggling into his coat. 'I'll come at once.'

It took a few minutes to return to The Angel and there John found that John King, the landlord, had already started to organise a search party. They stood around in the entrance, looking determined and large and ready to take the town apart if necessary. The terrible reality of what they were searching for hit the Apothecary so hard at that moment that he groaned audibly. The eyes of several Cornishmen fixed on him and he saw pity in all of them. He felt then that he wanted the floor to open and for him to disappear into a black pit.

Mrs King was hovering nervously in the background. Seeing John, she approached.

'Oh Sir, will you ever forgive me? I promise you I only left her for five minutes.'

The Apothecary shook his head. 'How can I blame you? You did your best. But it suggests to me that you were being watched and the abductors chose their moment.'

'What do you mean, Sir?'

'Obviously they were in the inn, otherwise how could they have known that you had gone downstairs?'

Mrs King shivered. 'How horrible. Who do you think is responsible, Sir?'

'I would imagine that we won't have to look much further than Mrs Anstey and her friends. I think they kidnapped Isobel Pill and their latest victim is my daughter.' He turned to go. 'God help the poor child,' he added in an undertone.

They set out. The majority of the party looking in every corner, every outbuilding, everywhere it would be possible to conceal a small being. But John and Trethowan, their faces stern and set, went in pursuit of the members of the satanic coven.

None of them was staying at The Angel; after consulting the landlord that much was clear. Yet they had to have a base to which they could retreat. John racked his brain, trying desperately to remember where the Colquites lodged, but no answer came up.

'I shall knock on every door in Helstone till I find them,' the Constable announced grimly.

'And I'll be beside you,' John announced. 'We've got to find her. I love the child. She's all I have left now.'

'You stay close, Sir, and we'll discover where those witches are hiding.'

'I forgot to tell you and I apologise for it. Lord Lyle – the head of them – has been murdered. I found him in his house above Loe Pool earlier this evening.'

Trethowan stopped walking and turned to stare at him. 'Murdered you say? Are you certain?'

'He had been strangled with a black scarf. He was struck from behind while he was sitting in a chair. But the interesting thing was that the house was deserted. Not a servant or soul about. It was almost as if he had ordered everyone to go and leave him.'

The Constable pulled at his nose thoughtfully. 'That would mean the entire coven are moving on.'

'Then why should they choose this moment to abduct Rose? And who wrote the letter to me?'

But even as he asked the question the Apothecary knew the answer. Into his pictorial memory came a vision of Sayce's frantic expression when last they had spoken. He had been aware of what was planned and he had not approved.

'It was Sayce,' he continued. 'I'm certain of it.'

'Then we must find him fast,' answered Trethowan. 'Maybe he holds the key to the entire mystery.'

As they talked they had been proceeding down Church Street and now found themselves in front of Nick Kitto's house.

'No use knocking here.'

'I think we should, William. Nick can help us search.'

'Very well.' Trethowan applied his great hand to the knocker and the door was answered a few minutes later by the aged servant. 'We're making enquiries about a missing child. May we see your mistress if you please.'

'She's gone to bed, Constable. But Master Nick is still up.'

And even as he said the words Nicholas strode into the hall. Seeing the Apothecary and his companion, he stopped short.

He opened his mouth to speak but John forestalled him.

'Listen, Nick, we need your help, and urgently at that. My daughter, Rose, has been abducted, we think by the coven of witches who infest this place from time to time. Every able-bodied man has been summoned to search for her. The Constable and I are going from house to house to try and find where the coven are staying. Please can you assist us?'

'Of course. Have you told my...the Vicar?'

'No, do you think we should?'

'Most certainly. You go on knocking down the street and I'll run to the vicarage.'

'I think most of the people who have houses close to the church are God-fearing folk,' put in the Constable.

'You never know,' Nick answered cryptically, and pulling on a cloak vanished into the night.

Half an hour later, when every dwelling in Church Street had been called upon, the Constable decided that it was too late to go knocking people up and said he would continue in the morning.

'We'd best go and join the search party,' he said.

John did not answer, indeed his lips had almost ceased to work. He was in a state bordering on hysteria, so full of tension that the slightest thing made him jump. First thing this morning he had witnessed Kathryn's terrible suicide. This followed by an evening unlike any other he could remember. His nervousness at Loe Pool had been heightened by the discovery of Lord Lyle's body, alone in that deserted house. Then to return to learn of Rose's abduction had been almost too much to bear. All the misery and pain that Emilia's death had brought him now returned, only this time it was doubled. He felt that his life had reached a turning point from which there was no escape. He knew that if he could not rescue his daughter he would retreat from the world, experiment with his herbs, become something of a recluse. Oh God, let me find her, he prayed.

As they walked back to The Angel they were joined by Nick

and the Reverend Robinson, the latter wearing a purposeful expression and bearing a large crucifix about his neck.

'This demonic gang must be broken up once and for all,' he announced.

'I think they may be already moving on,' John answered, and told the newcomers of his discovery of Lord Lyle's body in the empty house.

The reverend gentleman turned immediately to Nick. 'I must go up there at first light and conduct a Christian ceremony within the house. It is my duty to do so.'

'I'll go with you, Sir. Indeed I could not allow you to venture there unattended.'

Mr Robinson gave him a grateful glance. 'Thank you, my son,' he answered.

The Constable interceded. 'I cannot permit anyone to enter the place until the body has been removed. And that will have to wait till morning now. Indeed, Mr Rawlings...' He turned to John. '...it is getting almost too dark to search.'

'The rest of you can stop. I intend to continue all night.'

'And I'll help you,' Kitto answered immediately.

The rest of the searchers were called off until daylight but throughout the dark hours John continued with a type of insane eagerness. With Nicholas Kitto working alongside him they peered into every conceivable nook and cranny, every bit of broken wall, every outbuilding, every pigsty, up and down every street, in fact they searched everywhere but inside people's private residences.

As dawn came up, Nick turned to look at John and saw that during the night tears had run down the Apothecary's face making little pale rivulets through the dirt and grime ingrained there.

'Be of brave heart, my friend,' he said. 'Soon the Constable will start searching houses again and then Rose will be found, I feel certain of it.'

It was then that John realised that this new event was just what young Kitto had been looking for, something entirely different to get his mind off the murder of Diana Warwick. Almost as if he could read his thoughts, Nick spoke.

'That night you got us all together, the night we played cards and were interrupted by the ritual at Lord Lyle's house, what did you want with us?'

'Just to check the times you saw Miss Warwick.'

'I see,' Nick answered quietly. He looked at the ground and when he looked up again his eyes were full of questions. 'Tell me, did you ever discover who murdered her?'

'Yes,' John answered.

'And which one of us was it?'

'Mrs Pill killed herself this morning. Did you know?'

'Yes, the servants were gossiping about it. But what has that...' And then suddenly Nick understood and turned a terrible face in the Apothecary's direction. 'Oh God's holy life, don't tell me she was responsible?'

John nodded. 'I'm afraid so.'

'Jealousy,' stated Nick bitterly. 'What a poisoned worm it is, to be sure.'

'Yet have you not suffered from it as have I?'

Nicholas sighed deeply. 'I am a true offender. I was even jealous of my own father,' he added more quietly.

'Of Lord Godolphin?' John asked, wondering how this was going to be received.

Nick stared at him blankly. 'Lord Godolphin?' he repeated.

'Yes.'

The younger man burst out laughing, so loudly that the sound seemed to echo round the sleeping town and out to the distant hills.

'He's not my father,' he said, wiping his eyes. 'Whatever made you think so?'

'I just imagined...' John answered feebly.

'Well, you were wrong. My father is the Vicar. Mr Robinson.'

The Apothecary thought that if he hadn't felt so wretched, so down, so utterly hopeless, he would have joined in the laughter at his own idiocy. But instead he just felt a complete fool, a numbskull, a jumper-to-conclusions. He sat down suddenly on the kerbstone with all the stuffing knocked out of him. Nick crouched down beside him.

'I'm sorry to shock you like that. I was conceived when he was still a curate, you see. It was my mother who wouldn't marry him. At the time she was very pretty and she had her heart set on someone else. It's almost impossible to believe when you see her now, but those are the facts.'

At that John wept, where normally he would have just seen the silly side of the explanation. He had never felt so weak or so miserable in his life. The thought that Emilia and now Rose had been taken from him was almost too much to bear.

'Come on, old chap,' said Nick quietly. 'Let's go back to The Angel for a while. We have searched everywhere possible at night and we can start again in an hour or so. You need some food meanwhile.'

And suddenly it was so comforting to be led back to the inn and put to sit down in a parlour while Nick Kitto, enjoying his role as a consoler, went off in search of breakfast despite the earliness of the hour.

Chapter Thirty-One

Unable to eat a thing, John consumed several cups of tea and then his eyes closed and he fell asleep, his head rolling backwards, his mouth open. But it was not long before he felt a hand on his shoulder and, returning to consciousness, instantly knew that something was wrong. Just for a minute he struggled to remember what it was then the truth came vividly to mind and he jumped to his feet.

'What time is it? How long have I slept?'

The craggy face of William Trethowan appeared. 'It's five o'clock, Sir. Daylight. Time you went searching again, that is if you feel up to it.'

'Of course I do. I must find my daughter.'

'Right, Sir. Then I suggest you try Meneage Street. I'm afraid that I have a grisly duty up at the Loe Pool house.'

For no reason that he could possibly describe, the Apothecary was reluctant to go into town, preferring to do the kind of searching that he and Nick Kitto had carried out during the night.

'If you'll forgive me I think I would rather look round the place than go from door to door.'

'But, Sir, only you know who these children of Satan actually are. Apart from Sayce and Mrs Anstey I couldn't possibly identify them.'

There was undeniable logic in this but John immediately saw the weakness in the argument.

'But I have no authority to search people's houses.'

'I will send a deputy constable with you. He will have the necessary credentials.'

Yet again John had the feeling that he would rather stay in the locality. 'Then let him go alone.'

'You're not thinking, Sir. He will have even less idea of the identities of these accursed people than I have.'

The Apothecary bowed to fate. 'Very well. I'll go.'

At that moment who should walk in but Tim Painter,

dressed in black but other than for that bearing no outward signs of mourning. Indeed he was grinning quite cheerfully.

'Good day,' he said, taking in the assembled company and giving a small bow.

'You're up early, Sir,' commented the Constable.

'I'm catching the stage to Truro so I thought I'd make a reasonable start.'

'Tim,' said John urgently. 'I was wondering if you could help me. My daughter has gone missing – abducted I fear – and I was hoping that you might join the search party.'

Painter looked thoughtful. 'It would mean delaying my departure.'

'Perhaps you would consider it.'

'My dear friend, for you of course. Anything. Don't give it another thought.' He turned to the Constable. 'Now, my good fellow, what would you like me to do?'

'Perhaps you would care to accompany Mr Rawlings and my deputy in the search for members of the coven.'

'So they are involved,' said Tim knowingly. 'I might have guessed.'

John drained his cold tea cup, then turned to Nick. 'Thank you for everything you've done. I shall always be grateful to you.'

Nick eyed Tim disdainfully. 'I don't feel like leaving now. Do you mind if I continue to search?'

'By all means,' said the Constable, taking charge. 'Perhaps you and the other men would like to retrace your steps of last night.'

They set off about their various tasks, Tim strolling along in sprightly fashion beside John, who now had lack of sleep to add to his other torments.

Dropping behind the deputy constable, a short, bull-headed man called Pascoe, John whispered urgently, 'I wanted to search with the others, not go house to house.'

Tim stopped walking and John did likewise. 'Do you think she is still alive?'

'I can't be sure. I've always been so close to Rose, ever since she was born. I feel that somehow – if she is alive, that is – she would try and contact me.'

'But how can she? You don't know where she is.'

'I mean some mental kind of message. I can't explain further.'

But at that moment John saw Tim quiver, then he seized the Apothecary by the arm. 'Look, there's Sayce going for an early stroll.'

Despite the fact that his body ached with tiredness, John broke into a run. 'Sayce,' he called out. 'Stop! I want a word with you.'

Sayce glanced over his shoulder, and John had a vision of that melon-faced man looking thoroughly frightened. Then as best he could, the heavily built fellow broke into a lumbering run. Like two greyhounds John and Tim pursued him and, a second later, they heard the solid tread of Pascoe as he, too, joined in.

'Stop!' shouted John once more.

But they were gaining on him and at the Guildhall Sayce ran out of breath and came to a gasping halt, leaning against the wall. Instantly the Apothecary was on him, shaking him like rat.

'You bastard,' he hissed. 'You sent me that letter, didn't you. Where is she? What have you done with her?'

'Now then, Sir…' started Pascoe.

But the Apothecary ignored him, squeezing Sayce's throat until his eyes began to bulge. Vaguely aware that Tim Painter was trying to loose his hold, John knew that if the man refused to answer him he would kill him.

'Let him go, Sir. He can't speak while you've got him in that stranglehold.'

And Pascoe also started to beat John over the wrists, none too gently. Eventually the truth of what was being said began to dawn on him and John loosed his grip suddenly and leant against the Guildhall wall, panting.

'Now, Mr Sayce, you must make a statement,' said Pascoe firmly.

'Yes, you dogface. What have you done to Rose?'

Gasping for breath, Sayce spoke over damaged tonsils. 'I knew they were after her. I did my best and wrote warning you, Sir. You have me to thank for that.'

John flew at him again. 'How dare you try and justify yourself to me. You beastly old prick. If you have damaged her you shall pay for it. I'm telling you.'

Tim Painter spoke up. 'John, let him be. He can't speak when you're shaking him like that.'

Reluctantly the Apothecary released his hold and Sayce, under the belligerent eye of the deputy, began to blurt out his story.

'The coven like to make a sacrifice occasionally. That's what was planned for Isobel Pill but somehow the child managed to elude us. Heaven knows where she is.'

'Speak not of heaven,' John murmured deep.

'Anyway, their eye fell on your Rose. But I learned of their plan and could not tolerate such a thing going on. That's why I wrote to you, Sir. I wanted no evil to befall the child.'

'Where is she? What has happened to her?'

John would have rushed at the fellow a third time but was restrained by Tim.

'Sir, I cannot help you. I do not know the answer. If I did I would swear by all I hold dear that I would tell you. But the coven no longer trust me and told me nothing. And now, Sir, I am going to church to pray for forgiveness. I believe that I am a lost sheep that can return to the fold and that God will find it in His heart to receive me back and forgive me for all my wickedness.'

The three men stared at his retreating form as he panted up the street towards St Michael's.

'Can't you arrest him?' Tim asked Pascoe.

'Not really, Sir. After all, he did his best to save Miss Rawlings. Of what does he stand accused other than being a repentant member of a coven?'

'Of being a foolish old cock-brain, that's all,' Tim put in.

John turned to the other two. 'Listen, Tim knows who the coven members are. Let him go with you, Pascoe. I feel I must see what the other searchers have come up with.'

'Very well, Sir.'

John ran back to The Angel, the sweat lively on his face. As he ran he found himself saying words inside his head.

'Rose, can you hear me? Just give me a sign that you are alive, sweetheart, and I swear I will find you.'

And clear as a stream as he entered the doors of the inn, he heard – though only in his mind – Rose's voice say, 'Help me, Papa.'

There was no one around, everyone had gone out searching and John was quite alone. 'Mrs King,' he called out – but nobody came.

'Oh Rose, if only I knew where you were,' he muttered, as if by saying her name he could conjure her up.

And then of their own volition his feet turned to the yard lying beside the hostelry and he was out there and looking round him. An hostler worked in the deep confines of the stable block, mucking out and laying fresh straw. An unusual white dog lay asleep in the morning sun, ignoring the hens who wandered about it pecking at seeds. It was a calm scene, quiet and peaceful, and yet John was in turmoil.

'Where are you?' he said silently.

And then, suddenly, he knew. Sprinting to the well that stood there, the well that supplied water for the inn, he gazed down into its inky depths. One of the buckets had been lowered on the rope which, he noticed, had fractured, so that only one pail was in use. It hung nearby, idle and unused.

'Rose,' he called, leaning over the wall and cupping his hands. 'Rose, are you down there?'

He heard nothing but inside his head her voice said, 'Yes.'

His heart leapt wildly. 'Be steady, darling. I'll find someone to help. You stay exactly where you are.'

He turned round desperately and then, to his amazement, he saw Gideon come into the yard carrying the monkey. John hurried to him.

'Gideon, my daughter is down the well but the rope of her bucket has broken and I can't bring her up. What am I going to do?'

The tambourine player stared at him. 'I don't know, Sir. Nobody would dare climb down. It's so deep.'

'The monkey might go if we lowered him in the other pail,' John said slowly.

'He might at that.'

'But how will he know to carry up the broken rope?'

'If your little maid were to tie it on him. He won't be able to do it otherwise.'

'Please let's try. Otherwise I'll have to be lowered down myself.'

'You would never succeed, Sir. You're too big – as are we all.'

John leant over the well's side and shouted, 'We're going to lower Wilkes in the other bucket. You're to tie the broken rope on to his coat. Do you understand, my darling?'

Yet again, in his head, he heard the word, 'Yes.'

With Gideon standing beside him they placed Wilkes in the pail and started to turn the ancient handle and slowly, slowly lowered the wretched animal into the terrifying darkness. All the while John kept staring into the black circle of the well whose bottomless depths rose and fell in accordance with the weather.

In his mind he could see his daughter, sitting in the bucket with the broken rope, greeting Wilkes with a joy that only a true animal lover knows. And he could picture the monkey, soft and compliant, allowing Rose to tie the useless cord to him.

When he felt he had allowed enough time to elapse, the Apothecary, aided by Gideon, started to haul on the ancient handle and the bucket appeared in view. Inside sat Wilkes, shivering with fright but for all that triumphant, holding the piece of broken rope in his withered little claws. John immediately seized it and started to pull Rose up by hand, regardless of the rope burns on his palms.

And then, eventually, he was rewarded by a flash of red hair some thirty feet below him. He sobbed, he couldn't help himself, so that when finally his daughter came to the surface, pale and shivering and clutching a cotton nightgown around her small body, sitting in a bucket as big as she was, he was weeping with sheer emotion.

She flung her arms around his neck. 'Oh Papa. I was so frightened.'

'My darling girl, I swear you will never suffer anything like that again.'

'They were chasing me and I hid in the bucket, but the rope broke and I crashed down.'

'Sweetheart, when was this?'

'Last night, I think. But Papa...'

'Yes?'

'Isobel Pill is down there. That's where she must have fallen.'

The futility of all the searching, all the heartbreak looking for Kathryn's daughter, bore in on John and he sighed a great sigh.

'Poor child,' he said, and cuddled Rose close.

They brought Isobel up at sunset. Tim Painter, looking suitably grim, witnessed the scene but found it hard to identify the body, other than for the dress she was wearing. She had lost the skin off her fingers and every bit of the child's colour had drained away. Her face, already showing signs of the inevitable swelling which took place on contact with the air, was devoid of eyebrows, whilst the pigmentation of her eyes was gone. In their place were two glazed orbs gazing fishily into infinity.

'Cover her up and get her coffined fast,' ordered the Constable wearily. 'She'll swell up like a bladder in half an hour.'

At that Tim made a retching sound and hurried out of the courtyard and into the street. John, too exhausted to go and help him, merely turned his head away as the last mortal remains of Isobel Pill were removed from The Angel.

Inside was his daughter, safely ensconced with Mrs King who had promised not to leave her in any circumstances whatever. Outside another child, not so lucky, was being taken away for burial. Another day was at long last over.

Chapter Thirty-Two

Two days later the public stage left for Truro. This was a great event in Helstone and many people, especially those with relatives travelling to the big town, turned out to see it, though as yet the stable yard of The Angel was empty except for the coach itself, which was slowly being prepared for departure. This was scheduled for nine o'clock in the morning, but by eight John and Rose Rawlings, together with Tim Painter, looking incredibly handsome and finely dressed, were ready and finishing their breakfast.

'So you're off to see your lady friend, John,' stated Tim, putting down his newspaper.

'I am going to call on Elizabeth but as you know I'm actually bound for London,' the Apothecary answered primly.

'Oh yes, of course, you did say,' Tim said, grinning.

The Apothecary would have liked to have asked him what he was smirking about but decided against it in view of Rose's present company, full of ears and questions as she was. Looking at her he thought that his daughter had recovered completely from her ordeal, reinforcing his belief that the child had inherited his own resilience. He dropped a swift kiss on the top of her head.

'You're fond of her,' said Tim, still smiling.

'Yes, indeed I am.'

'I wonder if I'll have any children, legitimate that is.'

'I doubt you could ever settle with a woman long enough.'

'I don't know. I spent years with Kathryn – in a way. And now she's rewarded me. I'm going to be rich.'

Fortunately this line of conversation came to an abrupt halt as through the open window John saw the Gaffer, complete with all his band, haggling over the hiring of a cart. He turned to Tim.

'Please keep Rose under your closest eye, Tim. I just want to step outside and say farewell to the blind fiddler.'

'Very well – but don't be too long. I wish to say certain adieus of my own.'

Out in the yard momentum was beginning to gather. One or two passengers, complete with anxious relatives had arrived, while the horses – four jolly looking beasts – were being backed into the traces. John stood for a moment, watching the fiddler, thinking about what he had seen three nights before when the man had proved quite categorically that he was not blind at all. Silently he went up behind him and tapped him on the shoulder.

The Gaffer jumped and whirled round. 'Who is it?'

'John Rawlings, but I think you know that.'

The fiddler made no response and the Apothecary continued, 'May I have a brief word in private?'

'Well, Sir, I'm right busy with organising the cart to take us away.'

'I'm sure that one of the others will be able to manage. What I have to say will only take a few minutes. Come.' And John put his hand beneath the Gaffer's elbow and started to lead him away.

Young Gideon came up, bearing the monkey. 'Everything all right, Gaffer?'

'Everything is well. Just tell the others to offer the man half of what he wants and we might reach a compromise.'

Drawn by John's persuading hand, the fiddler stepped into The Angel and into a small snug, empty at this early hour of the day.

'Take a seat, Gaffer,' said the Apothecary. 'There's one right behind you.'

The fiddler sat down and turned his black spectacles in John's direction. 'Now, what was it you wanted to say?'

'I was in Meneage Street the other night and I saw you. You were looking for Wilkes the monkey.'

The Gaffer nodded but did not reply.

'I won't waste your time, nor mine,' John continued, the ruthless side of his nature suddenly showing itself. 'It was perfectly obvious to me that you could see. Gaffer, tell me, why do you adopt this pose? Is it to gain sympathy, perhaps?'

Very slowly the fiddler removed his glasses and gave John a long dark look from deep blue eyes. 'You're a clever young man, aren't you?'

'Not really. It was pure luck that made me guess about you.'

'But I've noticed you watching me from time to time with such a shrewd expression on your face. I thought perhaps you had worked it out long since.'

'No, I was deceived. And yet I had the feeling that you were hiding something from the real world, and I'm not referring to your blindness.'

The Gaffer laughed and John saw that underneath all the hair and grime he was really quite attractive. 'Well, as you're such a curious fellow I'll tell you my story – except that I've already told it to you.'

The Apothecary was frankly amazed. 'You have? When?'

'That night in Redruth. You remember me mentioning a certain game of cards which was played many years ago? A game of cards in which the Marquis of Dorchester lost everything but his title and disappeared that very night?'

'Yes, I do,' John answered, as he recollected the incident.

'Well, I used to be the Marquis before I was presumed dead and my cousin inherited. That night – the night I lost everything – I went away to blow my brains out but instead I picked up my violin and walked out of London and put the past behind me.'

John sat amazed, not having anticipated anything quite so dramatic.

'I'd had quite a talent for the instrument as a child and, indeed, as a young man. I went in to my home to find a pistol but instead I saw my violin. The rest you know.'

'What an extraordinary tale,' said John. Then he added, almost as an afterthought, 'You know that Lord Lyle is dead, by the way?'

'Oh yes,' said the fiddler, and he chuckled. 'You see, I killed him.'

John was totally bereft of words. He sat staring at the Gaffer and for once in his lifetime could think of nothing to say.

'Let me explain why. I thought for many years that he was another dull citizen with a penchant for gambling. But I learned in Redruth how wrong I could be. It was there that I discovered that he was the head of a coven, a disciple of Satan. He used that power to win everything off me at cards that night. But that's all in the past. What concerns us now is the present. I hear a lot as people think I am blind and talk freely before me. And I heard in the alehouse that your daughter had been snatched. Knowing it was on his orders I went up to his house and strangled him with a scarf. And good riddance.'

John shook his head. 'Are you going to report these facts to the Constable?'

'Are you?' asked the Gaffer, and in that question turned everything that John believed in on its head.

'No,' the Apothecary answered after a long pause.

'Well, let's say no more about it.'

'I've just one question. Why was Lord Lyle's house empty?'

'Because he was afraid. He was aware that it was only a matter of time before he was unmasked and probably arrested. He had sent the servants on to one of his many other residences. The rest of the coven have scattered and gone.'

'But why was he particularly scared now? What caused that?'

'Because, my dear young friend, I wrote and told him that I knew. I thought he was about to kill your child and it was too much for me to bear. So I sent him a letter and warned him off – and I signed it Dorchester.'

John stood up. 'May I ask your future plans?'

'I shall take to the road again, playing hither and thither.' A blue eye gave a slow wink. 'It's a good thing I learned the violin, isn't it?'

'A very good thing indeed,' John answered quietly

Half an hour later he entered the coach with Rose beside him. As usual, it was jam packed with people, some sitting on the roof, others beside the driver. Tim Painter, who had made much of bidding farewell to Gypsy Orchard, squeezed in beside a large lady and politely did his best to bow in the cramped conditions, a salutation which she returned with much interest. Meanwhile the gypsy was calling something to John who couldn't hear her and stood up and lowered the window.

'Reckon Rose was protected by her charm,' she said, giving him a look from her clearwater eyes.

John turned to his daughter and grinned. 'Reckon you're right,' he said.

And then he saw something and his blood turned to ice. Coming into the inn yard, clad from head to toe in deepest black, was that most reprehensible of women, Anne Anstey. Large and pale, her lecherous gaze for once dark and resentful, she headed purposefully for the coach and raised her hand. The Apothecary stared in pure horror as she opened her fingers to display what lay within them. It was a waxen image of himself, there could be no doubt of it. Drawing back her lips in a travesty of a smile she made to wring its neck but was forestalled by the gypsy woman, who merely made a gesture with her hand and watched as the poppet fell to the ground from whence she scooped it up immediately. John, for no reason that he could possibly name, felt in his pocket and discovered in its depths the golden hare that Elizabeth had given him. Drawing it out he held it aloft. The effect on Mrs Anstey was quite remarkable. She turned away and was suddenly lost in the crowd who had gathered to watch the coach depart, vanishing totally from his sight.

'Till we meet again,' called the gypsy, and the last view John had of her was waving one of her long tanned arms over her head, and laughing.

Two days later, travelling slowly and doing a little sight-seeing as they went, John and Rose arrived in Exeter, where they hired a man with a trap to take them to the great house that towered above the river Exe, the home of Elizabeth, Marchesa di Lorenzi.

Even as he approached it the Apothecary thought of all that had taken place within its walls, of the friendship that most remarkable of women had shown him, of the love of which she was capable but yet would never admit to.

He turned to Rose. 'We can't stay here long, my dear. We must get back to London and to reality.'

'Won't you miss Mrs Elizabeth, Papa?'

'A little,' he answered.

But in fact he would miss her desperately, finding life without her presence empty and dull. Was it his fate to be alone? he wondered. Was he destined to meet and fall in love with wonderful women only for them to be snatched away from him?

The trap dropped them outside the front door, situated as it was behind rising steps on either side. But no Elizabeth came out to greet them, only a footman answered John's suddenly urgent ringing of the bell. He bowed before them, and John suddenly felt very small and unimportant, covered with the stains of travel, his little daughter similarly grubby standing beside him.

'Mr Rawlings, Sir. We have been expecting you.'

'Thank you. Is Lady Elizabeth in?'

'No, Sir. Lady Elizabeth has been unwell and has gone to Bath to take the waters. She left instructions should you arrive that you could stay as long as you pleased. Kindly enter, Sir.'

Suddenly everything seemed very sad and somehow dismal. John shook his head.

'Thank you, but no. My daughter and I will return to Exeter. We catch the London stage tomorrow. Please give my kindest regards to her ladyship when she returns.'

'She will be sorry she missed you, Sir. Do you have any message for her?'

'Just send her my warmest greetings and thanks. Come Rose.'

He was just in time to catch the trap's owner who was

turning his vehicle in the carriage sweep.

'Exeter, if you please, my friend.'

'Lady of the house not there, Sir?'

'No,' the Apothecary answered sadly, 'I'm afraid she wasn't.'

'Never mind, Papa,' said Rose. 'I feel certain you will see her again.'

The Apothecary hugged her, realising that in his daughter lay Emilia's sound good sense and sweetness of nature. 'Yes,' he replied slowly, 'perhaps it is fated that some day I will meet Elizabeth once more.'

And with those words the trap completed its turn and John and Rose Rawlings set off for London and all that lay ahead of them.

Historical Note

John Rawlings, Apothecary, really lived. He was born circa 1731, though his actual parentage is somewhat shrouded in mystery. He became a Yeoman of the Worshipful Society of Apothecaries on 13th March, 1755, giving his address as 2, Nassau Street, Soho. This links him with H D Rawlings Ltd. who were based at the same address over a hundred years later. Their ancient soda syphons are now collectors' items and are sold on the internet. Helston, that quaint old Cornish town, is, of course, the place where the Furry or Floral Dance is performed annually. I went there in January, 2005, and had a good look round, staying at The Angel Hotel – formerly known as The Angel Inn – and was very intrigued by the ancient well, now part of the saloon bar, which has been built over the old stabling area. As yet I haven't seen the Floral Dance but I intend to put this right in May, 2006. It is heartening to know that these ancient traditions continue in this computer-ridden age.